BOOKMARKED FOR DEATH

BOOKMARKED FOR DEATH

LORNA BARRETT

WHEELER
CHIVERS

This Large Print edition is published by Wheeler Publishing, Waterville, Maine, USA and by BBC Audiobooks Ltd, Bath, England.

Wheeler Publishing, a part of Gale, Cengage Learning.

A Booktown Mystery.

The text of this Large Print edition is unabridged.
Other aspects of the book may vary from the original edition.
Set in 16 pt. Plantin.
Printed on permanent paper.

LIBRARY OF CONGRESS CATALOGING-IN-PUBLICATION DATA

Barrett, Lorna.
   Bookmarked for death / by Lorna Barrett. — Large print ed.
   p. cm. — (Wheeler publishing large print cozy mystery)
   "A Booktown mystery"—T.p. verso.
   Originally published: New York : Berkley Prime Crime, c2009.
   ISBN-13: 978-1-4104-1762-6 (pbk. : alk. paper)
   ISBN-10: 1-4104-1762-X (pbk.: alk. paper)
   1. Women booksellers—Fiction. 2. Large type books. I. Title.
PS3602.A83955B66 2009
813'.6—dc22   2009013308

BRITISH LIBRARY CATALOGUING-IN-PUBLICATION DATA AVAILABLE

Published in 2009 in the U.S. by arrangement with The Berkley Publishing Group, a member of Penguin Group (USA) Inc.
Published in 2010 in the U.K. by arrangement with The Berkley Publishing Group, a member of Penguin Group (USA) Inc.

U.K. Hardcover: 978 1 408 45678 1 (Chivers Large Print)
U.K. Softcover: 978 1 408 45679 8 (Camden Large Print)

Printed in the United States of America
1 2 3 4 5 6 7 13 12 11 10 09

ACKNOWLEDGMENTS

I don't work in a vacuum — at least I hope I don't. Therefore, I'd like to say a public thank-you to my writer chums who've been so generous with their time and expertise. My friend and fellow Berkley Prime Crime author Sheila Connolly is wonderful when it comes to brainstorming. She shared some pictures with me that were the inspiration for two of the subplots within the book. (To see them, check out my Web site — where you can also sign up for my periodic newsletter: lornabarrett.com.) She's a great pal and a wonderful critique partner.

Thank you to Sharon Wildwind for sharing her medical knowledge, as well as tidbits on a half dozen other subjects; to Hank Phillippi Ryan for her tips on reporters and how they behave; and to Sandra Parshall and the rest of my Sisters In Crime chapter, the Guppies, for answering so many of my questions — at all hours of the day and night. Jeanne Munn Bracken let me pump her for information on librarians, and her friend Richard Putnam provided local color. Marilyn Levinson, Shawn McDonald, and Gwen Nelson were my beta readers and gave me great input. Thanks, guys!

Thanks, too, to my agent, Jacky Sach, and to Sandra Harding at The Berkley Publishing Group. I couldn't have done it without them!

ONE

Crowded behind a table with her two employees and her guest author, Tricia Miles, owner of the Haven't Got a Clue mystery bookstore, held the left end of the sheet cake and flashed her most winning smile. "Cheese," she called along with the others.

"Oh, darn," Frannie Mae Armstrong said from behind her digital camera. As the only member of the Tuesday Night Book Club who owned such a camera, Frannie had been designated the group's official photographer for all signing events.

Behind her, Tricia's older-by-five-years sister, Angelica, flapped her hands in the air, encouraging them all to smile brightly. Her grin was positively demonic.

Tricia fought the urge to deck her.

A sigh from her near right and the muttered "Get on with it" also grated on Tricia's nerves.

Historical mystery author Zoë Carter

turned her head and sighed as well, her patience waning — not with Frannie but with her assistant, who shifted from foot to foot. "Kimberly, please!"

Kimberly Peters, a skinny, bored, twenty-something in a wrinkled gray suit, ran a hand through her shaggy straw-colored hair, and sighed.

Frannie laughed nervously, pressed the button, and the flash went off. Tricia's facial muscles relaxed as Frannie studied the miniature screen on the back of the camera.

"Oh, Mr. Everett, you must've blinked. Let's go for another one." She moved the viewfinder back against her eye.

In his late seventies, William Everett was Tricia's oldest yet newest employee. He gave her an anxious glance.

"Do you mind?" Tricia asked the best-selling author.

"Of course not," Zoë said patiently. "I'm here for all my fans."

"Say cheese!" Frannie encouraged in her strongest Texas twang.

Dutifully, Tricia, Zoë, Mr. Everett, and Tricia's other employee, Ginny Wilson — at twenty-four the baby of the group — complied. The flash went off and Frannie inspected the results. "Perfect!"

A round of applause from Angelica and

the members of the Tuesday Night Book Club greeted her announcement. Zoë's talk had gone well, if not spectacularly. Though she'd spoken in little more than a monotone, the twenty or so shoppers who'd crowded into the narrow bookstore for what was the last stop on Zoë's first and only national book tour had listened politely. Most of them had also picked up more than one copy of the book — for friends, family, and, in some cases, to put away and never be read. Signed first editions could be valuable, even for *New York Times* best sellers like Zoë Carter.

Stoneham's master baker, Nikki Brimfield, and her assistant, Steve Fenton, took charge of the eats table, assembling napkins, plates, and plastic cutlery.

Zoë sat down behind the stack of books on the larger of the two tables, away from the frosting and punch, and picked up her gold Cross pen, ready to sign. Kimberly leaned back against a bookshelf and folded her arms over her chest, looking aggrieved.

Frannie was the first in line, clutching three copies of Zoë's last book, *Forever Cherished*. She thrust her free hand forward, shaking Zoë's arm so forcefully the petite woman was nearly pulled from her chair. "I sure am glad to meet you at last, Miz Carter. I'm the receptionist over at the Chamber of Commerce. My boss, Bob Kelly, has spoken to you a number of times."

"Uh, yes. I believe I remember him," Zoë said, with a hint of scorn in her voice.

Frannie missed it. "I just started reading mysteries a few months back, after meeting Tricia," she said, flashing a grateful smile in Tricia's direction. "Of course, my very favorite author is Nora Roberts. What a storyteller, and you're guaranteed at least three books a year from her — not counting the ones she writes as J. D. Robb."

Kimberly rolled her eyes. "That hack? A reader can get dizzy from all that head hopping. And her prose — ? Don't get me started."

Frannie's jaw dropped, and Tricia stood by, both aghast at this assault on one of the romance genre's icons.

"Kimberly, why don't you go outside for a cigarette break?" a tight-lipped Zoë suggested.

"It's cold. And, anyway, you know I'm trying to cut down."

"But — but —" Frannie sputtered around the wad of gum in her mouth. "But I like Miz Nora's books. And millions of other people do, too."

"There's no accounting for taste," Kimberly said. She indicated the bright green palm fronds on Frannie's long Hawaiian shirt over a turtleneck and slacks. "And what's with the getup?"

Frannie looked down at herself. She longed to retire to the Aloha State one day, and her attire was the closest she could get to it while living in the great state of New Hampshire. "Getup?" she echoed, puzzled.

But Kimberly had already forgotten about her and rummaged through the handbag hanging off her shoulder, turning up a crushed pack of smokes. She moved away.

Frannie's jaw tightened, her mouth a thin line. She glanced down at the books still cradled in her left arm.

"I apologize for my niece's deplorable behavior," Zoë said. "Kimberly's been with me since her mother died, about ten years. I'm sad to say she never left her rebellious teen years behind her." She reached for the first of Frannie's books. "Here, let me sign that for you. Could you spell the name, please?"

Frannie sniffed. "Frannie — with an I-E, not Y."

Zoë bent down, picked up her pen, opened the book to the title page, and wrote: *To Frannie, I hope you enjoy Jess and Addie's last adventure. Fondly, Zoë Carter.* The words were written in tight cursive script. No flourishes, no embellishments. Just like Zoë herself.

"Thank you," Frannie said, a wan smile crossing her lips. She handed over the other two books. "Could you make the second one out to my sister? It's her birthday next month."

"I'd be delighted."

Tricia looked up to see Ginny at the register, ringing up a sale. She tossed back her long red hair and gave Tricia a wide grin and a thumbs-up. The event promised to be the best author signing Haven't Got a Clue had hosted since it opened exactly twelve months before.

As the next person in line offered Zoë a book, Tricia caught a whiff of perfume as a hand on her elbow pulled her away. Angelica.

"What are you doing just standing around?" she hissed. "This is your opportunity to sell the rest of your stock. Make the most of it."

Tricia's jaw clenched. Her sister had been in the bookselling business only five months; her own store was next door. Under Angelica's ownership, the Cookery had never held a book signing. In fact, in the six months since she'd moved to Stoneham, this was the first book signing Angelica had bothered to attend at Haven't Got a Clue.

"Why don't you just back off and take notes, and we'll compare strategies later," Tricia suggested.

Angelica shook her head, not a moussed hair on her blond head moving. "These events are supposed to boost sales."

"And they do. Go help Ginny at the sales counter and you'll see for yourself."

Angelica frowned. "I was really hoping to speak to Zoë for a few minutes."

"What about?"

"Oh, you know, the craft of writing. The publishing world. Stuff like that."

Angelica had never been interested in those subjects before. Tricia looked back toward her guest, who was signing a book for Tuesday Night Book Club newcomer Julia Overline. "I'm sure Zoë would be glad to talk to you for a few moments, but can't it wait until the end of the signing? I'd rather she give the most attention to paying customers. That is, after all, what she's here for."

"Oh, all right," Angelica groused. She and Ginny were not the best of friends. In fact, Tricia had had to break up more than a couple of spats between them. Still, Angelica turned and headed toward the cash desk.

Ginny looked up, saw her approach, and glowered.

Tricia turned her attention back to her guest author and the line of fans awaiting her attention. Elderly Grace Harris, her short white hair perfectly coiffed and always as poised as her first name, stepped up to the table with two copies of the book nestled in the crook of her left arm, offering her right hand to Zoë.

"It's nice to meet you once again, Ms. Carter — this time in happier circumstances." She didn't elaborate, and Zoë continued to smile sweetly. "I've read every one of your books at least three times. You deserve every award you've received," Grace said, her voice carefully modulated.

"Thank you so much. Believe me, I feel so honored to have those two Edgar statuettes and my three Agatha Award teapots. Historical mysteries usually aren't as popular as, say, a Tess Gerritsen thriller or the forensic novels of Kathy Reichs and Patricia Cornwell, but I don't mind being in such good company."

"I was disappointed to hear you've decided to retire the series. Isn't there anything your fans can do to change your mind?"

"I'm afraid not. It's time to move on, literally and figuratively speaking. I'm selling off the old Stoneham homestead. My winter residence in North Carolina will be my permanent home base."

"I'm surprised a woman your age still lives in this climate," Kimberly cut in, returning pink-cheeked from her smoke break outside.

"I have ties here," Grace said, taken aback. "And I like the changing of the seasons."

"Highly overrated. And a fall on the ice could be fatal for someone your age. That's why I can't wait to get Aunt Zoë out of this backwater. And what is it with all the goose poop around here?" She lifted her right foot to examine the bottom of her shoe, where some of the offensive goop still clung, then wiped her feet on the carpet, staining it.

Tricia stepped forward. "I'm terribly sorry. Lately the geese have gotten out of hand. We make an effort to clear the sidewalk several times a day, but —"

"Obviously, you're not doing a very good job of it."

Tricia clamped her teeth together, trying to hold onto her patience. Kimberly could have wiped her feet on the natural bristle doormat just inside the entrance, instead of grinding the droppings into the rug.

Zoë turned in her chair, lowered her voice. "If you're going to continue to be this disagreeable, Kimberly, why don't you just

15

go home?"

"It's my job to take care of you, Auntie dear. To see to your every need," Kimberly simpered.

The cords in Zoë's neck distended alarmingly, and Tricia was afraid she was about to lose her temper when a voice rang out from behind her.

"Shall we cut the cake?"

Tricia turned, grateful for the interruption. Nikki held a cake knife in one hand, a stack of paper napkins in the other. Though younger than Tricia by ten years, at thirty-one Nikki looked older — probably because she worked so hard. As manager of the Stoneham Patisserie, her baking prowess was renowned. She'd insisted on bringing the cake, her contribution as a member of the book club. And who in their right mind would turn down one of her fabulous creations?

But Zoë hadn't finished with Kimberly. "Go. Now."

Kimberly's cheeks flushed. "I'll go. But how will you get home, Auntie dear? You can't walk the dangerous streets of Stoneham — all four blocks of it — back to the house." She bent lower, but her words were still audible to a handful of onlookers. "Not with your blackmailer lurking out there."

16

The color drained from Zoë's face. "I'm sure I can prevail on someone to take me home."

"Y-yes, of course," Tricia stammered. "I'd be delighted."

"I'd be glad to take Ms. Carter home," Mr. Everett volunteered eagerly. She'll be quite safe with me."

Zoë looked as if she was about to protest, but Kimberly spoke again. "I may not be there when you get back. And you forgot to take your medication earlier, so you'd better take it by at least eight o'clock. I wouldn't want you to keel over and get hurt." She turned on her heel, marched to the door, and yanked it open. Tricia was glad she didn't slam it — otherwise she'd probably need to replace the glass. Twenty or so pairs of eyes stared at the exit.

Embarrassed for Zoë, Grace turned away, and the next person in line held out a book for the author to sign.

Tricia turned to Nikki and found her looking at the door where Kimberly had exited, her expression thoughtful. "She's a nasty piece of work."

"And how." Tricia let out an exasperated breath. "Thanks for breaking the tension."

"No problem. But I didn't mean to rush the evening along, either," Nikki said, making the first cut. "It's just that I really need to get home and get to bed. Three thirty comes awfully early. I already told Steve to head on home."

"Three thirty? Is that when you guys have to get up?" Tricia asked.

"It's the only way to have fresh bread and pastries available for our customers at eight a.m."

"Then it's well worth it — at least for your customers. Any news on the bank loan?"

"Not yet. I've got my fingers crossed it'll be either tomorrow or Thursday. Then the Stoneham Patisserie will be mine, all mine." The power of her grin could have lit a hundred lightbulbs.

"I'll keep my fingers crossed, too. What does Steve think?" Steve Fenton was well known around town as "the weirdo who doesn't drive." He had a reputation as a loner who was often seen riding his bike or jogging around the village — and sometimes hitched a ride to nearby Milford and surrounds. Maybe ten years older than Nikki, he was also her only employee and as knowledgeable about baking as Ginny was about bookselling — and just as valued.

"He says he'll rough up the bank manager if I don't get it."

"You're kidding."

"Steve is. He's all bluff and bluster, but I'm glad he's on my side."

Steve could be called scary. Tall, brawny, head shaved bald, sporting a do-rag and gold earring, and his muscular arms covered with tattoos, he fit the description of a biker, but without the motorcycle.

Tricia glanced down at the sheet cake. Zoë's book cover had been reproduced in exact detail, but now was marred by the cake's dissection. "Too bad cutting the cake ruins the picture. Just how did you transfer the cover onto the frosting?"

Nikki shrugged. "I snatched the picture off her Web site. It's much the same process as an inkjet printer — only with edible inks. Not my favorite way to decorate a cake, but for occasions like this it works well."

"And what's the surprise?" Tricia asked knowingly.

Nikki's eyes sparkled, subtracting a few years from her face. "Mocha chocolate cake with rum-infused white ganache filling."

"Sounds heavenly," Tricia said. Her stomach growled. She hadn't had dinner, and although cake wasn't her favorite food, she was willing to eat just about anything to stave off hunger pangs.

Already the book club members and the others who'd shown up for the signing were lining up in front of the eats table, their eyes wide in anticipation. "Let me get out of your way," Tricia told Nikki, just as the little bell over the entrance jingled. Russ Smith, editor of the *Stoneham Weekly News,* entered the store. A Nikon digital camera dangled around his neck, and he grasped it in anticipation of taking a shot. He looked across the crowded shop, found Tricia, and made his way through the throng.

"Am I too late?"

"Nikki's just cutting the cake."

"I mean to interview the big-time author." He didn't roll his eyes, but his tone suggested he'd thought about it. He glanced in Zoë's direction. "Not much of a looker, is she?"

Tricia, too, had been surprised by the author's appearance. A plain Jane dressed in what could've been a nun's habit — black skirt and shoes, and a white blouse. No headgear, of course, and the chain around her neck was unadorned as well — no gold cross hung from it.

"Now, Russ," Tricia chided, reaching up to straighten the collar on the plaid flannel shirt beneath his denim jacket. His brown hair curled around the base of his neck. No matter how often he got a haircut, it always seemed like he needed another in short order.

"No, really, Tricia. I don't need to be here."

They'd been over this before. She had to agree that in a town full of booksellers, another author signing was hardly breaking news, although Zoë was perhaps the biggest name to come through town in quite a while. Still, despite his budding relationship with Tricia, it was only the enticement of a slice of Nikki's cake that had sealed the deal and lured Russ away from his evening with ESPN. "You told me that the last few times you've written about Zoë, you've received a lovely thank you note, and even a couple of review copies over the years."

He nodded, resigned. "You're right."

The cake line snaked around the table, and a number of people clutched their signed copies as they oohed and aahed over Nikki's to-die-for confection. What was left of the book's icing cover now looked like a mosaic, and Nikki heaped another slice onto a waiting plate.

"I saw Frannie leaving. She wasn't exactly happy," Russ said.

"No, and I'm afraid she's not my only unhappy customer. Zoë's been great, but that assistant of hers should have her mouth washed out with soap."

"Assistant?" Russ asked, looking at those assembled.

"Zoë's niece. She sent her home a few minutes ago. That young woman was really obnoxious." Tricia caught sight of Grace speaking to Mr. Everett, pointing at where Kimberly had stood, and frowning. "Despite the fact this is probably the best author-signing I've hosted, I'm afraid Kimberly may have spoiled the evening for more than a couple of people, and that could be a bad reflection on the shop."

"Time will tell. What is this, your fourth, fifth signing?"

"Thirteenth."

"Well, that explains it," Russ said and laughed. "Thirteen is an unlucky number. And you are —"

"Don't even mention that 'village jinx' business to me again." A few unfortunate events some six months before had saddled Tricia with that irritating label.

Russ shrugged, his gaze wandering over to the rapidly diminishing cake.

"Tricia?" The timbre of Ginny's voice conveyed her growing annoyance.

"Get your cake — and be nice to Zoë," Tricia told Russ.

"If you say so."

Tricia hurried over to the register to save her employee from her sister. "Ginny, why don't you help Nikki with the cake," she suggested. "She's got to get up awfully early tomorrow morning and really needs to leave."

"Gladly," Ginny grated, scooted around the counter, and stalked away.

"Ange," Tricia admonished.

"I was just trying to help Ginny with that last customer. Honestly, she has no marketing savvy at all."

"Ginny is the best assistant in the entire village, and you know it. Why don't you go pester your own help?"

Angelica threw back her head and sighed theatrically. "Samantha quit this afternoon." Which would account for Angelica's sour mood. "She wasn't of much use, but I don't know what I'm going to do tomorrow at the store."

Stay busy and out of my hair, Tricia hoped.

Bursts of light drew Tricia's attention back to Zoë, who posed, pen in hand, for Russ. Again and again the camera flashed. Printing one of the shots in the *Stoneham Weekly News* wasn't going to bring in a horde of customers after the fact, but it wouldn't be bad for business, either.

Another customer stepped up to the

23

counter. Tricia took Ginny's vacated spot at the register while Angelica bagged two copies of *Forever Cherished* and a couple of paperback thrillers from the bargain shelf.

"That'll be fifty-seven thirty," Tricia said and finally looked up. "Deborah!" She'd been so preoccupied she hadn't even noticed her customer was also her best friend in Stoneham, Deborah Black. "Thanks for coming."

"Believe me, it's my pleasure. Little Davey's teething. I had him with me all day at the shop — it's his dad's turn to deal with him." Deborah ran the Happy Domestic, a boutique specializing in new and gently used products, how-to books, gifts, and home decor. Her son had been born some seven months before. Between running her shop and taking care of the baby, the poor woman had been worn to a frazzle. For the past few months, Tricia had been consulting her on redecorating — softening the industrial-looking exposed-brick walls — in her loft apartment. At least that was the excuse Deborah had given her husband for her Wednesday "girls' night out" dinner with Tricia.

"We still on for lunch tomorrow?" Deborah asked. Unfortunately, she couldn't make dinner this week and they'd already made alternate plans.

"I wouldn't miss it."

"Lunch?" Angelica piped up hopefully. "Mind a straggler joining you?"

Yes, Tricia was tempted to blurt, but instead said, "You can't go anywhere. You lost your sales force this afternoon."

"Darn."

"See you at the diner at noon — or as close to as possible," Deborah said, picked up her purchase, and headed for the exit.

Deborah's departure seemed to trigger a mass exodus of guests, who'd abandoned their paper plates and plastic forks on just about every flat surface, and headed for the checkout or exit, some having escaped without purchasing a book.

The crowd had thinned by the time the rush was over, leaving just Ginny, Grace, Mr. Everett, Russ, and Angelica on hand.

Ginny glanced at her watch. "Eight fifteen. People didn't stay as long as we thought they would."

"No." Tricia took in the stacks of unsold books still sitting on the author's table. Zoë was nowhere in sight. "Nor did they buy as many copies of Zoë's backlist as I'd hoped."

"I told you so," Angelica piped up. "And I haven't had a chance to talk to Zoë yet. Where is she, anyway?"

Ginny ignored her, turning back to Tricia. "How much stock will you have her sign?"

"All of it. Besides being a best seller she's a local author, even if she is abandoning Stoneham."

"Let's hope you can sell them to tourists. Her handler turned off a number of the locals we'd managed to lure in here tonight."

Tricia sighed. "What did Kimberly say to you?"

"Nothing too insulting. Just implied my career aspirations must be pretty low to 'settle' for a job in retail. I had to bite my tongue to keep from mentioning that I didn't have to depend on nepotism to keep me employed."

Tricia looked around the shop. "Where is Zoë? As soon as she signs that stock, I can shut the door and scrounge some dinner." She hadn't even managed to snag a piece of Nikki's cake, of which only crumbs remained — not that she was often seduced by sweets or desserts. Too hard on the figure.

"I didn't see her go," Ginny admitted.

Mr. Everett and Grace were rounding up icing-stained forks and plates, depositing them in a big black plastic trash bag. "Did Zoë leave?" Tricia asked them.

Mr. Everett shook his head, pointed to the

coat still slung over the back of one of the signing table's chairs.

"I think she went to the restroom," Grace said. She frowned. "Didn't that awful niece of hers say she needed to take her medication at eight o'clock?" She glanced at the diamond watch on her wrist. "Oh, my, she's been in there quite a while."

They looked uneasily at each other. "I'll go see," Tricia said.

Tricia had sacrificed her utility closet to add the small washroom a couple of months before. Most of her clientele arrived via bus tours, and one of the first stops the mostly elderly ladies and gents wanted to make was a bathroom. Since the front of her store had been outfitted to look like the Victorian facade of Sherlock Holmes's beloved 221B Baker Street, Tricia had carried out the decoration of her restroom in the same manner, with an antique pedestal sink and an oak mirror overhead, a high-tank toilet, dark beaded board, and reproduction hunter green flocked wallpaper. Unfortunately, she was the one who got to clean the little room every evening after the shop closed. Not the most glamorous part of owning her own business. In lieu of the closet, she'd had a wall erected to hide the boxes of stock and dollies, and had added shaker pegs higher on the wall for herself and her staff to hang their coats. Simple, but effective.

Tricia passed the last of the bookshelves and felt a draft. Bypassing the washroom, she hurried to the back of the shop, noticing that the rear door, which was always locked except for deliveries, was open a crack. Thank goodness her cat, Miss Marple, had been banished to her loft apartment during the signing. If she'd gotten out . . .

Tricia quickly closed the door and threw the deadbolt. Shoplifters had used the back exit for an escape route before, but the security system should have alerted her when the door was opened during business hours. It wasn't likely Ginny or Mr. Everett had circumvented the system, but whenever Angelica was around, unusual things seemed to occur.

Remembering why she'd come to the back of the store, Tricia stepped over to the closed washroom door. The little sign on it said OCCUPIED. She bent close and listened.

No sound.

She knocked.

"Zoë? Is everything all right in there?"

No answer.

Tricia leaned in closer, listening harder.

Still no sound.

Ginny approached. "Anything wrong?"

"I don't know," Tricia said. She rested her hand on the door handle. It turned. Since the room was tiny, the door opened out.

Tricia's breath caught in her throat and she backed away, bumping into the wall behind her.

Zoë Carter was seated on the lid of the commode, her dark skirt pulled primly over her knees, her mouth stuffed with paper napkins, and her face mottled a shade of purple Tricia had never seen. Scrapes marred her wattled neck, and some fingers from both hands were caught in the kelly green bungee cord that was knotted at her throat.

Two

Sheriff Wendy Adams glowered at Tricia. "You have a penchant for finding dead bodies, Ms. Miles." She referred, of course, to the body Tricia had found in a neighboring store some seven months before.

Tricia looked away from the tall, bulky, uniformed woman who towered above her. Seated in one of the upholstered chairs in Haven't Got a Clue's readers' nook, she held a cardboard cup of cold coffee in one hand, a balled-up, damp tissue in the other. "Believe me, Sheriff, finding a body is not on my top ten list of things to do." She closed her eyes, and found the image of Zoë's distorted face imprinted on her mind once again.

"What is it with you, Sheriff? Do you find pleasure in badgering traumatized witnesses?" Angelica asked.

Tricia opened her eyes to see that her angry sister had insinuated herself between

Tricia and the sheriff.

"Now, dear," Bob Kelly murmured, resting a gentle restraining hand on her arm, but Angelica shook him off. Bob had shown up — late — intending to take Angelica to dinner. Instead, he'd declined to leave once he saw the sheriff's patrol car outside and, as the head of the Chamber of Commerce and one of Stoneham's leading citizens, no one had asked him to leave.

"Back off, Bob," Angelica ordered, unaccountably surly. To Tricia's knowledge, Angelica had never said a cross word to her "good friend," as she called him. She folded her arms across her chest, and Tricia allowed herself a twinge of sisterly pride at the sight.

"Why don't you wait outside, Mrs. Prescott," the sheriff said, her spine stiffening. "I'll get your statement in due time."

"Sure, I'll just go out on the sidewalk and stand in the goose poop that the Board of Selectmen hasn't been addressing," she growled. "And by the way, I am no longer Mrs. Prescott. I've taken my maiden name once again. You may call me Ms. Miles."

Sheriff Adams jerked a thumb in the direction of the exit. "Outside. Everyone. You'll get your turn to give me your sides of the story. Placer" — she addressed the deputy — "don't let them talk about the crime. I want to hear everyone's story in their own unique way, without them contaminating each other."

The deputy stepped forward to usher everyone outside. Dutifully they filed out, sans coats, which were hung on pegs at the back of the store, next to where the body was still located. Once the door closed, the sheriff turned her attention back to Tricia. "Well?"

Tricia heaved a sigh. "I found her. Just like —" She risked a glance over her shoulder. "Like she is."

"And you didn't kill her."

Tricia's jaw dropped. "Of course not. She was my guest."

"Did she argue with anyone tonight?"

"No." She thought about it. "Although she had a little tiff with her niece, Kimberly Peters. And Kimberly did leave in a rush. I suppose she could've come back, snuck in through the open back door and . . ." The thought was too terrible to contemplate. A family member killing for — what? Money, revenge? Weren't they the usual motives?

"Kimberly also let it slip that her aunt was being blackmailed."

The sheriff raised an eyebrow, and Tricia explained.

"Was she teasing or serious?"

"That I couldn't say."

Wendy Adams grunted. "I'll need a list of everyone who was at the signing tonight."

"I can't give you one. I mean, I don't know everyone who came. I sent press releases to the *Stoneham Weekly News* and the Nashua newspaper, and advertising circulars. We had a good crowd. Maybe twenty-five people in all."

"Give me a few for instances."

Tricia exhaled again. "My sister, Ginny Wilson, Mr. Everett, Russ Smith, and Grace Harris, of course. Then there were Deborah Black, Nikki Brimfield, Frannie Armstrong, Julia Overline —" She thought about the faces . . . but no other names came to mind. "That's all I can think of. Ginny or Mr. Everett might be more helpful. They've lived in the area longer and are more familiar with the locals."

The sheriff's expression said *not helpful enough.* "Had you noticed anything out of the ordinary with the victim?"

"Her niece said Zoë had to take her medication at precisely eight o'clock. I thought that was a little odd, but apparently that's about the time she disappeared. I think I was on the register at the time. I sort of lost track."

"The victim didn't disappear. She died. In your bathroom, and not from taking any medication." It sounded like an accusation.

"I assure you, I had nothing to do with her death. And I don't know why anyone else would want to kill her, either."

"Do you recognize the murder weapon?"

Tricia blinked. She'd never thought of a bungee cord as a weapon before. Her insides twisted. "I . . . think . . . it could be one of the shop's. I don't know. I bought a bunch of them at the dollar store in Nashua some time ago. There were three or four in the package."

"Where would you keep them?"

"On one of the dollies in back."

Sheriff Adams bent down, grasped Tricia's elbow, and hauled her up. "Let's go have a look."

One of the deputies stood outside the washroom, taking digital photographs of the room and the victim from every angle. Tricia averted her gaze, feeling every muscle in her body tighten as they passed the tiny room and its deceased occupant.

The dollies were lined up along the wall near the back exit, two piled with boxes of books, one empty. Another deputy was crouched before the door, dusting for fingerprints, but straightened as his boss approached. "Only one or two clear prints." He eyed Tricia. "She said she touched it — they're probably hers."

Tricia swallowed her annoyance. Getting angry or protesting in her own defense would only cause them to think she could be guilty. But there was no way. This time she had witnesses.

"Where do you keep these bungee cords?" Sheriff Adams asked.

Tricia pointed to a rack of shaker pegs on the wall where a red and a yellow pair of bungee cords hung, along with an old umbrella, one of her zippered sweat jackets, and Ginny's, Angelica's, and Mr. Everett's coats.

"And you think there may have been a green one among them?"

She nodded. "Mr. Everett or Ginny might know for sure."

The sheriff's sour expression and general attitude relayed her unspoken belief that Tricia was clueless about her own property. But honestly, was she supposed to account for every pushpin, paper clip, and bungee cord on the premises?

"Just to be clear, because Ms. Carter was a famous person, Stoneham is likely to be inundated with press from Nashua, Manchester, and probably even Boston as soon as this breaks. I don't want you talking to anyone about what you saw in that bathroom."

"Russ Smith saw Zoë's body, and he's a reporter. He's sure to write about it."

"Yes, but he won't give his scoop to another news outlet, and by the time the next issue of the *Stoneham Weekly News* comes out, the story will be as stale as week-old bread."

Tricia swallowed her resentment. "Can I reopen in the morning?"

Sheriff Adams shook her head. "Not a chance. This store is a crime scene."

"But I also live here."

"Not tonight. And maybe not for a few days."

"But I have customers. Haven't Got a Clue is participating in the book fair and statue dedication this weekend. I have to be ready."

"If the Sheriff's Department is finished with its investigation, there'll be no problem. If we're not —" Wendy Adams's smile was positively wolfish. "Too bad."

"What about my cat? Can I at least retrieve her, some clothes, and other personal items?"

"Sure. And a deputy will accompany you as you gather these things."

Did the sheriff think Tricia had already stashed some kind of evidence upstairs? That she needed to retrieve it to avoid prosecution? Tricia couldn't keep the sarcasm out of her voice. "Thank you, Sheriff."

The streets of Stoneham had been deserted for hours by the time the last of the witnesses had been interviewed by the sheriff and her staff. Standing on the damp pavement outside Haven't Got a Clue, Tricia, Angelica, Ginny, Mr. Everett, and Grace, who were finally given permission to retrieve their coats, had assembled to talk about the near-term future.

Ginny's lower lip quivered. "We aren't going to reopen? But — but I can't afford to lose even one day's pay," she said, alarm creeping into her voice. "We need a new roof. The water heater sprang a leak. And now the dryer is on the fritz —"

Ginny's newly purchased, darling little cottage in the woods — all appliances included — had turned into a gigantic money pit.

Tricia had saved the bad news about closing her bookstore until the sheriff had questioned everyone who'd remained after the signing. By then, it was nearly eleven o'clock. Zoë's body still hadn't been removed, but the sheriff assured Tricia she'd take care of securing the premises.

"Don't worry, Ginny, you can come work for me for a few days," Angelica suggested, her voice oozing with sweetness. "You, too, Mr. Everett. I'm a bit short of help this week, and it would solve everyone's problems."

"Not mine," Tricia said, and shivered. She was hanging onto her purse, an overnight bag, her laptop computer case, and the cat carrier. Beside her on the sidewalk were a bag of litter, the cat's box, and a grocery bag of food, bowls, and kitty toys.

Angelica leveled a glare at her sister. "We'll all regroup at the Cookery tomorrow at nine thirty. See you then!" She gave Ginny a shove toward the municipal parking lot. Mr. Everett and Grace Harris followed reluctantly.

Angelica looked around hopefully. "Isn't Russ going to help us with all this stuff?"

"He went back to his office. Said he wanted to get started on the story. He might even put out an extra edition if he can't stop the presses on the current issue," Tricia said, and grimaced. "Right now his top story is Stoneham's mounting goose poop crisis. What happened to Bob?"

Angelica pulled a key ring from her jacket

pocket. "Damage control. He said something about calling the Chamber members to fend off any bad publicity that may come from this." She unlocked the door to her shop, turned back, and eyed the little gray cat. Miss Marple gave an indignant *Yow!*

"I'm not touching that cat box. I'll take your other stuff," Angelica said, and grabbed the purse, overnight bag, computer case, and grocery bag, leaving Tricia with the cat carrier, the litter, and the box.

Tricia followed her sister into the Cookery, both of them having thoroughly wiped their feet on a bristle doormat before entering the store. The Canada goose population had exploded in the past few weeks, with migratory birds joining their fellows who'd decided to winter near the open water of Stoneham Creek, local retention ponds, and the water traps in the neighboring Stoneham Golf Course. The result had been traffic snarled by wandering geese, and sidewalks littered with the birds' droppings.

Tricia followed her sister through the shop and over to the little dumbwaiter at the far end of the building. "We can put most of this stuff in there. That'll save trudging up all those stairs with it," Angelica said.

"Not Miss Marple!"

Angelica shrugged. "Suit yourself. But

you'll be banging that carrier into your knees for two flights, and probably give the cat motion sickness. And I am *not* cleaning up any cat barf."

Tricia looked up the brightly lit stairwell. What Angelica said made sense. "Okay, but don't send it up until I get upstairs and can unload her. I don't want her terrified by the ride."

"All right."

Miss Marple didn't travel light; it would take two trips on the lift to bring up everything.

Angelica pulled her keys from her pocket. "Here's the apartment key. Holler when you get upstairs, and I'll send up the lift."

"Okay." Tricia trudged up the stairs, opened the apartment door, flicked on the lights, and breathed in the ever-present smell of Angelica's perfume. She tended to use too much scent, making Tricia glad she wasn't prone to respiratory problems.

Angelica's loft apartment was completely different from her sister's next door. Where the stairs up to the third floor opened directly into Tricia's kitchen, Angelica's opened into a narrow hallway which ran the length of the building. Near this end was the bedroom. Beyond was a spacious living room. Or, rather, it would have been spacious if it weren't stacked with cartons and furniture. Angelica had reopened the Cookery with great fanfare in time for the Christmas rush only six weeks after acquiring the property. The loft conversion had taken over three months. A rented bungalow at the Brookfield Inn had been Angelica's home during that time.

In the time since Angelica had moved in, she'd been working ten-hour days in her store, which hadn't left her a lot of time to set up her home. Retaining employees had quickly become her single biggest problem. Angelica blamed them all for laziness, but it was her own perfectionism (or perhaps anal retentiveness) that had them quitting in droves. The fact that she'd lost five employees in the past two months should have given her a clue as to what the problem was.

Miss Marple survived the trip in the dumbwaiter just fine, and Tricia had unloaded everything and sent the lift down for the rest of her baggage, which made the return trip in record time. She'd carried some of it into the living room by the time Angelica made it to the third floor.

"Throw your stuff anywhere," she told Tricia as she picked up the last few items and headed for the living room, but there wasn't anywhere to put it.

"I need to set up Miss Marple's litter box. And it's way past her dinnertime."

Angelica frowned. She was definitely *not* a cat lover. "The box can go in the bathroom. You can put her food and water bowls on the kitchen floor — some place I won't step on them, if you please."

Tricia looked around the warehouse of a living room. She hadn't seen the apartment in at least a month, but it didn't seem to have changed a bit. "Where am I going to sleep?"

"The couch is a sofa bed . . . but I don't think there's room to pull it out. It would take too long to restack these boxes. And anyway, I have no clue where the sheets and blankets are. In one of these boxes . . . somewhere. I have a king-size bed. You can either bunk with me or sleep on the floor."

"Ange, how can you live like this? It's so not you."

"Tell me about it. I haven't exactly had all the time in the world to sort through everything and find a home for it. And there's no one around here I can hire to do it. Believe me, I've asked."

Soon a wary Miss Marple had been freed from her carrier and shown where to find her litter box and her food. But the cat had concerns other than eating, and disappeared among the jungle of boxes to explore the confines of her temporary home.

The kitchen overlooked Stoneham's quiet main drag, but Tricia was drawn to the center island with its low-hung, Mission-inspired chandelier and its high-backed stools. Though not the most comfortable places in the world to perch for any length of time, the chairs at the dining table currently offered the apartment's only functional seating. The alternative was the bed, and Tricia was too wired to sleep. "Got any wine, Ange? After what I saw tonight, I need something."

"And I'll bet you haven't eaten all day. I'll whip you up some comfort food. What would you like?"

"Something totally bad for me. Fried chicken."

Angelica turned to inspect the refrigerator's interior. "No can do. How about I make you an omelet? At least the eggs came from a chicken."

Too weary to suggest anything else, Tricia nodded. She plunked one elbow on the counter and rested her head in her hand. "What if the sheriff keeps Haven't Got a Clue closed for a week? That woman hates me," she groused.

Angelica pulled out a carton of organic

brown eggs and a half-empty bottle of char-donnay, shoving the fridge door shut with her hip. "Well, you did steal her boyfriend."

Tricia sat bolt upright, remembering the incident from the previous September. "I did not. I had lunch with him. Once. It wasn't even a real date."

Angelica shrugged, snagged a couple of glasses from the cupboard, poured, and handed Tricia the wine. "What do you want in your omelet? Veggies? Cheese? A big scoop of pity?"

"Hey, be nice to me. You said yourself I've been traumatized by finding poor Zoë dead on the toilet."

"Not where I want to be found when it's my turn," Angelica said, and opened the fridge once again. "I've got cheddar or moz-zarella. Which do you prefer?"

"Mozzarella. It's gooey and probably more fattening. Toss in peppers, onions, and anything else you'd find on a pizza."

"Right. Mushrooms, and I think I've got a tin of anchovies in the cupboard."

Tricia shuddered. "Let's not get too crazy." She tapped her right index finger on the granite counter. "The sheriff is going to make this as unpleasant for me as she can."

"Then I suggest you hold onto your temper," Angelica said, as she grabbed a knife from the block to chop an onion.

"I don't have a temper."

"No, but it wouldn't be hard to develop one if you're forced to interact with Sheriff Adams for any length of time." She waved the knife in warning. "I don't care how long she keeps your store closed. Don't rile the woman. I'll talk to Bob. We'll let him handle it."

"What?" And be beholden to him? "No way."

"Yes, way! Or do you want Wendy Adams to shut you down indefinitely?"

"She can't do that."

"Do you really want to take the risk?"

Tricia looked away. No, she didn't. Somehow, she'd have to make nice with the sheriff, or be prepared to wait a very long time to reopen her shop.

THREE

The telephone rang at six a.m., waking both sisters. Angelica groped for the bedside phone. "H'lo?"

Tricia rolled over onto her stomach, squeezing her eyes shut.

"What?" Angelica said, sounding a bit less sleepy. The bed jostled as she sat up. "Yes, I was." Pause. "No, I didn't." Pause. "She's my sister, why?"

Tricia opened one eye.

"Oh. Well, okay. Yes, I will. Have a nice day," she replied by rote and hung up the phone.

"What time is it?" Tricia asked. The clock was on Angelica's side of the bed.

"Six oh two."

"And what was that all about?" Tricia asked.

The telephone rang again.

"The *Manchester Union-Leader*. They wanted to know about —"

46

"Zoë's death," Tricia finished for her, and pulled herself into a sitting position.

"Yes." Angelica reached for the phone again.

"Don't answer that!" Tricia said, and swung her legs over the side of the bed.

The phone bleated again.

"If I were you, I'd unplug the thing. That is, unless you're willing to be interviewed again and again — and again."

"They're certainly not catching me at my best," Angelica said, and pulled at the cord, which led her to the jack just above the baseboard by the side of the bed. She unplugged the phone, but the extension in the kitchen continued to ring. "You take your shower first, Trish, while I go unplug the kitchen phone and get the coffee started."

"Deal."

Fifteen minutes later, and still toweling her hair dry, Tricia entered the kitchen to find Angelica bent over the kitchen island, coffee mug in hand, reading the morning paper.

Angelica straightened, her expression wary.

"What's wrong now?" Tricia asked.

"Why don't you have a nice cup of coffee," Angelica offered sweetly, and stepped

47

around to the countertop to grab a clean cup from the cabinet.

Tricia hung the towel around her shoulders and moved to take Angelica's former position. "I suppose they've already got all the dirt about the murder," she said, and folded back the front page of the *Nashua Telegraph.* There, in full color, was Zoë Carter's smiling face — and the blouse she wore looked very familiar. Tricia squinted to read the photo's copyright. "Russell Smith?" she read in a strangled voice. "Russ — my Russ — sold one of the photos he took last night to a competitor? Talk about blood money."

"Now, Trish, dear, you don't know that he sold it."

"Well, I'm sure going to find out."

Tricia stomped over to the phone, which lay on the counter where Angelica had left it after wrenching it from the wall. She picked the thing up, trying to find the connector, and mashed it against the wall. It immediately started to ring. She lifted the receiver and set it down again, effectively cutting off whoever was on the other end, then snatched it up again and punched in Russ's telephone number.

It rang and rang. Either it was off the hook, or he was conversing and ignoring his call waiting.

She slammed the receiver back onto the switch hook. The phone started ringing once again.

Angelica pushed her aside, yanked the offending instrument from the wall once more, and set it aside. "How about that coffee?" she asked cheerfully.

"I don't get it. He was worried about how it would look that his paper had no news on the murder, and now his photo appears in a rival paper."

"Don't you think you ought to talk to him before making all these assumptions? And anyway, what's so bad about that? People are curious. They'll want to see the last pictures taken of a dead celebrity. Although, let's face it, she's not half as newsworthy as old Anna Nicole was when she took a dirt nap."

Tricia stared at the photo. What was she so angry about, anyway? That Russ had betrayed her trust? Exactly how? She'd known those photos were going to be reproduced in a newspaper — she just hadn't figured it would be used in such a sordid way, or that it would appear so quickly.

"How about that coffee?" Angelica asked once more, wrapping Tricia's hand around a warm mug. "I have a feeling it's going to be a very long day."

■ ■ ■ ■

A lumbering, Granite State tour bus passed by the Cookery at nine fifty-five. Within minutes, the horde of book lovers would descend upon the village, charge cards in hand, and Haven't Got a Clue would not be their destination. The red CLOSED sign and yellow crime scene tape around the door would handle that. Any inquiries by telephone would be handled by the new outgoing message Tricia had recorded earlier that morning.

Behind the bus trailed a WRBS News Team Ten van, its uplink antenna neatly folded down the side. Tricia moved away from the Cookery's big plate glass display window, farther into the interior of the store. She'd deleted the messages from newspapers and TV stations on her voice mail, but doubted she'd make it through the day unscathed. And she hadn't been able to get hold of Russ, either at his home or via his office or cell phone.

Across the store, a tight-lipped Ginny, clad in a yellow Cookery apron, stood beside the register, getting her orders from Angelica, who fired them off like a drill sergeant. Ginny had worked in the store under its previous owner, and it had not been a happy experience. And as for Mr. Everett, in an effort to beef up his limited culinary repertoire, he had shown up for all the cooking demonstrations under the old administration, but since he never bought anything, his attendance at these minilectures had made him customer non grata.

Tricia wandered over to the horseshoe-shaped food demonstration area that dominated the center of the store, unsure what her role was to be. Too many workers in the shop would only get in the way of customers, and as cooking was the least of her domestic skills, she wouldn't be able to make thoughtful recommendations. Still, she'd learned a lot about bookselling in the year since she'd opened her store. Time to put that knowledge into action for her sister . . . and hope the effort would be appreciated.

But that's not what she wanted to do. She had no doubt Sheriff Adams would keep Haven't Got a Clue closed for as long as possible, just to spite her. With nothing to read — she'd forgotten to bring along the newest book in the Deb Baker Dolls to Die For mystery series that sat on her bedside table — she'd lain awake half the night listening to Angelica softly snoring on the other side of the bed. She'd spent a good portion of those hours going over her limited options. The sooner the crime was solved — or at least a suspect was identified — the sooner she could reopen. It was up to her to expedite the process.

And how was she going to gracefully exit the Cookery to do so?

Finishing with Ginny and Mr. Everett, Angelica moved her gaze, zeroing in on Tricia. Did cartons of heavy books need to be shelved, or did the washroom need cleaning? Tricia didn't want to find out. Instead, she went on the offensive. "Hey, Ange, have you thought about offering your customers cookies? You've got that beautiful demonstration area just sitting idle. Or maybe I could just nip on down to the patisserie and get some for you."

"Are you kidding? Now that I have competent help —" Angelica threw a glance in Ginny's direction — "I intend to make my own." She grabbed a book from one of the shelves, *Betty Crocker's Cooky Book.* The former owner had disdained that entire line of cookbooks, but once confided to Tricia that they were among her best sellers. Apparently Angelica had discovered the same thing. "Should I go for plain old chocolate chip, or maybe some blond brownies? The aroma will drive people nuts, and I'll sell a stack of cookie books."

Tricia resisted the urge to roll her eyes. "What ingredients are you missing? I could whip on up to the store for supplies."

"Good idea," Angelica said, still flipping pages. "But not the convenience store. I'll bet they rarely sell flour. Their stock probably has weevils. You'll have to go to Milford."

That hadn't been the direction Tricia had planned to go, but she was more than ready to make her escape.

Angelica headed for the register and grabbed a piece of scrap paper. "Hold on, I'll write up a list."

Tricia wasted no time waiting for Angelica to change her mind, and retrieved her jacket. Five minutes later, however, she was feeling uncomfortably warm as Angelica added yet another two or three items to her list. "Come on, Ange, you're making a couple of batches of cookies, not feeding a regiment."

"I know, but I'll need supplies for several days. With Ginny and Mr. Everett here, I can go back to my first love — cooking!" She checked over her list again.

The News Team Ten van rolled by the shop once more.

"Ange, if the media calls looking for me, remember I've got no comments on Zoë Carter's death."

"Right," she said, still distracted by her list. "But you don't mind if I comment, do you? Free press for the shop is free press."

"Ange!"

Angelica looked up. "Hey, there is no such thing as bad publicity. And now that I've had time to think about it, I can really milk the story."

Tricia grabbed the list before Angelica could think of anything else to add — and before she could strangle her. "Be back in an hour or so." Or longer.

Tricia headed for the back of the store and passed Mr. Everett, who was sorting misplaced books. She waggled a finger and bade him to follow.

"Mr. Everett, there's a news van that keeps circling the village. I want to avoid them."

"The hounding press," he said, and nodded. "They can be relentless."

"I can disable the Cookery's alarm, but can you reset it for me?"

"Of course. It's the same system we have at Haven't Got a Clue."

Tricia blinked. Yes, it was the same. That hadn't registered before. "Thank you." She searched the old man's face. "And thank you for showing up to help Angelica today. I know this is usually your day off, and you like to spend your time with Grace."

He held up a hand to stop her. "Grace had to leave town rather suddenly this morning."

"Oh?"

"Yes. I believe her sister has taken ill."

"Oh, I'm so sorry."

"I am, too. I must admit these past few months I've grown rather used to her company. I shall miss her."

"If you hear from her, please let her know she's in my thoughts."

"I shall. Thank you."

"Okay. I'll see you in an hour or so. And thank you again for helping Angelica."

"It's my pleasure."

Tricia disabled the alarm and watched as the door closed behind her.

Tricia sidled through the narrow passage between the Have a Heart romance book-shop and the Stoneham Patisserie, turned the corner, and peered through the front window. Already tourists jammed the store, loading up on cookies, scones, and other portable pastries. Nikki brushed back a loose strand of hair and took an offered bill, ringing up a sale at the register. Harried but happy was an apt description of her. She looked up, saw Tricia, and flashed a smile. Had she heard about Zoë's death? Probably not, but now was not the time to break it to her. It had been Nikki who had suggested Tricia invite the author. No doubt she'd feel terrible — possibly responsible — to learn of her death.

Tricia gave a quick wave and moved on. She crossed her fingers, wishing Nikki good luck with the bank loan, and headed down the street to the crosswalk. She looked left and right for traffic, waited for a green pickup truck to pass, and gave a mental sigh of relief that the WRBS news van was nowhere in sight.

So far, so good.

Frannie Armstrong was not one to gossip about the members of the Chamber of Commerce. She'd made it clear that putting her job as a receptionist in peril was something she would not consider. But none of the players in last night's drama had been members of the Chamber, except for Russ, Angelica, and Tricia herself. As the eyes and ears of the Chamber, Frannie came across an inordinate amount of useful information. From painting paneling to renting farm and other equipment, Frannie

56

knew where to go or how to do it, and if she didn't, she could direct you to someone who did.

Tricia pushed open the bright, red-painted door and entered the charming little log cabin that served as the Chamber's head-quarters. It had once been the home office of Trident Log Homes, which had gone bankrupt a decade before. Though it wasn't her taste in architecture, Tricia could ap-preciate the charm of the chinked walls, the timbered beams, the daylight flowing through the skylights and brightening the whole interior, and the way its designer had chosen to incorporate a soaring cathedral ceiling instead of a second-floor loft.

She found Frannie dressed in a blue and white calla lily Hawaiian shirt over dark slacks. Thanks to posters of the fiftieth state lining her workspace wall, she needed only a flower lei to look like she was auditioning for a community theater production of *South Pacific*.

Frannie was on the phone, but waved a cheery hello in Tricia's direction, then motioned for her to seat herself on one of the comfortable leather couches. On a little wooden stand near a rack of brochures was a self-serve airpot of coffee. The plate of store-bought cookies next to the pot reminded Tricia what her real mission was supposed to be. She pushed down the guilt and took one of the tea biscuits, nibbling on it while she waited for Frannie to finish her conversation.

A minute later, Frannie hung up the phone. "Hey, Tricia, I tried calling you this morning, but the answering machine kicked in saying Haven't Got a Clue is closed. Isn't it a shame about poor Zoë?"

"Yes." And about the sheriff shutting down her store, too, although she kept that opinion to herself.

Frannie shook her head and *tsk-tsk*ed. "I heard you found her. Was it too awfully terrible?" The gossip network was obviously working at peak capacity.

"It wasn't fun."

"I feel just terrible for you. And after what you went through last fall, too." She *tsk-tsk*ed again. "Have they arrested that appalling niece for Zoë's murder?"

"Not that I've heard. In fact, I haven't heard anything. I was hoping you might have."

Frannie allowed the barest hint of a smile to touch her lips. "Well, I do like to think of myself as being well-informed, but the gossip mill hasn't really had a chance to get started on this one yet. For my money, it's that nasty niece. You heard the way she talked to her aunt."

"And the way she talked to you," Tricia reminded her.

"And me," Frannie said. She shook her head ruefully. "I've lived in this town almost twenty-one years, but I never ran across that young woman before. Then again, why would I? I never had kids, so I never met many. Except the children of Chamber members, of course, at the annual picnic, et cetera."

"Had you met Zoë before?"

Frannie thought about it. "I suppose I must have, but it's nothing I remember. The people I know best are affiliated with the Chamber, or work at the library or the grocery stores in Milford. Other than that —" She shrugged. Then her expression shifted, and a sly glint entered her eyes. "Course, they say Miz Carter was mixed up in the whole Trident Homes disaster."

"Oh?"

Frannie leaned forward, lowered her voice. "Embezzlement."

"Zoë Carter?"

Frannie nodded. "I don't have the whole story, and it seems to me it was all rather hushed up. I mean, if it wasn't — wouldn't I, of all people, know?"

Yes, she would. "What happened to Zoë?"

"She didn't go to prison. Seems to me she got off with a suspended sentence. And it wasn't long after the whole sordid incident that she got published."

If Zoë didn't go to jail, there had to be mitigating circumstances. But this was at least ten years ago, and if the town gossip didn't know the details, who would? Russ had owned the *Stoneham Weekly News* only three or four years, but he did possess the bound volumes of years past. Had the former editor chronicled the story? She'd have to check.

"I wonder if Zoë was well-known at the library," Tricia mused aloud. "Her historical mysteries had to be researched somewhere."

"Lois Kerr is the head librarian. Have you met her?" Trisha shook her head. "She's a bit stern, but that's because she's old school. Still, she's the one who pushed for the village budget to include Wi-Fi access at the library. She's a real whirlwind of energy."

"I believe I've spoken to her on the phone, but . . . I haven't even had time to get a library card. I mean . . . I really only read mysteries, and I order everything I want and then some from distributors, as well as buy from people willing to sell their collections."

"It wouldn't hurt for you to talk to Lois

in person. Maybe get yourself a library card. Libraries are the best value you can get for your tax dollars."

"Yes, ma'am," Tricia murmured with respect.

Frannie laughed. "Any other questions?"

"Who would know Kimberly Peters?"

Frannie frowned. "Her high school teachers, I suppose. I don't know much about her. Russ Smith might, though. I mean, if she ever got in trouble — and it wouldn't surprise me, with that attitude of hers — it would've ended up in the *Stoneham Weekly News* crime blotter." That column was often only a paragraph or two long — if it even ran.

"You might also try Deborah Black," Frannie added. "She's only a few years older than Kimberly. Maybe she remembers her from school."

"Great idea. Thanks."

Frannie craned her neck to look beyond Tricia. "There they go again," she said, and shook her head.

Tricia turned to see a line of Canada geese marching down the sidewalk, no doubt heading for Stoneham Creek. It was the only running water in the area, and it seemed to be the attraction that kept luring the geese from the relative calm of the outlying retention ponds.

"Can't the Chamber pressure the Village Board to do something about them?" Tricia asked.

"They could get the state and the federal government to approve roundup-and-slaughter operations," she said matter-of-factly.

"What?" Tricia asked, horrified.

"Yup, that's what they call it. They wait until the geese are molting and can't fly, then they herd those poor birds into boxes and gas them with carbon dioxide."

"But I thought they were protected — and that's why the population keeps growing."

"Hey, it's happened. In Washington State, Minnesota, and Michigan. I read about it on the Internet," Frannie said, her voice filled with disapproval. "I'm willing to put up with a little inconvenience — cleaning off the sidewalks — if it'll save just one of those beautiful birds."

Tricia was not fond of the job, but when she thought about it, she felt the same way.

"Is the Chamber actually considering killing the geese?"

"It's an option."

"Who told you this?"

"Bob. Bob Kelly."

The phone rang. "Break time over," Frannie said, and stepped across the room to the reception desk. She picked up the receiver. "Stoneham Chamber of Commerce, Frannie speaking. How may I help you?"

Tricia gave a brief wave before she closed the door behind her. Sure enough, she was going to have to step carefully in the wake of the geese.

The early April sunshine held no warmth, and Tricia pulled up her collar against the wind. Since she was supposed to have lunch with Deborah today, she could ask her about Kimberly Peters. In the meantime, Angelica would be hopping mad if she didn't show up with flour, walnuts, and chocolate and peanut butter chips within the next half hour.

Reluctantly, Tricia headed for the municipal parking lot and her car. Preoccupied with the search for her keys in her purse, she didn't spot the WRBS van parked at the edge of the lot until it was too late. A brunette in a camel hair coat and calf-high black boots, clutching a microphone, made a beeline for Tricia.

Panicked, Tricia dropped her keys, fumbled to pick them up, and stood, finding herself looking into the lens of a video camera.

"Tricia Miles?" asked the brunette. "Portia

McAlister, WRBS News. I understand you found the body of best-selling author Zoë Carter in your store's washroom last night."

"Uh . . . uh . . ." Mesmerized by the camera, Tricia couldn't think.

"She was strangled with your bungee cord."

"I'm — I'm not sure."

"About what?" Portia pressed.

"If it actually was my bungee cord." She turned, pressed the button on her key ring and the car's doors unlocked. "I really have to go." Good sense — and Sheriff Adams's order not to talk to the press — clicked in. "I've got no more comments."

"She was found on the toilet. What was the state of the body? Was she fully clothed? Had she been sexually assaulted?"

Appalled by the question, Tricia slid into the car, slammed the door, buckled up, and started the engine. The cameraman swung around to block her exit.

Tricia pressed a control, and her window opened by two or three inches. "Please," she implored, "I have to be somewhere."

The microphone plunged toward her again. "Where are you going? Will you be talking to a lawyer?"

A lawyer? She hadn't done anything that warranted talking to a lawyer!

Tricia jammed the gearshift into drive, letting the car move forward a few inches. The cameraman didn't budge. She honked the horn furiously, edged forward a few more inches. What if he didn't move? If she hit him, then she'd have reason to speak to a lawyer.

"This is harassment. If you don't leave me alone, I'll call the sheriff!"

"Back off, Mark," the reporter said, and the cameraman immediately obliged, lowering his camera. "We'll speak again, Ms. Miles," Portia said as Tricia pulled away.

It sounded like a threat.

FOUR

The ten-minute drive to Milford helped calm Tricia's frayed nerves, and she steered directly for the biggest grocery store in town — the better to find bitter chocolate, she figured. Angelica's list of ingredients was long and varied, and Tricia had doubts she'd find everything her sister wanted.

Once inside the store, Tricia pushed her shopping cart down the various aisles until she found the baking section. She paused, scanning the bags of flour, and frowned. She didn't bake, hadn't even attempted it since she was a Girl Scout too many years ago. Should she buy all-purpose flour? Self-rising? Would wheat flour make a healthier cookie? And Angelica's list said brown sugar, but even that came in two choices. Should she buy the dark or the light?

Carts and people pushed past her as she contemplated the myriad choices. Should she take a wild guess, or break down and call Angelica? But if she did, she was likely to get a lecture for taking so long on her errand, and get the same again when she returned to the Cookery. It would be far better to get that dressing-down only once rather than twice.

"Tricia?"

She looked up at the sound of her name, instantly recognizing the voice. "Russ, what are you doing here?"

"Looking for you." Russ pushed his cart forward, pausing when he reached Tricia's. He nudged his gold-tone glasses up the bridge of his nose. "Angelica said I'd find you here. I've been waiting for almost an hour. Do you know how boring a grocery store can be when you have an hour to kill?"

"Sorry," she said, but wasn't sure it was true. And judging by the nearly full grocery cart Russ pushed, it looked like he'd found plenty to occupy his time.

"No, *I'm* sorry," he said, and sighed. "I didn't mean to blow you off last night and run to the paper. I didn't realize the sheriff would toss you out of your home. Why didn't you call? Why don't you come stay with me?"

"I want to be near my store — my home. It's more convenient for me and my cat to stay with Angelica."

"But Angelica doesn't even like Miss Marple."

"Everybody likes Miss Marple," said a voice behind them. An elderly woman bundled up in a parka and wearing a plastic rain bonnet stood behind a grocery cart. "Can I get through please? I need to get a cake mix."

Tricia and Russ moved aside. "I tried calling you for over three hours this morning. There was no answer," Tricia said.

"Sorry. Every news outlet in the state has been calling me for an interview."

"Yes, and I see you talked with someone at the *Nashua Telegraph* last night," she said, her tone cool.

"It was too late to stop my press run. I figured I may as well cut my losses and get some exposure for the pictures I took last night."

"Did they pay well?"

"No, I gave them to a buddy of mine on staff. I owe him, and this was a way to pay him back. Now I can feel free to call upon him some other time I need a favor."

That still didn't make it right in Tricia's eyes, but at least she felt better knowing he hadn't made money from Zoë's death. It was time to turn the tables. "Russ, what do you know about Zoë Carter's part in the downfall of Trident Homes?"

He blinked at her. "Nothing. Why?"

"A little bird told me that Zoë was prosecuted for embezzlement."

"That's interesting. When did all this happen?"

"Before she became a best-selling author."

"Maybe that's a reason she never wanted publicity."

"Indeed. Would the *Stoneham Weekly News* have covered this?" she asked.

He exhaled a long breath. "Possibly. But Ted Moser, the former owner, wasn't known for printing anything that reeked of scandal. He was a real cheerleader for the village."

Not unlike Bob Kelly, Tricia thought.

"I'll have a look at the archives, see what I can come up with."

"Thanks. Meanwhile, I have to get this stuff for Angelica," Tricia said, waving the grocery list in the air. "She's going to have a fit because I've already been gone so long."

"Come back to Stoneham and have lunch with me."

She shook her head. "I'm having lunch with Deborah today."

"Then have dinner with me tonight."

"Where?"

"My dining room."

"You're going to cook?" she asked.

He shrugged. "Let's face it, I'm better at it than you."

She nodded in reluctant agreement. "Deal." She thought about her encounter with News Team Ten. "It just so happens I may need some . . . professional advice."

He leaned, as far as he was able, over the grocery cart. "I'm intrigued."

Tricia's attempt at a seductive smile was interrupted by the cake lady. "Can I just grab a bag of brown sugar? I'm making a caramelized frosting for my son-in-law's thirty-fifth birthday. It's his favorite."

Tricia forced a smile. "How nice." Then her brain clicked into PR mode, and she almost started a pitch for books as gifts before she remembered Haven't Got a Clue was closed.

"You were saying?" Russ prompted.

She frowned.

"Professional advice?" he pressed.

"Oh, how to keep the press from bugging me."

"Why, what happened?"

"A TV reporter named Portia McAlister cornered me at my car in the municipal parking lot not half an hour ago. Talk about persistent. The sheriff told me not to speak to the press —"

"What about me?" he asked indignantly.

"She doesn't consider you important."

"Thank you very little, Wendy Adams."

Tricia ignored his feigned injured pride. "Anyway, she rattled me."

"The sheriff?"

"No, Portia McAlister. Before I knew it, I'd said more than I intended."

"She got what she wanted — throwing you off guard so you'd blather. As long as the camera was rolling, she got something she can broadcast. It'll placate her boss — for a few hours. But don't be surprised if she keeps popping up to bug you. Zoë's death is big news in these parts. Unless a bigger story comes along, she's going to keep at it."

"I was afraid you'd say that."

"Now, on to more important things. Like dinner. Is seven thirty okay?"

"Yes."

The cake lady had retreated, so Russ sidled closer, planted a light kiss on Tricia's lips. "Until later, then."

Angelica was in a foul temper by the time Tricia arrived with two paper sacks full with groceries. "Look at *this!*" she growled, pointing to the opened bakery box piled high with cookies in the shape of daisies, and frosted in pastel shades, that sat on the

Cookery's sales counter.

"You went out and bought them after sending me all the way to Milford and the grocery store?" Tricia asked, irked.

"No! Nikki Brimfield sent them over for *you!*"

"Me?"

"Yes. She heard about Zoë's murder and you finding her, and felt sorry for you. So she sent these over to cheer you up."

"Why are you so angry?"

"Because *I* wanted to bake. I want my customers to enjoy *my* food, not mass-produced *bakery* food. If I use a recipe from a book in stock, I've got a good shot of selling that book. But not with *bakery,*" she emphasized it like it was a dirty word, "items."

"Oh, come on. Everybody says Nikki's goodies are to die for."

"Yeah, well, I don't need a death in my store like you had in —" She cut herself off, looking horrified. "Oh, Trish, I didn't mean that . . . it's just, why does she have to sell cookbooks in her bakery?"

"It's a patisserie," Tricia corrected.

"I don't care what she calls it. She's a baker, not a bookseller."

"Ange, Stoneham is known as a book

72

town. Can you blame her for capitalizing on it?"

"Yes! Would you feel so generous if another store sold mysteries?"

Tricia didn't answer. Truthfully, she hadn't considered the equation from Angelica's perspective.

Tricia eyed her sister for a long moment. "I think sending me cookies was an extremely nice gesture on her part, and I'm going to make sure I thank her for her kindness. And, by the way, if they were sent to *me,* why are they open on *your* sales counter?"

Angelica frowned. "You can't eat all those cookies. You don't even like sweets all that much, Miss Perennial Size Eight."

Tricia exhaled, her nerves stretched taut. She and her sister had been battling the same demons for years, and things were improving too slowly. Angelica still drove her crazy. The fact that she hadn't kept her girlish figure was just one example of the continuing conflict between them.

She glanced at her watch. "We'll have to discuss this later. I'm supposed to meet Deborah for lunch in two minutes. In the meantime, if you don't want to serve the cookies to your customers — *don't!*" She left the store and walked briskly down Main

Street to the Bookshelf Diner.

The restaurant's lunch crowd never really thinned until the last bus of tourists left. But after waiting ten minutes, Tricia snagged a table in front, sat with her back to the window that overlooked the street, and perused the menu, trying not to dwell on her little altercation with Angelica. Was it a tuna salad or a ham on rye kind of day? It was definitely a hot soup day, but today's offering was cream of broccoli. Scratch ordering soup. Tricia had a personal policy against eating anything that looked as if Miss Marple might have coughed it up after a binge of grass eating.

Tricia was on her second cup of coffee when a wind-blown Deborah barreled through the diner's front door. She fell into the booth seat, scooted in, and pulled off her blue woolly hat. "So much for spring," she breathed. She signaled Hildy, the diner's middle-aged, early-shift waitress, and ordered coffee and a bowl of chili. "That ought to warm me up," she said, wriggling out of her jacket.

"I'll have tuna on whole wheat," Tricia said.

Hildy nodded and took off toward the kitchen.

"Sorry I'm late," Deborah said, "but I had

74

to do some cleanup in front of my shop. That goose poop is slicker than black ice, and if you fall in it, you may as well burn what you're wearing. Why can't the geese just stick around the water? Why do they have to walk up and down Main Street like they own the place?"

"I agree, but I can't be outside my store all day, shooing them away, either. Have you seen how big they are close up?"

"Yes. Some of them can even look right into my shop window." Deborah leaned across the table and whispered, "Never mind the geese, everybody's talking about your murder last night."

"Don't call it *my* murder."

"Well, it happened in your store. Hey, did that pushy reporter from Boston corner you yet?"

"Yes, just as I was getting into my car to go to the grocery store. She wanted to know if Zoë had been sexually assaulted. I had to pull the old 'no comment' and drive away to get rid of her."

"I couldn't tell her much because I'd left your store before the body was found. I was hoping to put in a plug for my store, but she shut down the camera and lost all interest in me as soon as I told her."

Tricia shook her head. "Has the sheriff

spoken to you yet?"

Deborah nodded. "Last night. Woke us out of a sound sleep. It took hours to get little Davey settled down again. I'll tell you one thing, I'm not voting for that woman the next time she's up for reelection."

"I've only talked to Frannie. Otherwise, no one's said a word to me about it. Is it because they think I'm guilty?"

"Of course not. It's just —"

"Don't start that village jinx business again," Tricia warned.

Deborah didn't bother to try to hide her smile. "Two murders in less than a year — and you discover both bodies."

"Don't tell me *you* think I'm guilty?"

"Of course not. Everyone's saying it's Zoë Carter's niece. Odds are, as her only living relative —"

"That we know of," Tricia corrected.

"She might be in for a lot of money. Zoë's books were *New York Times* best sellers. You don't make that list without earning a few big bucks."

The food arrived in record time, and Deborah plunged her spoon into the steaming bowl of chili. Tricia took a bite of her sandwich, chewed, and swallowed. "Frannie says you were in high school about the same time as Kimberly. What do you know about her?"

Deborah's spoon hovered close to her mouth. "I don't know what Frannie's been smoking, but she must be one very mixed-up lady. I'm not even from Stoneham. I graduated from East Hampton High on Long Island."

"You don't have a Long Island accent."

She grinned. "That's what a good voice coach will get you."

Tricia put her sandwich half back on her plate. "Whatever could Frannie have been thinking?"

"She must've gotten me mixed up with someone else."

"I guess." Under the circumstances, Tricia didn't bother asking Deborah if she'd heard of Zoë's checkered past. "Frannie also suggested I talk to the Stoneham librarian. Do you know her?"

Deborah shook her head. "Who has time to read?"

"But you're a bookseller."

"Among other things. But I also have a seven-month-old baby. I haven't picked up a book to actually read since the day Davey was born, and my to-be-read pile nearly reaches the ceiling. I love him dearly, but I can't wait until he starts school and I can have a few moments to myself again."

Tricia picked up her sandwich half again, but didn't take a bite. "I need to get my store open again. Any ideas on how I can push the sheriff's investigation forward?"

Deborah shrugged. "I guess you'd have to talk to everybody who was at your store last night."

"Supposedly what the sheriff is already doing."

"Yes, but she's so intimidating, she'll probably frighten everyone into clamming right up. You're more subtle. You'll be able to get them to tell you what they remember."

"That's the problem. Nobody seems to remember exactly *when* Zoë went to the washroom. Nobody was paying attention. The security system was down, but it might've been disabled for hours. Truth be told, I usually set it and forget it."

"Me, too. I mean, most of my deliveries come in through the front door."

Tricia nodded, her gaze falling to her plate and the small pile of potato chips on it. "I want to talk to Kimberly. She's staying at Zoë's house here in Stoneham, but the phone number is unlisted. All my contact information for Zoë is locked in my store."

"Have you tried reaching Zoë's publicist

or agent?"

"No, but that's a good idea."

Deborah moved to one side, looking beyond Tricia and out through the diner's big, plate glass window. "There goes the News Team Ten van cruising down Main Street again. I wonder who she's going to try and nail this time?"

"I'm actually surprised we haven't seen more news trucks and reporters."

"Be surprised no more," Deborah said. "There goes another one. Channel Seven from Boston."

Tricia pushed her lunch away, no longer hungry. "If I was smart, I'd write a press release saying I can't make any comments, and just have Angelica hand it out to everyone."

"Why don't you? Then again, this can only last a few days. By then your store will be open again and things will get back to normal. Until the pilgrimages start, that is."

"Pilgrimages?"

"Of course. You run a mystery bookstore. A best-selling mystery author was murdered there. Her fans — if that's what you want to call anyone that ghoulish — will flock to Haven't Got a Clue in droves. And if she signed your stock, you can ask a fortune for those books."

"She didn't sign the stock."

Deborah shook her head. "Too bad."

Just as well, Tricia thought. Selling the books for an exorbitant price, making money off a dead woman, just wouldn't sit well with her.

Hildy stopped by the table. "Want me to box that up for you, Tricia?"

She nodded. "Thanks."

The waitress took away the plate and Deborah scraped the last spoonful of chili from her bowl, savoring it. "I suppose someone will find out I was at the signing last night and want to talk to me, too." She brightened. "Good promo for my shop."

Exactly what Angelica had said.

"At least you're still open."

"You'll be back in business in a day or so. Look how fast the Cookery reopened after the murder last fall."

"Different circumstances entirely." And besides, it had been six long weeks — a possible death for a going concern.

Deborah pushed her bowl aside as Hildy returned with a Styrofoam box and the check. She glanced at it, then dug into her purse for her wallet. "Hey, I wonder what I could get on eBay for one of the last copies of *Forever Cherished* that Zoë Carter signed?"

"Now who's being ghoulish?"

"I'm a businesswoman. It's my job to make money. For me!" She peeled off a five-dollar bill and set it on the table, grabbed her hat, then wiggled back into her jacket. "Call me later if you need to talk." And she was off.

Tricia stared down at the cold coffee in her cup, at the desolate little box with her partially eaten sandwich in it, and felt empty. *I want my store back. I want my life back.*

She put another five-dollar bill and a couple of ones on the table, donned her coat, and steeled her nerves to return to the Cookery, hoping Angelica's wrath had been soothed by the act of baking.

FIVE

Squish!

Tricia winced and looked down at her loafer and the gummy substance clinging to it. *Not again!* She hobbled to the edge of the curb to scrape the bottom of her shoe, cursing herself for not watching where she walked.

Mission accomplished, she started off again, but paused outside the Stoneham Patisserie. It was still crowded with customers; she'd have to thank Nikki for the cookies later.

Business was also brisk at the Cookery, and the air was laden with the heavenly aroma of fresh-baked peanut butter blondies. Nikki's box of bakery cookies was conspicuous by its absence. A smiling Angelica flitted about the store, paper-doily-covered silver tray in hand, offering sample-size morsels — along with paper napkins — to the grateful browsers. Mr. Everett helped customers while Ginny manned the cash register. Her smile was forced, but somehow she managed not to convey to Angelica's clientele her anger at being there, while exhibiting the helpful cookery knowledge she'd picked up while working for the former owner.

"Just a few more days," Tricia whispered to her as she bagged an order.

"I never want to see another cookbook again," Ginny hissed. "She *is* going to pay us, right? I mean, we haven't even filled out any paperwork."

"Angelica's good for it," Tricia assured her. "And you know I won't let you down if she isn't."

For the first time that day, the tension eased from Ginny's face. "Thanks, Tricia. You're the world's best boss."

"No, I'm not. But I've been where you are — in a new house that needs a lot of work, and with limited funds." Okay, that was a bit of a lie. Tricia had been extremely lucky and had never experienced a day of poverty or even strained finances in her life. But she had read Dickens, and that had to count for something.

"While you were gone, I sneaked a peek on Angelica's computer. There are already signed copies of Zoë's books, dated last night, for sale on eBay. With pictures and everything."

"You're kidding."

Ginny shook her head. "It says right on the screen, 'Item location: Milford, New Hampshire.' "

"Rats. I was hoping no one would try to cash in on her death. At least, not this soon."

"Hey," Ginny said, and shrugged. "It's human nature. Or should I say human greed?"

Tricia frowned. Deborah would have competition selling her copies of the book.

The door flew open, the bell over it jangling loudly. Kimberly Peters stepped inside, her face flushed in anger. "Where do you get off telling people I killed my aunt?" she demanded.

Ginny pointed to herself. "Me?"

Kimberly glared at Tricia. "No, her."

Several customers looked up from the books they were perusing, and Angelica turned so fast, she whipped her tray of blondies away from a woman who'd been about to sample one.

"Excuse me, but could you lower your voice?" Tricia asked.

Kimberly marched up to the sales counter. "No, I won't."

Tricia stood her ground, exhaled an angry breath. "For your information, I haven't ac-

84

cused anyone of killing your aunt, least of all you. Unless I'm very much mistaken, and that's always possible, I figured you were too smart to murder her after that display you put on last night."

It was Kimberly's turn to exhale loudly, although she did lower her voice. "I was a bit upset last night," she admitted. "But you're right. I'm not stupid enough to kill the goose that laid the golden egg. My aunt was very generous to me, and I'd be an idiot to exterminate my only relative and my employer. Now I'll probably have to go out and get a real job."

"You mean she didn't leave you every-thing?"

Kimberly's glare was blistering. "Not that it's any of your business, but no. She left me only a tiny portion of her estate. The rest will be split up among various charities. Believe me, the last thing I wanted was for the old girl to die."

So the bulk of Zoë's estate was going to charity. Tricia itched to know the circum-stances surrounding Zoë's embezzlement conviction — if indeed she *had* been con-victed. Embezzlers usually go to jail, as well as having to pay hefty fines. What about the investors who'd suffered losses when Trident Homes went under? Had Zoë's eventual plan been to give away all her worldly wealth as a final act of atonement before exiting this life?

Too many pairs of eyes still stared at them, and Tricia decided this wasn't the time to pursue Zoë's past with Kimberly. "So who's going around spreading vicious gossip about me?" Tricia asked, changing the subject.

"How do I know? I got an anonymous call on my voice mail. And they told me right where to find you."

"They? Man or woman?"

"A man."

Besides Mr. Everett and a couple of Angelica's customers, the only man Tricia had spoken to that day was Russ Smith, and it wasn't likely he'd be spreading that kind of gossip. Not if he ever hoped to woo her again.

Not knowing what else to say to that news, Tricia changed tack. "I'm very sorry about your loss, Kimberly. Your aunt's work was loved by millions."

"Yes," she said, yanking down her suit jacket — brown, and just as wrinkled as the one she'd worn the day before. "It was."

"It." Not "she."

"Were you serious when you mentioned blackmail last night?"

"Sort of."

"How can one 'sort of' be blackmailed?"

"There was no implicit threat. Just a strong suggestion that one should honor one's debts," Kimberly explained.

"And did your aunt owe someone a lot of money?"

Kimberly shrugged. "Not as far as I know. And anyhow, it's not my problem." And with that, she turned and stalked out of the store.

Not her problem? Only if the blackmailer gave up or Kimberly didn't care about her aunt's reputation, which was entirely possible.

Angelica hurried over to the sales desk. "What was that all about?"

"I don't think we need to do a rerun in front of your customers," Tricia whispered.

Angelica shoved the tray of blondies at Ginny. "Circulate the store, will you?"

"Please," Tricia admonished her.

Angelica glowered. "Just do it," she told Ginny, who followed Kimberly's lead and stalked away from the register.

It was Tricia's turn to get angry. "Ange, if this is how you treat your employees, it's no wonder they quit after only a couple of days."

"What are you talking about?" she asked, sounding truly puzzled.

Tricia shook her head. "I would appreciate it if you would treat Ginny and Mr. Everett with respect. I don't want either of them quitting on me because you've treated them badly."

"How have I treated them badly? I treat them just the same as I treat all my help."

"My point exactly."

"What did Kimberly say? What did she say?" Angelica badgered. "Denied everything, right?"

"Well, of course she would. But I don't think for a minute she killed Zoë," Tricia said. "I don't think she'd be that stupid."

"Unless that's what she *wants* you to think."

"Don't be ridiculous."

"I think you're discounting Kimberly far too easily."

"I'm not saying she doesn't have more to tell. But here in the Cookery wasn't the place for a meaningful conversation. I'll have to get her on her own — in a quiet setting. But first I need to find out more about both her and Zoë Carter."

"How are you going to do that?"

"By talking to people."

"Who?"

Tricia shrugged. "Townspeople. Her neighbors."

"You think a local person killed her?"

"Could be."

"You didn't know half the people who showed up at the signing last night. I suppose any one of those strangers could have strangled her."

"Maybe," Tricia said, consulting her watch. It was already after two. "I'd better get going."

"Will you come back to the store before closing time?"

"I don't know. It depends on how many people I can track down who knew Zoë. By the way, I hope you weren't expecting me for dinner. I'm going to Russ's."

Angelica frowned. "But then I'll be all alone with — with that cat of yours," she said with disdain.

"So? Miss Marple won't bite — unless you tease her. And you'd better not treat her the way you're treating your employees. Or else."

Angelica sniffed. "Perhaps I'll invite Bob over for dinner."

"Great. Maybe you can get him to help you unpack some of those boxes."

Angelica ignored the jab, narrowing her eyes. "Will you be coming home tonight?"

"Your apartment is not my home. And . . . I don't know. Probably." She thought about it — how she and Russ were so involved in their respective businesses that their time together was all too rare. If she stayed with him, they might finally get some quality time together. Then again . . . "We'll see."

It was no secret in Stoneham that Zoë Carter had lived on Pine Avenue most of her adult life. She was, after all, the little village's only real celebrity. But the house in question was no palace, and was in fact the plainest house on the block. Tricia parked her car and scoped out the neighborhood, looking for rogue Canada geese. Sure enough, several waddled down the sidewalk on the opposite side of the street, occasionally stopping to peck at the exposed grass, no doubt looking for something to eat. She should be safe enough.

Since she wasn't yet ready to talk to Kimberly, Tricia instead marched up the walk of Zoë's next-door neighbor to the north and knocked on the door. Almost immediately a burly man dressed in a paint-splattered blue MIT sweatshirt and jeans, and sporting a churlish expression, opened the door but didn't say a word.

Tricia adopted her most winning smile. "Sir, my name's Tricia Miles. I own the mystery bookstore in town."

"Where Zoë Carter was killed?"

"Uh, yes," she answered, already rattled. She hurried on. "I was wondering if you'd be willing to talk to me about Zoë?"

"You gonna give me fifty bucks? The reporter from WRBS gave me fifty bucks to tell her everything I knew about the old girl."

Taken aback, Tricia tried to remember how much cash she had in her wallet; a ten and a few ones? "I hadn't thought —" she started.

He waved a hand in dismissal and stepped back to close the door.

"Wait!" Tricia called, but the door slammed in her face.

She tried across the street, but no one answered her knock, despite the fact that a pale blue minivan sat in the drive. She'd canvass the whole street if she had to. But first she'd check Zoë's neighbor to the south. She crossed the street and walked past Zoë's home, once more noting that it was the least attractive house on the street. Not that it was run-down, but no spring flowers or landscaping brightened the drab exterior, its curb appeal nil. Only the green and gold FOR SALE sign gave the yard any color. No car stood in the drive. Was Kimberly home, parking whatever car she drove in the one-car garage, or was she out, possibly making funeral arrangements?

Tricia passed Zoë's home and headed up the walk to the house next door on the south. By contrast, this white clapboard house with pink shutters welcomed her. Scores of sunny daffodils waved in the slight breeze against a backdrop of well-tended yews, and empty window boxes promised more color come summer. A grapevine wreath was intertwined with silk flowers and painted wooden letters in pastel hues that spelled out WELCOME.

Tricia lifted the brass knocker and tapped it three times. The door sprang open and a diminutive, elderly woman dressed in slacks, sweater, and a frilly white apron tied at her waist stood just inside the door. "Yes?"

"Hello," Tricia said and explained who she was and how she'd known Zoë Carter. "Do you mind if I ask you a few questions?"

"Do you have some kind of identification? I mean . . . those TV people wanted me to talk about Zoë, and I don't want anything I say to end up on television or in the newspapers."

"I can assure you, it won't." Tricia dug into her purse and brought out not only her driver's license but also a business card for

Haven't Got a Clue that she handed to the woman.

The older lady examined both items before returning Tricia's license. "I'm Gladys Mitchell," she said, taking Tricia's offered hand. Gladys shook her head. "It's all very sad, but I don't think I can help you. Although Zoë and I were neighbors for nearly thirty years, we were hardly more than acquaintances. She kept to herself, didn't have much personality. Wasn't interested in chatting or getting to know any of the neighbors."

"She seemed personable enough to me," Tricia said, knowing she was pushing it. On a scale of one to ten, Zoë might've mustered a four or a five on the personality scale.

"She was peddling her books at the time, wasn't she?"

Tricia nodded.

"Then I expect she learned to force herself to at least appear interested in those who showed up to buy her wares."

"Was Zoë friendlier before she was caught embezzling?"

The older lady pursed her lips. "You know about that?"

"I'm sure once News Team Ten finds out about it, that old scandal will make the story of her death even more titilating."

"I know she didn't go to jail." That confirmed what Frannie had said. "As far as I know, she had never been in trouble before that. And her niece had just come to live with her. I believe the girl had no other relatives."

"Did you ever read Zoë's books?"

The older woman shivered and crossed her arms across her chest, warding off the cold. "I took the first one out of the library. I was surprised it was so good. I wasn't expecting it to even be readable."

"Why?"

"Because *she* wrote it. It was actually interesting. The characters were believable. Look at her house. Would you think someone that talented would live in such an uninteresting house?"

No. Tricia thought about Zoë, sitting at the table in Haven't Got a Clue. She'd been dressed in a plain white blouse, a black skirt, and black pumps. She'd worn no makeup or flashy jewelry, and her short salt-and-pepper hair, cut to frame her face, would never be called stylish. But just because the outside package was unexciting didn't mean the woman couldn't have lived a vicarious life of adventure through her characters.

"Zoë wasn't a native of Stoneham, you

know," Gladys offered, disapprovingly.

"No, I didn't."

"She came from some little town in New York," the woman said, as though that was somehow despicable. What would she say if Tricia admitted she was originally from Greenwich, Connecticut?

Tricia decided she'd have to make nice with Kimberly and get inside that house, see where Zoë had created her much-loved characters Jess and Addie Martin. Then again, many a famous author had decided that staring at a blank wall — and piece of paper or computer screen — was far less distracting to the creative mind than a fascinating vista or seascape.

Tricia changed the subject. "Do you know Zoë's niece, Kimberly?"

Gladys pursed her lips. "She was a mouthy teenager. I was glad when she went off to college. At least I had peace during the school year."

"I understand Zoë lived most of her time down south."

"For the last couple of years, yes. I wasn't surprised when the FOR SALE sign went up the other day."

"Why now? She must've made a fortune on her books. Why do you think she didn't take this step before now?"

The old lady shook her head. "As I said, we weren't friends. You'll have to ask her niece that. As far as I know, she's the only one in town that Zoë ever trucked with." The old woman took a step back, allowing the door to almost close. "Oprah will be on soon. I really have to go." And with that she closed the door, leaving Tricia standing on the cold concrete step, staring at Gladys's WELCOME wreath and feeling anything but.

Few residents answered her knocks as she visited the rest of the homes along Pine Avenue. One angry goose charged at her, hissing and flapping its wings, when she tried to walk up one driveway, and Tricia had to abandon her task. By late afternoon, she was chilled and had little left in the way of stamina. Still, she had a few more places to look for the facts concerning Zoë's background, and she did not want to return to the Cookery to face Angelica — or worse, the wrath of her two employees, who were little more than indentured servants until Haven't Got a Clue could reopen. A call to the sheriff's office had not rewarded her with good news. Sheriff Adams was not available. Her message would be relayed. Thank you, and have a nice day.

Not!

It was nearly five when Tricia pulled into the Stoneham library's parking lot, which was nearly full. The library had once been in a quaint little Cape Cod house, but with the explosion of new tax revenue from the revitalization of Main Street, the village had built a new library — complete with retention pond for containing storm water runoff — only eighteen months before. The concrete walks and beautiful landscaping would have welcomed her as she stepped out of her car, except, like most of the rest of the village, the library hadn't escaped the onslaught of the Canada geese, who had left their messy calling cards.

Sidestepping the droppings, Tricia entered the low-slung brick building and strode up to the front desk to ask the woman behind a computer terminal if she could speak to the head librarian. She disappeared behind a wall festooned with posters encouraging one and all to READ and returned a minute later with an older, bespectacled, gray-haired woman in a drab brown woolen skirt and a crisp white blouse.

Lois Kerr looked as stern as any head librarian Tricia had ever met — until she smiled; then her expressive eyes hinted at the warmth of her personality.

Tricia held out her hand. "Hello, my name

is Tricia Miles. I own the mystery bookstore in the village, Haven't Got a Clue."

"Yes, I believe we've spoken on the phone several times. I'm very happy to meet you at last." Her smile waned. "I heard about the unpleasantness at your store last night."

"Extremely unpleasant," Tricia agreed. "One of the villagers suggested I come see you." She noticed several people at the checkout desk looking in their direction. "Is there someplace more private we could talk?"

Lois nodded. "My office has a door. This way."

Tricia followed the woman to a small office behind the circulation desk and took the chair the librarian offered. Lois sat down behind her desk and folded her hands on the uncluttered top. "How can I help you?"

"Did you know Zoë Carter?"

The old lady nodded, as though she'd expected the question. "Although not well," she admitted. "She'd come in here on Saturday mornings to read a week's worth of the *Wall Street Journal.*"

"What for?"

Lois shrugged. "It certainly didn't pertain to her writing. And I would've thought she could afford a subscription."

"I understand that before she became

published, she was a bookkeeper for Trident Log Homes." She waited to see if the librarian took the conversational bait.

"Yes, the Chamber of Commerce is now housed in what was formerly their main sales office. They went out of business . . . oh, maybe ten years ago."

Until today, Tricia had always assumed it had failed because there were so many log-home businesses located in New England.

"People seem to remember Zoë played a part in Trident's demise, but no longer remember the details. Embezzlement, wasn't it?"

The librarian lowered her gaze. "I believe so. I don't know the details, and even if I did, I wouldn't feel comfortable talking about it. It all happened a long time ago, and now the poor woman is dead."

"Yes. It wasn't long after the whole Trident affair that Zoë's first book was published."

Lois nodded, and seemed relieved to talk about something else. "That book always puzzled me . . . as did the ones that followed, if truth be told."

"Why?"

"Because Ms. Carter never came to us to help her with her research. I suppose for her later books she could have done it all on the Internet . . . but she could have read

99

the *Wall Street Journal* on her computer, as well. If she had one, that is."

"Did she read historical novels?"

"Not that I recall. In fact, I don't think she had a library card. She never showed any interest in fiction, or books for that matter, at all."

That was odd. Most authors were voracious readers. Then again, Zoë hadn't talked about her writing much at her "appearance" the night before. She'd been cordial, and spoke about the book, reading a passage and answering questions — but only what pertained to the book itself. She'd bragged about her awards to Grace, but she hadn't really talked about the work itself, or how she approached it. And she'd mentioned more than once that the series had ended with no hope of her returning to it.

"What are you really saying? That you think she had help writing the books?"

"I didn't mean to imply anything," Lois said, spreading her hands in a placating manner. "I'm merely stating what I know, and that's the fact that Zoë Carter didn't read fiction."

"Lots of people don't visit libraries to take out books. I haven't visited a library in years."

"Is that something you're proud of?" Lois

asked pointedly.

"No." Tricia quickly backpedaled. "It's just, I've always been lucky enough to have the means to buy every book I've ever wanted. And it's a large part of why my lifelong ambition was to become a book-seller — even if I embraced that career only in the last year."

"Sadly, for many people, the only means they have of reading a book — be it fiction or nonfiction — is through a library. Stone-ham is lucky the Board of Selectmen re-alizes the importance of a strong library. Without sufficient funding, we'd have to cut hours and staff. We could lose accreditation with the statewide system, which would hamper us in many ways, one of which is that we couldn't participate in interlibrary loans. We can't obtain every book published, and without interlibrary loans, our patrons would be cut off from borrowing works owned by other libraries."

"I didn't realize that."

"Sadly, a lot of people don't. A library is more than just books. These days, we're total media centers. And that takes money."

Duly chastised, Tricia cast about for another subject. "Um, do you know Zoë Carter's niece, Kimberly Peters?"

"Her," Lois said with contempt. "She was

banned from the library several times during her teenage years. Inappropriate behavior. She'd meet boys. They'd visit the more remote shelves and . . . let's just say they did their own brand of research on human biology."

"Oh, dear." Tricia sighed. "Zoë hinted that Kimberly had been a handful growing up. And after spending an hour or so with her last evening, I have to say she hasn't changed. They had a bit of a tiff, but it certainly wasn't anything worth killing Zoë over."

"Pent-up resentment perhaps? It doesn't take much to snap a fragile mind."

"Kimberly didn't give that impression. She seemed more bored and . . . maybe frustrated? She asked one of my employees why she worked in retail, intimating it was beneath her. I wonder if she felt that way about her own job as Zoë's assistant."

"Why don't you ask her?"

Tricia nodded. "I think I will."

"You might also want to talk to Stella Kraft. She taught English at the high school for over forty years. I'll bet she taught Zoë, and maybe even Kimberly."

Tricia blinked. "I was told Zoë wasn't a native of Stoneham — that she came from somewhere in New York."

102

The librarian sighed. "Some of our citizens are very territorial. The truth is, we can't all be from Stoneham. I myself am originally from Reading, Pennsylvania."

"Yes, I have noticed an 'us versus them' bias from some of the villagers."

"It might die out — in another couple of generations," Lois said with a wry smile. "That is, if they can keep the young people from escaping en masse. Already the majority of villagers come from other places."

Tricia smiled, too. "How can I get in touch with Stella Kraft?"

"She's in the phone book." Lois swiveled her chair, reached for the slender book behind her desk. Adjusting her reading glasses, she flipped through the pages of the phone book until she found the entry, grabbed a scrap of paper, and wrote down the number, then handed it to Tricia.

"Tell her I sent you to her. She'll talk to you."

Tricia stood. "That's very kind. Thank you."

Lois stood as well. "Kindness has nothing to do with it. I'm a bit of a mystery fan myself. I can't wait to see how this unravels."

Six

It was still too early to head over to Russ's house for dinner, so Tricia wandered the library, checking out its mystery section and finding a few books she'd never read. Since she'd left her to-be-read pile of books by her now inaccessible bedside table, her visit had proved to be a godsend. She applied for and received a library card, and settled down to start the latest book in the Jeff Resnick mystery series.

The next time Tricia looked at her watch, a full hour and a half had passed. She stuffed the piece of paper with Zoë's school-teacher's name and number between the pages as a bookmark, gathered up her purse and the other books she'd checked out, and headed for the door.

Tricia arrived at Russ's house ten minutes late, knocked on the door, and was soon rewarded with Russ's smiling face. "I wondered what happened to you. You're usually so punctual."

"I got sidetracked," she said, her nose wrinkling as she stepped across the entry-way's threshold. She detected a kind of fishy odor. "What is that . . . aroma?" she asked.

He brightened. "You like it?" Apparently he hadn't heard the touch of sarcasm in her voice. "It's my mother's specialty: tuna noodle casserole. I figured that after what you've been through, you might need some good, old-fashioned comfort food."

Tricia couldn't quite suppress a shudder. Her life didn't revolve around food the way Angelica's did, and there were few things she found truly unpalatable. Unfortunately, warmed-over tuna was one of them. Was it something to do with the canning process that changed the flavor of the fish when it was heated? On other occasions, Russ had made barbeque or splendid seafood pasta dishes. Why had he resorted to this? And since her mostly uneaten sandwich still sat in Angelica's little demonstration area's fridge, Tricia suddenly realized how raven-ously hungry she was.

"Let me take your coat," Russ said.

Tricia shrugged out of her jacket, glancing into the living room. Russ had assembled a plate of cheese and crackers on the chrome-and-glass cocktail table, and she made a

105

beeline for it.

"Can I get you a drink? Some sherry, perhaps?" Russ asked, over the squeal of his police scanner.

Tricia glanced across the room at the hated little black box that sat atop Russ's TV. She turned back to him. "I'd love it," she said, seating herself on the leather couch and grabbing the cheese spreader, smearing some Brie onto a butter cracker. She wolfed it down, glad Russ wasn't in the room to notice. Maybe if she filled up on crackers, she wouldn't have to eat the casserole.

Russ returned with a cordial glass of sherry for Tricia and his usual Scotch and soda, setting them down on the cocktail table and taking a seat next to Tricia. She was more interested in the Brie.

"You said you were sidetracked?" he said, raising his voice to be heard over the scanner.

"Yes. I've had a very long day," she shouted in response.

"Looking into Zoë's past, no doubt."

"I need to get my store open and running again, and I'm sure Wendy Adams won't be in any hurry to help me with that. She'd drag her feet for months on this investigation if she thought she could get away with it."

"What?" he asked, over the squawk of the scanner.

"Can you please turn that down?" she practically yelled.

"Sure thing." He got up and turned off the scanner, plunging the room into silence. He took his seat next to Tricia and daubed cheese on a cracker for himself. "What were you saying?"

She sighed. "I said Wendy Adams would probably keep my store closed forever if she thought she could get away with it."

"Aren't you being a little hard on her?"

"No. You haven't heard her tone when she speaks to me. She blames me for something I never did. There's no way I can change her misperceptions of the past."

"I guess," he said, and took a sip of his drink. "What else did you do today?"

"First of all, I had to soothe my employees' ruffled feathers. They're not happy working for Angelica, and I can't say as I blame them. My sister's managerial style is more militaristic than altruistic. I'm surprised she doesn't strut up and down her shop carrying a riding crop, in case one of them steps out of line. She gives them orders, then hovers over them, waiting for them to make mistakes. Not the best way to build trust."

"I can see why she loses so many employees."

Tricia nodded, and spread Brie on another cracker. "I spoke to Frannie at the Chamber. She's the eyes and ears of Stoneham, but even she hadn't heard much about the investigation into Zoë's death." She took a bite.

"So far there isn't much to tell."

Tricia swallowed. "Oh?"

"I have a few friends in the Sheriff's Department," Russ admitted, "but they're not talking, at least not about specifics. What else did you do today?"

"I spoke to a couple of Zoë's neighbors, and Lois Kerr at the library. Do you know her?"

"Only most of my life."

Tricia picked up the cheese spreader and had another go at the Brie. She wasn't about to tell Russ about the possibility that Zoë hadn't written the *Forever* books. Shocked? Yes. Appalled? Definitely. And how could it possibly be true? Could someone get away with that kind of deception for almost a decade? Still, both Gladys and Lois had known Zoë for years, if only from a distance, and had had plenty of time to observe her conduct and speculate what she was capable of, whereas Tricia had had only a little over an hour to observe her.

She took a sip of her sherry and noticed that the smell from the kitchen seemed to be growing stronger. She picked up another cracker and grabbed the knife again, overloading it with cheese.

"Whoa! Leave some room for dinner," Russ chided as Tricia bit into her seventh cracker.

Tricia sank against the back of the couch, swirling what was left of the mahogany-colored liquid in her glass. "At least I managed to avoid the press for the rest of the day. They just can't take no for an answer."

"I hope you're not including me in that statement," he said, moving close enough that his breath was warm on her neck.

"Can you take no?" Tricia asked, the hint of a smile creeping onto her lips.

He pulled back slightly. "Only if you really mean it."

Tricia sank against the back of the couch and exhaled, trying to coax her muscles to relax. "I didn't get a chance to see the news. Did Portia McAlister find out about Zoë's criminal past yet?"

Russ straightened. "It was the top story."

"Rats. I would have liked to have seen the report. I wonder if they'll post it on the station's Web site."

"Don't tell me you want to look right now?"

She did, but she didn't voice it. "Did you get a chance to look at the *Stoneham Weekly News*'s archives?"

"Yes, and as I suspected, Ted Moser brushed the story under the rug. There was a short article about Trident Homes going under, but no real detail."

Scratch an official record. Unless — "Where would the case have been prosecuted? Nashua?"

"Yes."

"I suppose I could go dig through old court reports, but I don't think I need that kind of detail."

"No," Russ said, and sidled closer once again. "What're your plans for tomorrow?" he asked, his voice almost a whisper.

Tricia sighed. "I'm going to try contacting Zoë's former high school English teacher."

"What for?" he said, nibbling her ear.

A flicker of unease wormed through Tricia, and she drew away. "Just looking into her background."

"Anything else?"

"I want to talk to Kimberly again . . . if I can track her down. Say, do you remember her ever getting into trouble when she was a teenager? Apparently she was a bit of a hellion."

"Again, that was before I took over the *Stoneham Weekly News.* I've already searched the archives once. You could do it, if you're that interested."

"I might be, thanks. Has there been any word on funeral arrangements for Zoë?"

Russ sighed. "I talked with my buddy Glenn at the Baker Funeral Home, who spoke to me off the record. When the body's released by the medical examiner's office, it's to be cremated. Nobody's contacted me or my staff about a paid-for obit in the paper. I'll go with what I've been working on, although it's really pretty skimpy. Fact-filled, but not personable."

"That's pretty much what I've picked up, too."

His smile was coy. "You'd have made a pretty good reporter."

High praise, or something else? Some quality in his tone put her on alert.

He leaned in closer once more, his mouth mere centimeters from her ear. "Tell me," he said breathlessly, "what were you thinking when you found Zoë Carter dead in your washroom?"

Tricia sat bolt upright. First the photos, now this! "Excuse me!"

111

Russ straightened. "I mean . . ." He hesitated. "Come on, Tricia. Everybody in the village is wondering. Zoë was Stoneham's only celebrity. You found her. It's news. And giving me an exclusive would be —"

Using the couch's arm, Tricia pushed herself to her feet. "I can't believe it. I can't believe you'd use me like this."

"I'm not using you. I'm tapping you — just like you just asked me about Kimberly Peters, Zoë's embezzlement charges, and even her funeral arrangements."

"It's not the same thing, and you know it."

He sat forward, pushing his glasses up his nose. "Hey, you're a source. What we have together has no bearing on the story I'm working on. And it's not like I'm going to splash it over the national news. I'm a crummy little weekly. Throw me a bone, will you?"

"I've just told you everything I know." Maybe that wasn't entirely true, but it was close. "You saw her body. Can't you tap into your own feelings? Why on earth would you have to know about and report mine?" She stormed off toward the entryway, wrenched open the closet door, and found her coat.

"Tricia, wait!"

After struggling into the sleeves, she opened the front door and stalked into the night.

"I'm sorry," Russ called after her. "Come back. We'll talk about it."

She turned. "I'm so angry with you right now, I'm not sure I want to talk to you ever again." She headed straight to her car, her anger intensifying with every step. She opened the car door, jammed the key in the ignition, and took off with tires squealing. It took nearly two blocks before her ire began to cool and she realized there was at least one consolation concerning her abbreviated evening with Russ: she wouldn't have to eat tuna noodle casserole.

Tricia parked her car in the municipal lot and walked the block to her store. It wasn't until she saw the crime scene tape still in place around the front door that she remembered she wasn't allowed in. She stepped back on the sidewalk to get the full effect of the storefront. She'd gone to considerable time and expense to duplicate a certain Victorian address in London, from its white stone facade to the 221 rendered in gold leaf on the Palladian transom over the glossy, black-painted door. The sight never ceased to please her.

She sighed, realizing she'd told Angelica she might not return that evening, and a quick glance around her confirmed that Bob Kelly's car was parked outside the Cookery.

It occurred to Tricia that although she had keys to Angelica's store and apartment, she might not be all that welcome if Angelica was . . . entertaining . . . her friend.

Bob Kelly had never been Tricia's favorite person. He looked too much like her ex-husband, albeit an older version, for her to feel comfortable around him. The fact that he could sometimes be a pompous ass had also colored her feelings in the past. She'd had to work at softening her dislike since Angelica had become romantically involved with the man.

It was with apprehension that Tricia pulled out her cell phone and punched in Angelica's number. One ring. Two rings. Three rings. *Hurry, or it will go to voice mail,* Tricia pleaded.

"Hello."

"Ange, it's Tricia. Can . . . can I come up?"

"Of course you can. Why would you think otherwi . . . oh." Her voice flattened. "Bob and I are eating dinner. Shall I set another plate?"

"Do you mind?"

"Of course not."

"I'll be right up." Tricia hung up the phone, extracted the key to the shop, and let herself in, locking up behind her. She was used to the three-flight walk and wasn't even winded as she reached the landing. Cautiously, she knocked on the apartment door.

"It's open," Angelica called.

Tricia hung her jacket in the closet and followed the lights and the heavenly aroma of garlic to the spacious kitchen. Several cartons had been flattened, their contents stacked on the end of the counter. So Angelica *had* enlisted Bob's help for unpacking. Only another half a million boxes to go!

"Hi, guys," Tricia said and took her seat at the table. Angelica passed the pasta bowl. Scampi, which looked as heavenly as it smelled.

"Good thing I always cook enough for an army," Angelica said. "What happened to your dinner date with Russ?"

"Oh, he was busy. Working." She hoped her tone indicated the subject was now verboten.

"I talked to Wendy Adams this afternoon," Bob started conversationally, digging at his pasta and plucking a fat shrimp with his fork. "Sorry, but she insists she needs more time to collect evidence in your store. She grudgingly suggested you could be open for the weekend. I tried to push her, but she doesn't appreciate how closing for even a few days can affect your bottom line."

"Amen. You got more out of her than I did. I appreciate it. Thanks, Bob." Tricia picked at her pasta. Angelica poured her a glass of wine and Tricia found herself staring at Bob. Bob, the head of the Chamber of Commerce, someone who prided himself on knowing everybody who was anybody in southern New Hampshire. And if the owners of Trident Homes had been members of the Chamber, he might have inside information. But would he share it? She'd have to tread lightly.

"Bob, did you know Zoë Carter?" Tricia asked casually.

He shook his head. "Although it was partly because of Zoë that Stoneham became a book town."

"What do you mean?"

Bob actually blushed. "When I had the great idea to invite all the booksellers, I naturally approached Zoë. Here we had a *New York Times* best-selling author living right in the village. I figured she might be interested in lending her name to our first few celebrations. She ignored my calls and

116

letters, and when I finally cornered her, she turned me down flat."

"Did she give you an explanation?"

"No. Just that she didn't do —" He put two fingers from each hand into the air and wiggled them to form air quotes, " '— those kinds of things.' I called her publisher and tried to get them to help me convince her. They were sympathetic. The woman I spoke to thought it was a great PR opportunity. We'd lined up press from Portland, Nashua, and even Boston, but Zoë refused to participate. Word got out that she wasn't willing to support the village. Ticked off quite a few people. I was shocked when Angelica told me you'd talked her into the signing. And just how did you do that?"

Tricia shrugged. "I e-mailed her from the contact page on her Web site. Got a note back from her niece, Kimberly Peters, saying the date and time were fine. That was that."

Bob frowned. "I couldn't figure Zoë out at all. Most of the authors I've run into are always looking for a chance at free publicity. This woman actually seemed afraid of it. I wonder why?"

Time to introduce a tougher subject. "Could it have been her indictment for embezzlement?"

Bob cleared his throat and frowned. "That happened a long time ago."

"It was only about a year before her first book was published."

"But turning Stoneham into a book town was years later. She could have lent her name in some capacity. Nobody would have remembered her past."

"Oh, but they did," Angelica said. "I heard it on the news."

Tricia and Bob turned to look at her. "They compared her to some other famous mystery author who was convicted of murder when she was a teenager. It was the parallels they pushed. Both were historical authors; both were convicted of felonies."

"The writer you're talking about was convicted in New Zealand, not the U.S. Do they even have felonies there?" Tricia asked. She shook her head.

"Well, whatever. The fact is, they both committed crimes."

"But no one died as a result of Zoë's crime."

Angelica shook her head. "It doesn't matter. Crime is crime. You, of all people, should know that."

It was Tricia's turn to frown. Should she mention that more than one person found it hard to believe Zoë had written the books? And passing them off as her own . . . was that another crime?

No, it was too soon to talk about Gladys Mitchell's and Lois Kerr's suspicions. Tricia needed facts, not innuendo, and it was just plain bad manners to spread unsubstantiated rumors about the dead. Still, the thought niggled at her brain. How could Zoë have gotten away with that kind of charade? Someone would have to have read the manuscripts — critiqued them. Very few authors worked in a vacuum.

Tricia poked her fork at her pasta, toying with a morsel of garlic. Was it possible the real author had been present at the signing just twenty-four hours before? That didn't seem likely, either. As far as she knew, none of the readers who'd arrived to meet Zoë had any literary aspirations; at least, no one had asked the kinds of questions author wannabes tended to ask. Like "Will you read my manuscript?" and "Can I have the phone number of your agent?"

Tricia thought back to the night before and remembered something Grace Harris had said about being glad to meet Zoë under "happier circumstances." It hadn't meant anything at the time.

She waited for a pause in the conversation before speaking to Bob. "Did you ever hear of an argument between Grace Harris and Zoë Carter?"

He frowned. "Not an argument. Grace was the chair of a citizens committee reporting to the Board of Selectmen. I believe she approached Zoë on behalf of them and asked her to participate in one or more of the grand openings. Like me, she received a cold shoulder. I consider my persuasive skills to be top notch, but nothing compared to Grace Harris, who, like Mame, could 'charm the blues right out of the horn.' "

Tricia blinked at that analogy, while Angelica fought to hold back a chuckle.

Okay.

Could the unhappy circumstances be as easily dismissed as Bob suggested? Could Zoë have been incredibly rude to Grace? She'd seemed anything but ruthless when Tricia had met her. A female milquetoast. From what she had seen and discovered in talking to others, Zoë had never mustered any kind of passion, be it love or anger.

"Speaking of the Board of Selectmen," Angelica said, "when are they going to deal with the goose problem here in Stoneham — and more importantly, how? I'm going to have to have the carpet in my shop shampooed again if this keeps up."

"It's a sticky situation — in more ways

than one," Bob said, laughing at his own joke.

"I don't think it's funny," Tricia said, and took another sip of her wine.

Bob ate another forkful of pasta. "No one can decide the best way to handle the geese. The problem is, they're protected under the Migratory Bird Treaty Act. You need special permission to hunt them. We just can't dismantle their nests or break their eggs. By law, you're not even allowed to harass them. Half the citizens of Stoneham want them shot — and as you know, hunting season ended in September. The other half want them humanely removed. The problem is, doing it humanely takes time, and I'm afraid the majority of business owners don't want to wait."

"I can't say I blame them," Angelica said, and poured herself more wine. "I'm out there cleaning off the sidewalk in front of my shop two or three times a day."

"What's the humane way of dealing with them?" Tricia asked.

"Scaring them, for one. The trouble is, they get used to loud noises, so that doesn't really work. A lot of communities have hired companies that use border collies to chase the geese. This works, but it, too, takes time. They chase away one group of birds and another flies right in. You have to keep it up. Then there's egg oiling."

"What does that involve?"

"Sealing the eggs so what's in them can't develop. But that just stops the next generation of birds, not the ones you've already got. And it's very labor-intensive. What we really need to do is make Stoneham unattractive to the birds. If they don't like where they are, they'll go away."

"And bother some other community," Tricia said.

"Possibly," he conceded.

"How do you make the village less attractive to them?" Tricia asked.

"Unfortunately, that's difficult to do. Today's zoning laws require the presence of retention ponds to handle storm water runoff, keeping it from messing up the sewer system. The birds don't know the ponds aren't real. And it doesn't help when every stay-at-home mom in the village ignores the signs that have been posted and takes her little tykes out to feed the geese."

"Boy, you really are into this," Angelica said admiringly.

"I need to be informed if I'm going to represent the Chamber members' interests."

"What about the immediate problem?" Tricia asked. "Isn't there some way the village can clean the sidewalks on a more regular basis?"

"And don't forget these birds are huge. I've had more than one frightened wisp of an old lady tell me the things charged and hissed at her," Angelica said.

"I know, I know," Bob said. "They're very territorial. That aggressive behavior could become a major liability problem. If someone gets hurt, the business owners could be financially responsible for injuries incurred."

"Not just business owners," Tricia said. "I was chased just this morning over on Pine Avenue — a residential neighborhood."

"Cleaning the sidewalks takes money," Bob said, getting back to the subject, "money that hasn't been budgeted. I'm sure the business owners wouldn't like to see taxes go up to pay for it."

"Not especially," Tricia said, "since it's *us* who pay them — not the building owners."

"You all knew that when you signed the leases," Bob said.

Yeah, and he owned half the buildings on Main Street, and had stipulated that his tenants pay those taxes when he drew up the leases.

"Frannie told me that one of the options is to 'round up and slaughter' them. She said it's under consideration."

Bob's eyes narrowed. "She had no right discussing Chamber business with you."

"She had every right. I'm a member of the Chamber, too, you know."

"Killing them en masse would be very controversial. A lot of people love the damn things. Exterminating them could prove to be a PR nightmare — the last thing the village needs."

And *that* was what he really worried about.

As though to avoid discussing that very subject, Bob launched into an update on the weekend book fair and statue dedication, but Tricia only half listened, her mind wandering back to Zoë and the ramifications of everything she'd learned today. All the facts and innuendo swirled around in her mind in a disconnected mess.

"Something wrong with the shrimp?" a concerned Angelica asked, once Bob had wound down. "Maybe I shouldn't go so heavy on the garlic."

Feeling contrite, Tricia gave her sister a wan smile. "It's perfect, Ange." She took another bite and savored the taste, once again thankful she wasn't sentenced to eating tuna noodle casserole.

SEVEN

After dinner, Tricia retired to Angelica's bedroom with her laptop and the pile of library books to comfort her. The computer looked distinctly out of place in the girly boudoir, the only room devoid of boxes, with its gilt-edged French provincial furniture and the stacks of sumptuous lace pillows lined up against the ivory velvet-covered headboard.

Angelica's vanity sported scores of perfume bottles and colorful nail polishes. One cobalt blue bottle stood out among the crowd: Evening in Paris talc. Tricia removed the cap and breathed in a much-loved memory of her grandmother. Where had Angelica found it? They hadn't made that scent in decades. A bigger mystery was the thought that Angelica might possibly have loved their grandmother as much as Tricia had. It wasn't something she'd ever considered, and yet Angelica had once mentioned that it was their grandmother's cookbook collection that got her interested in cookery. Either way, grandmother had inspired a love of books in both of her grandchildren.

Recapping the bottle, Tricia replaced it and settled on the bed, delighted that the little computer sniffed out a wireless connection — probably tapping into the signal from her own home next door. After a few minutes Miss Marple showed up from the depths of the living room's box jungle, settled herself next to Tricia, and purred deeply as Tricia Googled the News Team Ten Web site.

As she'd hoped, Zoë's murder was still a top story. Portia McAlister had stood in front of Zoë's home late that afternoon, judging by the shadows behind her, and dragged up Zoë's past indiscretions, as well as her literary triumphs.

"Before her fame as a mystery author, Zoë Carter lived a life of mystery herself. A life that included an indictment for embezzlement," she said with deadly seriousness.

Tricia listened intently, then hit the reload button and played the video again. As a bookkeeper for Trident Log Homes, Zoë had participated in a scheme to defraud the investors. With phantom vendor accounts, she'd channeled hundreds of thousands of dollars to Thomas Norton's pocket. Norton, the company's married CEO, had had a brief fling with Zoë, whom he declared at the trial to be naive and delusional. Zoë, he asserted, had been under the impression Norton would leave his wife, and that it was her idea to divert the funds.

That story fell apart when prosecutors showed it was Norton who squirreled away the missing funds in an offshore bank account, not Zoë. Zoë had never had so much as a speeding ticket, and was the sole support of her recently orphaned niece. Her testimony was enough to convict Norton, while she got off with a suspended sentence, a hefty fine, and an order to make restitution. While out on appeal, Norton skipped the country and died in a car accident in the Austrian Alps — no doubt on his way to tap a Swiss bank account.

Tricia shook her head, folding down her laptop and setting it aside. It sounded like the plot of a bad movie.

Miss Marple scolded Tricia for disturbing her, but settled right back down as Tricia grabbed her library copy of *Dead In Red* and picked up where she'd left off reading some hours before. Sometime later, the sound of Miss Marple's purr lulled her to sleep.

Much later in the night, Tricia awoke to

find her book removed and her cat gone, the lights out, and Angelica on the other side of the bed, once again snoring quietly. She rolled over and fell back into an exhausted sleep.

When she awoke in the morning, Angelica was gone, Miss Marple was back, and the aroma of freshly brewed coffee filled the air. Tricia found her robe, grabbed her book, and staggered into her sister's kitchen.

"Well, good morning, sleepyhead," Angelica said, pouring a cup of coffee and handing it to her sister.

Tricia sat on a stool at the kitchen island and took a deep gulp of the fortifying brew.

Angelica scrutinized her face. "Okay, what's up?"

Tricia refused to meet her gaze. "Nothing."

"You ate your dinner and snuck off to bed. And the corners of your mouth never lie. Something's making you unhappy. What did Russ do that you couldn't tell me about in front of Bob?"

Tricia ignored the question. "I'm sorry I showed up on your doorstep, especially after I told you I probably wouldn't. I must've spoiled your plans for the evening."

Angelica waved her hand in dismissal. "Don't give it a thought. I already told Bob that as long as your business is closed and you're staying with me, there wouldn't be any fun stuff going on here."

Tricia eyed her sister. More information than she wanted to know. She turned her attention back to her coffee.

Angelica, still clad in a robe, headed toward the bathroom. "I'm off to take a shower. Help yourself to anything you want. There's oatmeal, eggs —" Whatever else she suggested was lost in Doppler echo as she disappeared down the hall.

Tricia looked around the otherwise spotless kitchen, still cluttered with the booty from the emptied boxes. She missed her nice, uncluttered home. She missed her favorite blend of coffee. She even missed her treadmill.

Beethoven's Pastorale Symphony chimed from inside Tricia's purse. She whipped her head around, wondering where she'd left it and if she *could* find it before she missed the call. Aha! She located it on one of the stacks of boxes lined against the wall. She flipped open the phone and stabbed the button. "Hello?"

"Tricia. It's Ginny." Her tone was as cold as an iceberg. "What is it going to take to reopen Haven't Got a Clue? I don't think I can stand another day with your sister at the Cookery. He hasn't said so out loud, but I think Mr. Everett feels the same way."

Tricia's stomach roiled. Angelica had been so kind to her during the past thirty-six hours and yet she didn't seem able to engage that gene when it came to her — or Tricia's — employees.

"I don't think we're going to see the store reopen until at least the weekend. But I'll speak to Angelica. Again."

"Will you be at the Cookery today? She isn't as mean to us when you're there."

Tricia thought about her quest to speak with Zoë's ex-high school English teacher. She could probably do it by phone, but her results weren't likely to be as satisfying. Selfishly, she knew that if Ginny and Mr. Everett didn't show up, she'd have to stay at the Cookery all day and help until Angelica could hire yet another clueless temp from the Milford employment agency.

Another truth was that the subject of food preparation bored Tricia to tears. The colorful photos in many of the books were great, she supposed, if you were into that kind of thing, but they couldn't hold a candle to the magic of losing oneself in the pages of an enthralling story.

"Tricia?"

"Don't worry, Ginny. We'll work something out. See you in a little while."

"Bye," Ginny said, and disconnected. She didn't sound pacified.

Tricia put her phone away, then searched the fridge and found some whole wheat bread for toast. She was nibbling her second slice, her nose in her library book when Angelica reappeared in her robe, her head swathed in a peach-colored towel. "That looks good. Put a slice in for me, will you?"

"We have to talk," Tricia said, extracting bread from the wrapper and pushing the lever on the toaster. "You're about to have a mutiny on your hands if you don't treat Ginny and Mr. Everett nicer."

Angelica looked aghast. "Moi?" she asked innocently.

"Oui, toi," Tricia countered. She softened her voice. "Ange, you've got a big heart. Why do you lose it the minute you walk into your store?"

Angelica turned her back on her sister, grabbing her coffee cup and pouring the cold contents down the sink. "I'm a perfectionist. Is it wrong to demand the same from the people I hire?"

"When you're paying them minimum wage or just above — yes. If you're lucky, you've got two more days with Ginny and Mr. Everett, but if things don't improve this morning, they're ready to walk."

"But Ginny said she needs the money."

"She apparently doesn't need it that badly."

Angelica poured herself another cup, leaned against the counter, and sighed. "Okay. I'll play nice."

"Good. Unfortunately, I have some errands I have to run today, and may not be available to play referee. So make sure you keep your promise, or they *will* walk out."

"What kind of errands?"

"First off, I want to talk to someone who knew Zoë back when. Someone who might have influenced her . . . writing career."

"And who would that be?"

"Her high school English teacher."

Angelica nodded. "Makes sense. Where did you come up with the idea?"

"From the village librarian. You know, for such a small town, Stoneham really has a nice library. Cutting-edge, I'd say."

"I've only driven by it. Looks nice."

"It's the best value you can get for your tax dollars," Tricia said.

Angelica blinked, looking confused. "What?"

Tricia laughed. "Frannie told me that."

Angelica took another swig of her coffee and swallowed. "Okay. What else have you got on tap for today that's going to keep you from helping me in my shop?"

"The thing I don't want to do is run into that TV reporter, Portia McAlister. She hunted me down yesterday morning in the municipal parking lot." The memory made her shudder.

"She hasn't come to talk to me," Angelica said, sounding miffed. "I wish she would. I'd love to get in a plug for the Cookery."

"Call the station. I'm sure they'd be glad to give you Portia's cell number."

"Maybe I will. After all, I was at the scene of the murder. I'm sure I can add loads of color to her story."

"But you didn't actually see anything. Not even Zoë's body."

"Yes, but you did. Maybe I can milk that angle."

"Please don't. That'll only get her interested in talking to me again."

Angelica shrugged. "Oh, all right. I suppose two days later the story is old news anyway."

She drained her cup and put it into the dishwasher. "Better get dressed," she advised. "Time is money." She turned and headed toward her bedroom.

Tricia eyed the telephone, then the clock on the wall. It was after nine, surely late enough to call a retired schoolteacher. Abandoning her stool, she picked up the slip of paper with Stella Kraft's number that she'd been using as a bookmark, crossed the kitchen, picked up the receiver, and dialed.

As promised, Angelica was on her best behavior, greeting both Ginny and Mr. Everett like old friends about to begin a new adventure. They eyed their temporary employer with suspicion, but dutifully donned the Cookery aprons and began the day with, if not enthusiasm, at least not scorn.

Tricia's appointment with Zoë's former teacher was for eleven, and the four of them started the workday by restocking shelves, dusting, vacuuming, and getting ready for an anticipated glut of customers, who arrived right at opening time.

At ten forty-five, Tricia was just about to duck out when Ginny cornered her. "Tricia, we need to talk about Saturday."

"Saturday?" Tricia echoed.

"Yes, the statue dedication."

Tricia smacked her forehead. "Rats! I forgot all about it."

Ginny pulled a piece of paper from her apron pocket. "I managed to get a few minutes free yesterday and made some calls.

I hope I'm not going to get in trouble about it when Angelica sees it on her phone bill."

"What kind of calls?"

"About the extra books. I hope you don't mind, but I didn't know if we'd be open. I took the liberty of ordering copies of all of Zoë's books. I had them expressed, so they should arrive no later than tomorrow morning. I talked to Frannie and confirmed the tent, and wrestled the promise of a borrowed cash register if we can't bring our extra one. It's a shame we can't raid some of our used stock, but if you'll download the flyer from your laptop, I can get more of them and our newsletters printed before Saturday morning."

Tricia swallowed as guilt coursed through her. She'd been so caught up in learning about Zoë that she'd neglected her own business. "Ginny, you've just earned yourself a big bonus. What would I do without you?"

"Just doing my job," Ginny said shyly, her gaze dipping to the floor.

"And then some." Tricia glanced at her watch. Time to go. "I've got to leave right now, but I promise, as soon as I get back, we'll talk some more about this and make more contingency plans." She reached out to touch Ginny's arm. "Thank you."

Ginny smiled and turned back to the

register. Tricia waved for Angelica's attention and promised to be back in time to give the others a lunch break. Since Stella lived only two blocks from Stoneham's main drag, Tricia decided to make up for the lack of her treadmill and walk the distance.

A carefully printed sign on the front door directed visitors to the back entrance of the little house. The woman who answered Tricia's knock looked about 108, with deeply wrinkled, leathery smoker's skin, a husky voice, and sharp eyes that didn't miss a trick. "Miss —" or was she a Mrs.? "— Kraft?" Tricia asked.

"Come on in," the old woman encouraged, and held the door for Tricia to enter. The dated yet immaculate kitchen was swelteringly hot, the air stuffy, smelling like boiled potatoes with an underlying scent of mothballs. Tricia was ushered past a worn white enamel table, but declined the offer of coffee or tea.

"I heard all about Zoë Carter's death," Stella said.

"She was a student of yours?" Tricia asked.

"Oh, sure. Until I retired, just about every kid who graduated from Stoneham High passed through my classroom at least once."

"But I thought Zoë wasn't from Stoneham?"

Stella shook her head. "Neither am I. Some people in this town think that if you weren't born here, you don't belong here. Just as many don't subscribe to that narrow thinking, thank goodness."

"Did you teach her niece?"

Stella frowned. "Yes, I had her niece, too. Now that one was a piece of work. Smart, but didn't apply herself." She padded down the hall, motioning Tricia to follow her into the living room. Every wall had a bookcase, and it was all Tricia could do not to abandon her mission and study the hundreds — possibly thousands — of titles.

Stella gestured to the faded gold couch. "Sit, sit," she encouraged. "Sure I can't get you anything?"

Tricia shook her head, but took the offered seat while Stella commandeered a worn leather club chair.

"I know it was a long time ago, but do you remember what kind of student Zoë Carter was?"

Stella answered without a moment's hesitation. "Quiet little mouse of a thing. She had excellent math skills. She won a couple of prizes or something, so obviously she wasn't stupid. But I wasn't all that interested in her." She leaned forward and lowered her voice conspiratorially. "I probably shouldn't admit this, but I always had favorites among my students. And those with a quest to learn about literature, I doted on."

"So as a teenager Zoë showed no story-telling aptitude?"

"None at all. If I may employ a cliché, she couldn't write her way out of a wet paper bag."

"And yet at her death she was a *New York Times* best-selling author."

The old woman cocked her head, her eyes narrowing. "Interesting, isn't it?"

Tricia carefully phrased her next question. "What do you think brought her latent talent to the surface?"

"That's my point. The woman — or at least the student — had no writing talent."

"You don't think she wrote those books?" Tricia asked, hoping she sounded convincingly skeptical.

Stella shook her head. "Never in a million years. Someone like Zoë, who'd never really known love, could never have written such believable and heart-wrenching characters."

And how did Stella know Zoë was un-loved?

"Then who — ?"

The old woman looked away and sighed. "I've been asking myself that for the last decade. I wish I'd saved the papers of some of my more impressive students; I had a few that showed promise. But who's to say the author of those books even came from Stoneham?"

Who, indeed? "But Zoë still lived in Stoneham when the first book was published."

"Yes. And it's well known she never sought the limelight. She didn't want to go on book tours, and was practically a hermit when it came to promotional activities. It was word of mouth that sold that first book — nothing Zoë did."

"Sounds like you've followed her career closely."

"Stoneham High hasn't graduated any rocket scientists. Apparently Zoë was our only star."

"Have you shared your suspicions with anyone else?"

"In the beginning I might have mentioned it to a few of my former colleagues — I've been retired for almost eight years now. But who listens to the rantings of an old English teacher?"

I might, Tricia thought.

Now to spring the sixty-four-thousand-dollar question. "Do you think it's possible

139

the real author of those books murdered Zoë?"

Stella didn't even blink. "Why not? Stranger things have happened."

Time to play devil's advocate. "But why wait until the last book was published?"

"I've been pondering that same question. Zoë had been scarce in these parts since publication of the third book; I heard she moved down south. Rumor has it she only came back to Stoneham to sell her house."

"Yes, she mentioned that at the signing the other night. Wouldn't it be ironic if the person who wrote those books is still here in Stoneham and has been waiting all these years to take her revenge?" Tricia blurted, finally voicing the theory that had been percolating in the back of her mind.

The old woman nodded. "What makes you think it was a woman who wrote them?"

"The real author?" Tricia said, a bit surprised that Stella hadn't immediately refuted her idea.

"I assume you've read the books?" Stella paused and Tricia nodded. "Do you think a male author could've done justice to Addie's character, or the loss of her son in the mine cave-in?"

"That depends on the author," Tricia said, surprised a former English teacher would even voice such a sentiment. "But Kimberly Peters told me someone — a man — called her to say I was spreading rumors about her and her aunt. And let me assure you, I have not been."

"How do you know she was telling you the truth about the call?"

Tricia opened her mouth to protest, and then just as quickly shut it.

Stella nodded. "I'd be skeptical of anything *that* one tells you."

"But she knows more than she's telling."

"More than she's telling *you.* That's not to say she hasn't spoken to others."

Sheriff Adams in particular, Tricia thought. Still, that was good — if it meant solving the crime and getting her store back open.

"If all this is true, what could have happened that triggered the killer? If she wanted the glory, why wait until the last book was published to take revenge?"

Stella looked like she was about to say something, then thought better of it and shook her head. "I'd be careful about mentioning Zoë's lack of creative talent and the idea she might not have written the books."

"But wouldn't that be a credible motive for the killing? Giving the true author credit for those books?"

"Yes, but getting the credit will also land that person in jail. There's nothing to be gained — unless Zoë was killed out of spite." Stella shook her head. "Whoever killed Zoë will do everything she can to remain anonymous. If I were you, dear, I'd let the sheriff handle this one. You wouldn't want to be the killer's next victim."

EIGHT

It was almost noon by the time Tricia returned from Stella's house. She opened the door to the Cookery and Angelica pounced upon her immediately. "Big news," she cried. Tricia could practically feel the waves of exhilaration emanating from her sister.

Tricia wiggled out of her jacket. "Tell me about it before you jump out of your skin."

"Bob just called. They've decided to change the whole dedication ceremony on Saturday."

"Change how?" Tricia asked, heading for the closet at the back of the store.

"It'll now be a memorial service for Zoë Carter."

Tricia stopped. "What does that mean for the vendors?"

"Vendors?" Angelica said, confused.

"Yes. The dedication was supposed to be a celebration of books and how they saved

Stoneham. It'll look pretty tacky if we're all set up around the square selling books, hot dogs, and fried dough. It sounds more like a circus than a memorial service."

Angelica frowned. "Oh. Well, I'm sure Bob thought about that. He's a genius when it comes to PR. But don't you see, this is a great opportunity for you. Ginny said she'd ordered extra copies of Zoë's books. You'll make out like a bandit."

"I don't know about that."

"Um, Bob — or rather the Chamber — was wondering if you'd be willing to call some of Zoë's publishing colleagues and invite them to the ceremony. Like maybe Zoë's agent."

Tricia was about to blurt a definitive "No," then thought better of it. What better way to find out more about Zoë than from people inside the publishing industry? "Maybe you're right, Ange. Bob just might be a genius after all."

Since Ginny had gone out for a sandwich and was unavailable to talk about their Saturday plans, Tricia hiked the stairs to Angelica's loft apartment. A chatty Miss Marple met her as she opened the door, admonishing her for leaving her alone once again.

"I know, I know. But Angelica serves food in her store. No cats allowed."

"Yow!" Miss Marple protested.

"I'll relay your dissatisfaction to the Health Department," Tricia promised.

Miss Marple followed her to the kitchen, and Tricia filled her bowl with kitty treats.

With the cat placated, Tricia picked up Angelica's kitchen extension before scoping out the fridge in search of sustenance for herself. Despite its being lunch hour, Tricia called and found Bob in his office at the Chamber of Commerce. "Hi, Bob, Angelica said you wanted to talk to me about the dedication ceremony," she said, and it was no effort to keep a smile in her voice.

"Yes, the Chamber held an emergency meeting on it this morning, sorry you weren't able to make it —" Make it? She hadn't even known about it. But since she rarely went to Chamber meetings anyway, it wasn't a big deal. "Changing our focus to include a memorial ceremony for Zoë Carter is an opportunity we, as her adopted hometown, didn't feel we could pass up. And since we've already got everything set up for the dedication anyway, it's a win-win situation."

"But what about the words carved on the statue?" she asked, looking past the scampi leftovers to root around in the back of the fridge. It wasn't really a statue. Tricia had seen drawings of the proposed piece. A big block of marble with a carved open book on the top.

"Turns out they weren't able to do the engraving before the ceremony on Saturday, so we can still change what it says. How's that for luck?"

Tacky. But Tricia wasn't about to argue the point. She withdrew a bowl of what looked like homemade soup, removed the plastic cover, and sniffed. It still smelled good. "Ange said you wanted me to contact Zoë's colleagues," she said, and opened a drawer to find a spoon.

"Yes. They thought you, as a mystery bookseller, would have a better feel for who in the publishing world should be contacted."

Oops! Deborah had suggested Tricia do the same thing the day before — but with everything else that was going on, Tricia had completely forgotten about it. She put the bowl in the microwave and punched in ninety seconds. "Did you speak to Kimberly Peters about this?"

"Following in her aunt's footsteps, she declined to be involved, although she did say she'd at least show up," he said, his voice

146

conveying his disapproval. "Will you help us, Tricia?"

"Bob, I would love to. How soon do you need to know?"

"We'd like to have the guest list set by tomorrow. Is that a problem?"

"No. In fact, I'll start making calls as soon as I get off the phone with you."

"Thanks, Tricia. This is a big help to the Chamber. And I'll see what I can do to nudge Wendy Adams about reopening your shop. She's stubborn, but she can see reason when it's pointed out to her."

"I'd appreciate that, Bob. Thanks."

She took notes as he repeated the details surrounding the dedication, which pretty much matched what she remembered from the Chamber's previous communications.

"I'll get right on this and give you an update later today."

"Thanks, Tricia."

Tricia replaced the phone on its cradle and resisted the urge to rub her hands together with pleasure. Then reality set in. How the blazes was she supposed to get a hold of, let alone assure the attendance of, Zoë's colleagues? There was only one thing to do — hit the Internet to try to find some answers.

The microwave stopped, giving a resounding beep, beep, beep, to let her know her lunch was ready, but Tricia was too hyped to eat. Instead, she went in search of her laptop computer, set it on the kitchen island, and connected to the Internet. Her first stop, Zoë's Web site. She checked out the media page and found pay dirt. Zoë's agent was none other than Artemus Hamilton. Tricia had met the short, balding man several times at cocktail parties during her years in Manhattan.

A search of the Yahoo! Yellow Pages gave her Hamilton's office number, and she eagerly dialed the phone. An answering machine picked up after the third ring, directing her to leave a message. "This is Tricia Miles, owner of the Haven't Got a Clue bookstore in Stoneham, New Hampshire. I'm sorry to say that your client Zoë Carter died in my store on Tuesday night. Stoneham is having a memorial service in her honor, and we wanted to invite —"

The phone clicked in her ear. "Ms. Miles? This is Artemus Hamilton. Thank you for calling."

The man himself. No doubt he'd received some crank calls, or possibly had been hounded by the press since Zoë's death and found it necessary to screen his calls. Or perhaps his assistant was out to lunch and he was monitoring his own phone.

"I don't suppose you remember me, Mr. Hamilton. We met several years ago at one of Sylvia Cranston's parties."

"Sorry. I meet a lot of people." Oh, well. That was no doubt true. "What were you saying about a memorial service?"

"Since Zoë was a longtime resident of Stoneham, we naturally want to honor her. We hope you and some of Zoë's other colleagues could join us on Saturday for a memorial service."

"That's odd. I spoke with Zoë's niece this morning, and she said nothing about a memorial service."

"I'm sure at the time she wasn't aware of the Chamber of Commerce's plans. You know Kimberly Peters?"

"Yes, of course. I had dinner with Zoë and Kimberly on a number of occasions. Delightful young woman." He must've seen a side of Kimberly she hadn't bothered to show to the citizens of Stoneham. "What time is the ceremony?" he asked.

"Eleven o'clock. It'll be outside, as there's also a statue dedication."

"How on earth did you get a statue of Zoë made so quickly?"

"It's actually a statue of a . . . a book." Boy, that sounded lame.

"A book?" he repeated in disbelief.

"Yes. It's really very nice," she lied. She hadn't actually seen it. "It's a big block of white marble with an opened stone book on the top." She flinched at her own words. It sounded ridiculous even to her.

"Eleven's rather early to come up from New York. Perhaps I should arrive the night before. Is there anywhere decent to stay in Stoneham?"

"I can recommend the Brookview Inn."

"Can you e-mail me the particulars? I'll have my assistant book me a room as soon as she comes back from lunch."

"Fine."

"Where can I reach you in case I need to call?"

Tricia gave him Angelica's number and that of her cell phone. "We'd also like to invite Zoë's editor. Would you be willing to share that number, or would you talk to him or her and have them contact me?"

"I'll speak to him, and if he's interested he can get in touch with you. Thank you again for the invitation. I'll be in touch," Hamilton said and ended the call.

Tricia got her facts together concerning the inn and e-mailed Hamilton's office, then checked that her phone was fully charged before heading down to the Cookery, where

150

she found an impatient Ginny waiting for her.

"Oh, good. You're back," Ginny said, and glanced over her shoulder to see if Angelica was close by and listening in. "Whatever you said to Angelica must've worked. She's hardly yelled at us at all today. Makes me wonder when I'll feel the stab of pain in my back when she reverts to type."

"Ginny," Tricia chided.

"Oh, sorry," Ginny hastily apologized. "I keep forgetting she's your sister. Anyway, while there's a lull, we'd better go over the plans for Saturday. Did you know they were changing the focus of the celebration?"

"Yes. I've already talked to Bob Kelly about it, and he asked me to invite some of Zoë's colleagues. Her agent will be here on Saturday, possibly her editor as well. I'm waiting to hear."

"That's great. Several members of the Tuesday Night Book Club have stopped by or called to ask if we should do something special in honor of Zoë."

"You mean like flowers or something?"

She nodded. "They're taking up a collection and thought it would be a nice touch, since most of them were among the last people to see her alive."

And Tricia had been the one to find her

151

dead. She gave a little shudder and tried not to think about it.

"On our end," Ginny continued, "Mr. Everett managed to snag the UPS man and signed for the books for the dedication on Saturday. So at least we can set up shop and get a little income for the week."

Tricia glanced around the store, spotted Mr. Everett speaking with a customer, and smiled. "I am so proud of you two. You've made this whole unpleasant situation much easier to take."

"Thanks, Tricia. It's nice to hear a kind word." Ginny leveled a pointed glance at Angelica's back.

"Has the sheriff or her team been anywhere near Haven't Got a Clue today?" Tricia asked.

Ginny shook her head. "It doesn't seem like she's doing much in the way of investigating, as far as I can see, so why won't she let us reopen?"

"Pure and plain nastiness."

"Speaking of which," Ginny said, lowering her voice, her gaze wandering to a disapproving Angelica, who waited on a customer at the register. "Did you know Angelica threw away all of the gorgeous cookies Nikki sent over yesterday?"

Tricia frowned. "Why?"

"I think she was jealous. She said she wasn't going to serve someone else's products in her store."

Angelica had made that perfectly clear the day before. "Well, they weren't sent here to be served in her store," Tricia said testily. "They were sent to me."

Ginny giggled. "I hope you don't mind, but I grabbed a few before she tossed them in the Dumpster out back. I wrapped them up for later. Do you want a couple?"

Tricia sighed. "With everything that's been going on, I've kind of lost my appetite. You enjoy."

Ginny nodded. "So how are your inquiries going?"

Tricia looked around the shop, making sure no customers were in listening range. "Don't say a word, because I have no proof . . . but several people I've talked to don't think Zoë was the author of the Jess and Addie *Forever* series."

Ginny's eyes widened. "That's very interesting. And certainly a motive for murder."

"Exactly."

"Any hints on who did write them?" she asked, eagerly.

Tricia shook her head. "Uh-uh. Not until I have more information."

"Darn! Is there anything I can do to help you?"

"Thanks, but no. In the meantime, I need to talk to Kimberly again. To see if I can pin her down." Tricia remembered what Frannie had said about Deborah and Kimberly possibly being classmates. Deborah and Ginny both had long hair. Could she have gotten them mixed up? "You weren't in high school with Kimberly, were you?"

Ginny nodded. "But I didn't know her. She was a senior when I was a freshman — a much lower form of life. Eventually we all knew her by reputation, as the class slut."

Which supported what Lois Kerr had said. "Do you think any of her friends still live in Stoneham?"

"What friends? She slept with every decent-looking guy in the school. Not many of the girls would even talk to her."

How sad. Did she act out just to get attention — attention she didn't receive from Zoë?

"I'd like to call her, but of course Zoë's phone number is unlisted, and all my contact information is locked up inside Haven't Got a Clue."

Ginny pulled a little notebook out of her Cookery apron pocket. Tricia recognized it as one she usually carried in her Haven't

154

Got a Clue apron. "I've got Zoë's Stoneham number. Why don't you call Kimberly now?"

Tricia smiled. "Remember that bonus I mentioned earlier? It just got bigger."

Ginny positively beamed.

NINE

Tricia was glad Kimberly answered the phone after only two rings, though she quickly made it clear she had no desire to discuss her aunt. That is, until Tricia suggested they meet for dinner; then suddenly Kimberly was only too happy to oblige. They made plans to meet at the Bookshelf Diner at seven.

Tricia adopted her bravest smile and prepared to spend the next five hours hand-selling — she nearly shuddered — cookbooks.

But before she had a chance to dive into the world of cookery, a Milford Florist Shop truck pulled up outside and double-parked in front of Angelica's store. Tricia watched without interest as the driver got out, went to the back of the truck, and opened the gate. He consulted a clipboard, then pawed through his inventory and withdrew a large white box. He jogged to the door and opened it. "Delivery," he called.

Angelica rushed forward, her face flushed with pleasure. "Oh, that Bob! He's such a sweetheart." Her grin soon disappeared as she looked at the card on the top of the box. She turned, annoyed. "They're for you, Trish. Seems to be your week to receive gifts."

Tricia stepped forward, unsure she wanted to accept the box. They had to be from Russ, and she wasn't sure she was ready to accept an apology. She took the card, opened it, and frowned. *Please forgive me. Love, Russ.*

Love? He hadn't uttered that word to her in person.

She set the card aside and removed the red ribbon that bound the box. Drawing back the green tissue, she gasped. She'd expected roses, but instead found nine perfect calla lilies — her favorite. Had she ever told him? How else could he have known?

She glanced at Angelica, who seemed reluctant to meet her gaze. Was there a conspiracy in the works?

"Ooooh," Ginny cooed, coming up behind her. "Someone thinks a lot of you."

"Possibly," she said, trying to keep her voice neutral, and lifted the card to read it once again.

"I think I've got a vase in back," Angelica said, and disappeared to find it.

"Are you going to call him?" Ginny asked.

"Who says they're from a 'him'?"

"Oh, come on, Tricia, they've got to be from Russ."

Angelica returned with a tall, clear, pressed-glass vase. She stopped at the little sink in her demonstration area to fill it with water, then set it on the counter. "You are going to call and thank him, I hope."

Tricia blinked innocently. "Who?"

"Russ."

She frowned. "Why does everyone assume these flowers are from Russ?"

"Well, who else have you been dating for the past five months?"

Tricia turned up her nose. "I have a lot of admirers."

"Not in this burg," Angelica quipped.

The door opened, and several customers entered. Angelica and Ginny both sprang into action, leaving Tricia at the sales counter with her flowers. She lifted them one by one and placed them in the vase.

Love, Russ.

She didn't love him, at least not yet, but, she admitted to herself, she was quite fond of him. She didn't like there being tension between them. Still, she didn't want him to think he could buy her affection with a vase of flowers — beautiful though they might be.

Love, Russ.

She glanced around, saw Angelica, Ginny, and Mr. Everett were busy, and turned back to her lilies, allowing herself a small smile.

It was after six, and the sun hadn't yet begun to set as Mr. Everett buttoned his coat, getting ready to leave for the evening. Ginny had grabbed her purse and jacket. "Are we coming back here tomorrow?" she inquired, her voice almost a whine.

"I didn't hear from the sheriff that I could open tomorrow — so I guess we're stuck here at least one more day."

Ginny let out a long breath and almost looked like she wanted to cry.

Since there were no customers in the store, Angelica flounced around the bookshelves with her lamb's wool duster, humming happily.

"Today wasn't so bad, was it?" Tricia asked.

Mr. Everett looked to Ginny, who seemed all too ready to speak for the two of them. "No, but that's only because you were here. You will be here tomorrow, won't you?"

"As far as I know."

"I shall say good night now," Mr. Everett said. He called to Angelica. "Good night, Mrs. Prescott."

Angelica looked up from her dusting, and frowned. "That's Ms. Miles," she reminded him. "Good night. And good night to you, too, Ginny!"

"Good night," Ginny growled, and turned her back on Angelica. "I'd better leave before she finds one more thing for me to —"

"Oh, before you leave —" Angelica said, hurrying to the front of the store.

"Go!" Tricia ordered, and Ginny and Mr. Everett quickly made their escape.

"Hey," Angelica protested, "I wanted Ginny to post a couple of bills for me."

"I'll do it when I leave to go to dinner. I'm meeting Kimberly at the Bookshelf Diner."

"You're not eating here?"

"Kimberly insisted we meet there. I want to please her. If she's happy, she might be more open with me about her aunt."

"What more do you need to know about the woman? She's dead. Seems like you've talked to everyone in town who knew her. Whoever killed her isn't going to just walk up to you and say, 'Hello, I killed Zoë

160

Carter.' "

"Have you seen Sheriff Adams — or even a patrol car — roll by even once today, let alone enter Haven't Got a Clue?"

"No, but what's that got to do with — ?"

"As long as Wendy Adams isn't breaking a sweat to investigate this murder, it's up to me to do all I can. I want my store to reopen. *Now!*"

Angelica backed off. "Okay, okay!"

The door opened and Nikki Brimfield stepped inside. "Am I interrupting something?"

"Not at all," Angelica said with relief.

Tricia remembered yesterday's box of goodies and flushed with guilt. "Nikki — I meant to drop by and thank you for the cookies. That was so sweet of you."

Nikki waved a hand in dismissal. "I just felt so bad for you. What rotten luck. And I see the sheriff still hasn't let you reopen. Are you on for tomorrow?"

"No, which is what we were just discussing when —"

The door opened, the bell above it jingling. There stood Russ.

Angelica gave Nikki a nudge. "Let me show you this marvelous new cake cookbook that just came in," she said and grabbed Nikki's arm, pulling her away, apparently

161

willing to temporarily forget that Nikki competed for her customers.

Russ didn't even seem to know they were there. He stepped forward. "Hi, Trish," he said shyly.

"Hi," she answered.

His eyes were drawn to the flowers still sitting on the sales counter. "Oh, good. They arrived okay."

"Yes, thank you, they're lovely."

"Like you."

Their gazes held for a few long seconds, then Tricia turned to admire the flowers. She picked up the card. "I wondered about this. Did you mean it?"

He studied the card in her hand for a moment, then his gaze met hers. "I'm pretty sure I did."

"Pretty sure?" she asked.

"That's about as definite as I can be right now. How about you?"

"I'm not at all sure, but I'm willing to hang around to see if it happens."

He took her hands and pulled her forward, pressing a gentle kiss against her lips before pulling away. "Can we try dinner again?"

The thought made her throat constrict. "On one condition. No more tuna noodle casseroles — ever."

"I think I could pull that off." He smiled,

and tugged on her hand. "Get your coat. Let's go."

She stood firm. "I can't. I promised Kimberly Peters I'd have dinner with her tonight." Disappointment shadowed his eyes for a few brief seconds, and then they flashed. "No," Tricia said resolutely, "you're not invited."

"I didn't say a word," he protested.

"No, but I could read the thought balloon over your head. You're still working on your story," she accused.

"It's not much of a story until something breaks. Did you notice the Boston and Manchester TV vans have left town, although they might be back for the statue dedication on Saturday? Bob Kelly has sent press releases to half the East Coast news outlets."

"Only half?"

"He's still got another day," Russ added dryly. "When can I see you again?"

"I'm not doing anything for lunch tomorrow."

"I was thinking more along the lines of dinner, remember. How about Saturday?"

"Saturday's fine."

The corners of his mouth lifted. "And then maybe . . ."

"Maybe what?"

"We could . . . become friends all over again."

She felt the edges of the card still clutched in her hand. *Love, Russ.*

Out the corner of her eye, Tricia noticed Nikki and Angelica peeking around a book-shelf, eavesdropping. She cleared her throat, and they disappeared. Turning her attention back to Russ, she said, "Saturday night it is."

The Bookshelf Diner pulled out all the stops for its evening crowd, offering early bird specials and even lighting the miniature hurricane oil lamps that sat on each table. Kimberly was already seated in the last booth when Tricia arrived. She settled in the seat across from her, and shrugged out of her jacket. "Have you been waiting long?"

"No," Kimberly said, barely looking up from the laminated menu she consulted. She ran her finger down the list of appetiz-ers. "I haven't had a cigarette in two days, and I'm starved." She looked up. "You did say I was your guest, didn't you?"

She quit smoking? Obviously she wasn't stressed about the death of her aunt. "Of course."

A nasty little smile twisted Kimberly's lips. "So what was it you wanted to know about dear Aunt Zoë?"

So much for small talk. And Tricia wasn't sure she was ready to discuss what she knew — or at least thought she knew. "Several people I've spoken to wondered about your aunt's unsold novels." Not the truth, but not a total lie, either.

Again Kimberly looked up from her menu, her expression darkening. "Unsold?"

"It's a known fact that the first efforts of most authors usually aren't up to publishing standards. And for Zoë to burst out of the gates and not only win *the* major mystery award and hit best-sellerdom, she had to have a few 'practice' or trunk novels squirreled away. You know, things that she never thought would appear in print."

Kimberly ran her tongue across her lower lip. "Not that I'm aware of."

"But you were her assistant. Didn't she confide in you about her early work? Her dreams and plans for her future work?"

Before Kimberly could answer, Eugenia, the perky blonde, college-age night waitress, approached the table. "Good evening, ladies. What can I get you to drink?"

"I'll have a glass of the house red," Tricia said, noticing Eugenia had added a pierced brow to her already pierced nose and ears.

"Me, too," Kimberly echoed.

Eugenia nodded. "I'll be back to take your orders in a few minutes."

Tricia waited until she was out of earshot before speaking again. "The unsold books," she prompted.

Kimberly's attention was again focused on the menu. "I'd have to search her files. She may have left something in one of the file cabinets. She did most of her work in the Carolina house these past few years. Maybe I'll check when I get back home."

"You don't consider Stoneham your home?"

Kimberly looked up sharply. "This dump? Not on your life. I hate the winters. And besides, who can you meet here?"

If it was husband material Kimberly was talking about, Tricia had to agree. Most of the booksellers were married, and as Lois Kerr had pointed out, the majority of young people in the village seemed to move to Boston, Portland, or New York as soon as they could escape. "When will you be going home?"

"When I can find the gas money. All Zoë's accounts have been frozen until probate is complete. I'm not her executor," she reminded Tricia. "She didn't trust me enough for that."

"Who *is* her executor?"

166

"Until recently, it was her agent. Now it's some lawyer. At least he's given me permission to stay in either of the houses until they're sold. But it makes more sense to close up this one as soon as possible, since that's what she wanted. I never intend to live in, let alone visit, Stoneham ever again."

Why had Zoë changed executors? Did she have a falling-out with her agent? He'd sounded eager to attend the memorial service. She shook the thought away. If nothing else, it would look good for him to be there. But whom did he want to look good for?

Eugenia returned with their wine, and soon held her pen over her pad, ready to write. "All set to order?"

Kimberly nodded. "I'll have the twice-baked potato appetizer, French onion soup, the chicken pot pie with a side of mashed potatoes, and a slice of the cherry pie. Oh, and a Diet Coke."

Tricia folded her menu, wondering how someone as thin as Kimberly could eat such great quantities of food. She sighed. "I'll have the Cobb salad plate with peppercorn dressing on the side. Thanks, Eugenia."

Eugenia collected the menus, nodded, and headed for the kitchen.

Tricia addressed Kimberly once more. "At

167

the signing, you made a big point of reminding your aunt about taking her medication. Why?"

Kimberly shrugged. "The old girl was diabetic. She'd been known to keel over if her sugar dropped. We hadn't had dinner that night — just ran out of time. I'd gotten so I could pretty much gauge when she was going to need another insulin shot."

That sounded reasonable. Tricia thought about the big question that had weighed heavy on her mind. Despite Stella's warning, she decided to test Kimberly. "Your aunt told my customers she was done with the Jess and Addie series. Had she started another?"

Kimberly hesitated. "No. Like Margaret Mitchell and Harper Lee, my aunt only had one set of characters whose stories she cared to tell. Only in her case, instead of just one novel, it came out in a five-book arc."

"I've been talking with a number of people around the village. Some people find it hard to believe Zoë actually wrote the Jess and Addie mystery series."

Kimberly raised an eyebrow but said nothing, her expression bland.

Tricia decided to try a different approach. "You wouldn't want to tell me why you were so angry at your aunt the night of her death, would you?"

"For just that day, or do you want the full ten-year list?"

"Just that day will do," Tricia said.

Kimberly leaned forward, resting her arms on the table. "My aunt was very wealthy, but you wouldn't know it to see the way we've lived."

"But she had two houses."

"Two cheap houses. I worked my ass off on this book tour, but she couldn't — or wouldn't — acknowledge it. Good press? Oh, that was from the publisher — not from the interviews I lined up for her, or the coaching I gave her. She didn't like to fly. Who drove her ten thousand miles in the last two months?"

"Why didn't you leave?"

Kimberly hesitated. "Let's just say I had my reasons. But I was quickly running out of them. In fact, just before we came to your store, I told her I was ready to walk. She called my bluff, but not before dangling another carrot in front of me."

"And that carrot was?"

Eugenia chose that moment to set the appetizer in front of Kimberly, who plunged her fork into it with zeal.

"Would you like the soup with your entrée?" the waitress asked.

Kimberly shook her head, already wolfing down a bite. "Bring it now, thanks."

Eugenia shot Tricia a look that asked "What gives?" but Tricia could only shrug. She looked back at Kimberly. "Sure thing," she said, and headed back for the kitchen.

"What did Zoë offer you to keep you from leaving?" Tricia asked.

Kimberly shoveled in another forkful of potato before she set down her fork. She took a sip of her wine. "That's none of your business. But I'll be honest with you about one thing, Tricia. I'm broke. Flat busted. There's no food in Zoë's house, and I have no idea how I'm going to manage. I've even contemplated snagging one of those pesky geese roaming the village and roasting it. That would probably feed me for a week." She gave a half-hearted laugh, but soon sobered. "Until probate is settled, I've got a roof over my head but no income. This food," she pointed at her plate, "will have to last me a few days. After that . . ." Her mouth trembled, and her desperation was nearly palpable. "I don't know what I'll do."

Tricia resisted the temptation to reach out and comfort Kimberly, who probably wouldn't have appreciated it anyway. Kimberly's despair wasn't grief for her aunt — more for her own circumstances. And what could Zoë have possibly offered to keep her in a situation she found so miserable?

"What about the manuscripts? Can you tell me about them?" Tricia asked.

"What do you expect me to say?"

That Zoë didn't write them! she wanted to scream. Instead, Tricia struggled to keep her voice level. "What was Zoë's writing process? Did she write them on a typewriter or a computer — or even longhand?"

Kimberly stabbed her potato with her fork, and exhaled a long, slow breath. Evidently that question had hit a nerve. "I believe the original manuscripts were written on an old manual typewriter. I wasn't around when they were actually typed, so I can't be sure."

"Are you saying all the manuscripts were written before you came to live with your aunt?"

Again, Kimberly hesitated. "I was seventeen years old when I came to live with Zoë. My parents had just died. I'd never been close to my aunt, and I didn't much care about her or her hobbies. I didn't become interested in the books until my sophomore year in college, when I changed my major from humanities to English lit. One of our assignments was to read the first *Forever* book." She paused, and took a breath. "It changed my life. Those characters were so beautifully drawn, they inspired me. And that's when I first thought that I might want to write a book, too."

Tricia raised an eyebrow, surprised at Kimberly's candor. "Go on," she encouraged.

"Zoë was delighted I took an interest. She hired me during vacations to key in her manuscripts, read over her contracts, and help with publicity. It got her publisher off her back, and it was a great way for me to learn about the publishing industry. In some ways we actually became a team."

"But there was always a bit of animosity between you?"

Kimberly's gaze dipped, and she scraped cheese and flesh from the potato skin. "Zoë was a really private person. There was a lot she never wanted to talk about, things she didn't want to reveal, even to me. She'd be pissed to know I'm talking to you about her."

But that didn't answer Tricia's question, and she got the feeling they could dance around the subject for days and Kimberly wouldn't reveal what it was that Zoë had kept hidden all these years. She swallowed, abandoning that line of inquiry. "Tell me about those threatening letters Zoë received that you mentioned the other day."

Kimberly sobered, and then let out a resigned breath. "I only found out about it a few weeks ago, when a new batch of them came in. Apparently, she'd been getting them off and on for years."

"What made you think the blackmailer could be here in Stoneham?"

"Most of the letters were postmarked from Milford or Nashua."

"Did Zoë worry about them? Is that why she finally put the house here in Stoneham up for sale?"

"No. She blew them off as from a crank. Authors get a lot of oddball fan mail and solicitations. Someone always wants you to look at a manuscript or to give them your literary agent's name. Zoë hadn't been back to Stoneham in over a year, and she was tired of paying for utilities and for someone to look in on the house now and then."

"How did Zoë respond to these letters?"

"She ignored them."

"Did she keep the letters?"

Kimberly shook her head. "Just the last batch. Sheriff Adams asked me about them the night Zoë was killed. I had to turn them over to her. She seems to think they'll lead to the murderer."

Tricia bit her lip to keep from saying,

"Well, duh!" Then again, she wasn't sure Wendy Adams was capable of solving a petty robbery, let alone a murder. "Too bad. I would've loved to have seen them."

Kimberly's mouth twitched. "I thought you might say that. I brought copies." She reached for her purse.

Talk about a surprise. But still . . . "Why give them to me?"

"Because, besides the press, you're the only one who seems to care what happened to my aunt."

"Funny. I wasn't sure *you* did."

Kimberly leaned forward. "I didn't like my aunt very much. She could've helped me a lot more than she did. She interfered with friendships I'd made and kept me from seeing people I enjoyed. But she was all I had, and I guess I feel some kind of weird twisted loyalty to her." She brought out the papers. "If you don't want them, I can always get rid of them." She pulled the little oil lamp to the center of the table, removed the hurricane glass, and waved the papers over the flame.

Tricia's heart pounded. "No!"

The old Kimberly was back, and flashed another wicked smile. For a moment Tricia was afraid she'd actually set the pages on fire. Then the smile faded. She placed them on the table and shoved them toward Tricia.

Tricia swallowed, her hands shaking as she picked up the folded stack. Kimberly had just earned the price of her gargantuan dinner. Tricia read the first note and frowned.

An honest woman repays her debts. You've found riches in your new career, leaving behind those whose financial life you helped ruin.

Tricia scanned through the several sheets of paper. They were all like that, random sentences pointing the finger of guilt, but not specifying the crime nor demanding a set amount of cash.

But worst of all, she recognized the handwriting.

TEN

Tricia swallowed, and tried to keep her hands from shaking. "Can I keep these, or at least one of these?"

"You can have them all," Kimberly said. "I made more than one set of copies."

"Thank you."

Tricia couldn't tear her eyes from the familiar script. How many times had she seen that spidery scrawl on book requests and other forms at Haven't Got a Clue? It belonged to Mr. Everett.

She scanned the lines again. No, he'd made no mention of the books themselves, didn't accuse her of stealing another's work — just that she had unpaid debts. Why would he believe Zoë Carter owed him money? Had she known he was the one sending the letters? Was she shocked when she showed up at Haven't Got a Clue and found Mr. Everett at her signing?

Tricia thought back to that night. Mr.

Everett had barely spoken to Zoë. She couldn't swear on a Bible, but she also didn't remember him being in the vicinity of the washroom at any time before Zoë's body was found. In fact, he and Grace Harris had been pretty much inseparable that entire evening — as they usually were since they'd started . . . well, dating didn't seem the right word — since they'd renewed their friendship over the past winter.

"Are you okay?" Kimberly asked, pausing in her eating marathon. "You look a little pale."

"Perfectly fine," Tricia said, but she pushed her plate away. She'd completely lost her appetite.

Eugenia paused at the table. "Everything all right?"

Kimberly pushed her plates of uneaten food toward the waitress. "You want to box these up? I'll be taking them home."

"Sure thing." She placed the check face-down on the table, picked up the plates, and headed for the kitchen.

Kimberly pushed the check toward Tricia. "Thanks for feeding me for a couple of days. Got any ideas on how I can eat for the next six months?" she added snidely.

"I'm not your enemy," Tricia said.

"Yeah, and you're not my friend, either,"

Kimberly said. She stood up.

"If you can stand to play the part of the bereaved, you might be able to milk brunch out of the Chamber of Commerce on Saturday. It sure wouldn't hurt you to show a little respect for your dead aunt."

Kimberly raised an eyebrow. "Not a bad idea," she said, and managed a wan smile. "After all, I did minor in drama in college." She got up from the table, intercepting Eugenia and the bag of leftovers, and left the diner.

Tricia drained the last of the wine from her glass. If she'd thought her dinner with Kimberly was tough, an even worse situation awaited her — talking to Mr. Everett. She paid the bill, leaving Eugenia a generous tip, and headed for the door, dreading what was yet to come.

Tricia had never been to Mr. Everett's home before, although, as his employer, she knew his address by heart. She drove past the darkened house and saw that his car was missing from the drive. On impulse, she turned into a neighbor's driveway and turned around, then drove across the village to another, more impressive house in a more expensive neighborhood. She well remembered the pseudo-Tudor home from her previous visits, only now spring flowers nodded cheerily along the neatly tended walk, quite a difference from the forlorn and unkempt appearance it had sported the previous fall.

Mr. Everett's car sat in the drive, and the warm glow of lights made Grace Harris's home look inviting and friendly. Tricia parked at the curb, marched up the walk, and rang the bell. When no answer came in thirty or forty seconds, she rang again. Light burst from the copper sconces on either side of the great oak door, and it opened.

"Tricia! My goodness, what are you doing here?" Grace asked. "Come in. Come in from the cold."

Tricia entered the foyer, which had also undergone a transformation. A vase of fresh flowers graced the marble-topped table, and the polished floor positively sparkled. "May I take your coat?" Grace inquired.

"No, thanks. I really came to speak to Mr. Everett, if you don't mind."

"Certainly. William is in the living room. Follow me."

Tricia already knew the way. The last time she'd seen the room, it had been in a state of dishevelment. Grace's treasures had now been restored to their former places, and a gas fire glowed brightly in the once-dark hearth.

"Ms. Miles," Mr. Everett said, and stood at her arrival. He'd donned a beige sweater with suede patches at the elbows, and held a well-worn leather book in his heavily veined hands. A pot of coffee and two cups sat on a silver tray on the coffee table.

"Can I get you — ?"

Tricia waved a hand to forestall an invitation to join them for coffee. "I need to speak with you about a very important matter. May I sit down?"

"Go right ahead," Grace said, directing Tricia into one of the plush, brocade-covered wing chairs. Grace sat next to Mr. Everett on the loveseat, taking his hand.

"You've come about the letters, haven't you?" Mr. Everett asked.

Tricia nodded. She reached into the pocket of her jacket and brought out the copies, handing them to the elderly gent.

His gaze met hers, his eyes worried. "Are you going to fire me?"

Tricia blinked. "Of course not! But I suspect you may need to speak to an attorney. As your employer, I would be glad to vouch for you and help in any way I can."

"That won't be necessary," Grace said, her face growing pale.

180

"These aren't the originals," Mr. Everett said, shuffling through the pages.

"I'm afraid the sheriff has those. Kimberly Peters turned them over to her the night Zoë Carter died. I don't for a minute believe you killed her, but the sheriff hasn't been known for listening to reason."

Mr. Everett continued to look at one of the letters in his hand.

"Would you like me to explain, dear?" Grace asked.

He shook his head. "If you will recall, Ms. Miles, I once owned the only grocery store in Stoneham. My accountant used to chide me for giving credit to customers. Over the years I helped out many people who were down on their luck. Zoë Carter was one of them. After she lost her job at Trident Log Homes, she was in need of financial help. She was proud, but she had her niece to think of. She asked for and received credit from me."

"To the tune of over two thousand dollars," Grace piped in.

"It wasn't a lot of money, but when I was struggling to keep the store open, I asked all my customers to try to pay back at least some of what they owed me. Most of them rewarded me by shopping at my competition in Milford. Ms. Carter was among them. After she became a best-selling author, I approached her a number of times about repaying her debt. Even though the store had closed, I myself needed cash when my Alice took sick."

"I wish you'd come to me, William," Grace said, real tenderness in her voice.

"I didn't want charity. I only wanted to be repaid by someone who could now afford to do so. I never threatened Zoë Carter; I tried to appeal to her conscience. Sadly, I don't believe she had one."

"So she knew it was you who sent the letters."

"Of course. I always put my return address stickers on the envelopes — that was so she'd know where to send the money. I didn't even ask for interest — just what was owed me."

"And did you continue to send the letters even after your wife passed?"

He nodded. "Once or twice a year. Sadly, I can't live on only what you pay me. And Social Security only goes so far."

"I understand."

The silenced lengthened, only the ticking of the grandfather clock in the corner and the hiss of the gas fire making any sound in the quiet room. "You should tell the sheriff about this, if only so that she doesn't waste precious time when she could be going after the real killer. And I'm sure we both want to see Haven't Got a Clue reopen as quickly as possible."

Grace patted her friend's hand. "I'll call my attorney first thing in the morning and get his advice."

Mr. Everett shook his head. "No, Grace, I can't let you —"

"This is one time I won't let your pride keep you from accepting my help. You need competent legal advice, and I'm sure young Mr. Livingston will be glad to help you."

Tricia stood, unwilling to get into the middle of that discussion. "I'll leave it to you, then, to contact the sheriff."

Mr. Everett nodded, and then he, too, stood.

"I'll explain to Angelica why you won't be at work tomorrow. Between Ginny and me, we should be able to keep her happy."

"I shall apologize to your sister myself, perhaps on Saturday. Thank you again for not firing me, Ms. Miles. I enjoy working at Haven't Got a Clue and would miss the books, you, Ginny, and Miss Marple."

"Thank you, Mr. Everett. I'm glad you feel that way."

As Mr. Everett was not a touchy-feely kind of person, Tricia restrained herself from reaching out to hug him and instead extended her hand, which he solemnly shook.

Grace led Tricia back to the big oak door. "Thank you for looking out for William, Tricia. He's a good man. He's suffered a lot, what with losing his business and then his wife."

"Yes, I know." Tricia gave the old lady a smile. "I hope your sister is feeling better."

Grace frowned, looking puzzled. "Sister?"

"Yes, I understand she wasn't feeling well."

"Tricia, where did you get the idea I have a sister? I was an only child."

"But — ?" Tricia stopped herself. She wasn't crazy. Mr. Everett had told her Grace had left town the day after Zoë's murder to nurse an ailing sister.

If that was a lie . . . could she believe anything the old man told her?

Tricia parked her car in the municipal lot and walked the block and a half to her own store on autopilot, preoccupied with everything she'd learned that evening. She even had her key out, ready to open Haven't Got a Clue's front door, when the crime scene tape across it reminded her she was still shut out.

She turned, walked to the Cookery, and

took out that key. Entering, she locked up behind her and walked through the quiet store and up the stairs to Angelica's loft apartment, wishing she was taking the steps to her own home.

Upon opening the door, an eight-pound bundle of gray fur pounced, meowing frantically. "Miss Marple. Did you miss your Mum?"

"Yow!" the cat replied emphatically.

"Angelica? Angelica?" Tricia called, but there was no other sign of life in the darkened apartment. She flicked on the switches and padded down the hall to the kitchen. A note was attached to the refrigerator door. *Having dinner with Bob. Don't wait up for me.*

"Yow!" Miss Marple insisted.

"We're alone! Hurray!"

But Miss Marple was not about to be placated. Her dinner was late, and she'd been left alone for yet another day. Tricia busied herself and fed the cat, who tucked in with gusto.

Tricia stood in the middle of the unfamiliar kitchen and tried to think of what she should do next. She could unpack some of Angelica's boxes, which would either anger or delight her sister, but she was tired, and the thought of hauling around a lot of dusty, heavy boxes was not enticing.

Take care of your own business, said a small voice within her. Though she didn't have access to the store itself, voice mail continued to pick up the shop's incoming calls. Although the outgoing message said the store was temporarily closed, customers and creditors were still leaving messages that needed to be answered.

Tricia settled down on one of the stools at the island and keyed in the number to retrieve her calls. Sure enough, there were seven of them awaiting her attention. Three were from customers wanting to know the status of their orders; two were from buyers; someone was interested in selling her late mother's collection of mysteries; and the last was from Frannie. "Tricia, it's me," she said. No mistaking that Texas twang.

Miss Marple jumped up, landing on Tricia's lap, startling her, and nuzzled Tricia's hand for attention.

"Looks like Nikki didn't get the loan for the patisserie, and she is absolutely *devastated.* I've been talking to a bunch of the Tuesday Night Book Club gals, and we want to do something to cheer her up. We're thinking of going to brunch on Sunday at the Bookshelf Diner. Ten o'clock sharp. I know it would mean a lot to Nikki if you could be there, too. Give me a call to let me know if you can make it. Bye!"

Miss Marple wiped her damp gray nose across the back of Tricia's hand, demanding more of her attention. "You're not the only unhappy person on the planet, you know," Tricia chided, but Miss Marple was seldom interested in the goings-on in the world at large if they did not directly apply to her.

Tricia absently rubbed the cat's head. She actually did feel sorry for Kimberly. She felt sorry for Nikki, and despite the fact that Zoë might have misrepresented someone else's work as her own, Tricia still felt a pang of pity for the woman. Had Zoë accomplished so little of worth in her own life that she felt no qualms at passing off another's work as her own? At least at first. The fact that she had rebuffed the attention best-sellerdom could have afforded her, lived rather frugally, and left the majority of her estate to charity could attest that she had never felt entirely comfortable with the whole deception.

And now she was dead at another's hands.

"You wouldn't want to be the killer's next victim," Stella Kraft had told Tricia the day before.

No, she wouldn't. And yet someone she'd spoken to — perhaps someone she knew well — had a reason for killing Zoë Carter.

And now that Zoë was gone, there was a chance the killer would go to ground and never be discovered.

Over the years more than one friend or acquaintance had asked Tricia why she was so enamored of the mystery genre. How could she actually enjoy stories that celebrated violent death? They had it all wrong. The books didn't celebrate death, but triumph for justice. Too often real-life villains got away with murder, but in fiction, justice was usually assured.

Sometimes she wished life better imitated art.

ELEVEN

Friday dawned cold and wet. Typical April weather. And, Tricia reminded herself, rain was good for retail — it brought out shoppers. Too bad none of the shoppers would be visiting her store. No sooner had Tricia delivered the bad news to Angelica that Mr. Everett would be absent for the day, than her cell phone rang.

"Tricia, it's Ginny." Her voice sounded strained.

"Are you okay?" Tricia asked.

"No. I'm calling in sick." This troubled Tricia. Ginny *never* called in sick, especially now, when she so desperately needed the money for home repairs.

"What's wrong?"

"Food poisoning, I think. Your sister made appetizers yesterday, and I had quite a few."

"Are you sure that's what made you sick?"

"I didn't have anything else all day, and I spent most of the night huddled in the bathroom with cramps and diarrhea."

Tricia winced. More information than she wanted to know.

"Would you tell Angelica I'll be in this afternoon if I can? I really hate to lose a couple of hours' pay, but I think it's better if I stay home, at least for the morning."

"I agree. Take care, now."

"Thanks, Tricia."

Tricia hung up the phone. With Mr. Everett out for the day, and now Ginny, Angelica would be depending on Tricia to help out at the Cookery. That meant there'd be no extended breaks to look into Zoë's death. No chance to get away at all.

It was going to be a very long day.

Try as she might, Tricia's heart was not into selling cookbooks. Although the bulk of her own stock favored classic mystery, Tricia had been on a "cozy mystery" kick of late. Not for the first time she found herself telling Angelica's epicurean-minded customers about Diane Mott Davidson's Goldy Schulz culinary mystery series. Did Angelica's customers like chocolate? Then a Joanna Carl mystery was just the ticket. She made a beeline for a woman checking out *Martha Stewart's Homekeeping Handbook* to make a pitch for a Barbara Colley's "squeaky clean,

Charlotte LaRue" mystery series.

Angelica did not approve, and more than once interrupted one of Tricia's pitches. "Will you stop trying to sell things I can't supply?" she hissed. "Heck, you can't even supply them, since you sell mostly vintage stock."

"I know, but your customers would really *enjoy* those books. It wouldn't hurt you to start stocking them, either — especially since I don't."

"Don't even go there," Angelica said, straightening up so that she stood her full two inches taller than Tricia.

The Cookery's door opened, and Frannie Armstrong strode in. "Tricia!" She waved and charged forward. "I'm glad I found you. You're the last person on my list."

"List?" Tricia repeated.

"For the flowers."

Tricia stared at her, uncomprehending.

"For Zoë Carter's memorial service tomorrow. Or will Haven't Got a Clue be sending its own floral arrangement?"

Ginny had mentioned something about it the day before. "To tell you the truth, I hadn't thought about it."

Frannie blinked, obviously startled by this gaffe. "Oh."

"Is the Chamber providing flowers?" Tricia asked.

"Of course. They've ordered a beautiful Victorian mourning wreath that exactly duplicates the one Zoë wrote about in *Forever Gone* for Addie's beloved father, who died so tragically."

"Of course," Tricia echoed. "Who came up with that idea?" Surely not Bob. For all he'd done to bring the rare and antiquarian booksellers to Stoneham, she doubted he'd ever picked up a book to read for pleasure.

"Me, silly," Frannie answered. "It was fresh in my mind, since I just reread the book a few weeks back in prep for reading the new book. I finished *Forever Cherished* just last night." She shook her head sadly. "To think of all that talent gone from the world."

Or possibly still living among them — angry at Zoë for taking credit for work that was not her own. Angry enough to kill.

"Would it look tacky if I only contributed to the group fund?" Tricia asked.

"Not at all. In fact, two displays — one on either side of the statue — would give balance. Three wouldn't look as harmonious."

Unless someone else sent flowers. Considering Kimberly's financial situation, Tricia doubted there'd be an offering bearing a ribbon with BELOVED AUNT draped across a spray of gladiolas. Would Zoë's agent think to send flowers? Tricia had met Zoë exactly once — for a little over an hour — had barely spoken to her, and Frannie had offered the perfect out.

What was she thinking? She could well afford to spring for flowers. It was the proper thing to do. And yet — honoring someone who'd passed off another's work as her own just didn't set right with Tricia. So what if she didn't yet have proof? She believed it.

"So what do you think?" Frannie said.

"How's twenty dollars sound?" Tricia asked.

Frannie's eyes lit up. "That's very generous. Thank you."

"It's my pleasure."

Angelica ambled up to join them.

Frannie's gaze wandered around the Cookery. "My, you have done a beautiful job with this place."

"Thank you," Angelica said. "Would you like a tour?"

"Just a short one. I'm on my lunch break."

Tricia retrieved her wallet and extracted a twenty-dollar bill. After her tour, Frannie left with it, plus two Tex-Mex cookbooks, a miniwhisk, a nutmeg grater, and a jar of jalapeño pepper jam.

"Bye, Frannie," Angelica called as Frannie left the shop. She turned to her sister and grinned. "Feel free to invite your friends to my store any time."

Ginny showed up for work about two o'clock, looking pale, but willing. Instead of putting in hours for Angelica, though, she spent the bulk of time helping Tricia with the plans for the statue dedication and book fair set for the next day. Angelica would not be participating, and kept complaining — loudly — that she would not be able to handle the usual expected crowd that a Saturday would produce. Thank heaven Mr. Everett called to say he would return the next morning at nine forty-five sharp.

With Ginny there to help Angelica, Tricia didn't have to feel guilty about making a call she already felt was long overdue.

"Medical Examiner's office."

"Yes, I'd like to speak to the medical examiner."

"I can take a message. Your name — ?"

"No, I don't want to leave a message, I need to speak to someone in charge. My place of business was the scene of a crime. I've been shut down for days during the investigation. I need to know when I can reopen."

"Please leave your name and number, and someone will get back to you."

She did, but she didn't believe for a minute that anyone would.

She tried another tack and called her lawyer, Roger Livingston. He was actually available, and said he'd personally call the ME's office.

Tricia helped three customers look for books, and had rung up another two sales by the time her cell phone interrupted her. She glanced at the number on the tiny screen. "Ginny, can you finish up here? I need to take this call."

Ginny manned the cash register and Tricia stepped behind a shelf of books.

"Tricia, it's Roger Livingston."

"Thanks for getting back to me so soon, Roger. Good news or bad?"

"Good. I called in a favor and got to speak right to the medical examiner. You were right. His office finished with your store yesterday, and so have the county's crime scene investigators. He said there's no reason you weren't informed and allowed to reopen."

"I knew it. I knew Wendy Adams was just being ornery. She hates me."

"I can't comment on that, but I've got a call in to her office. It's getting late. We may

195

not get satisfaction today, but I'll follow up and make sure something happens by tomorrow."

"Thanks, Roger, you're the best lawyer in the world."

"That's true," he said, and she could picture him smiling. "And you'll receive my bill in the mail."

It would be well worth it to reopen the door to Haven't Got a Clue and be back in business.

A much happier Tricia kept an eye on the clock, and at five fifteen announced she needed to leave to pick up Zoë's literary agent at the airport.

"Why don't you bring him back here for dinner?" Angelica said.

"What for?"

"It doesn't seem very friendly just dumping him off at the inn."

"I'm not his friend," Tricia reminded her. "I'm doing him a favor."

"Well, you could be his friend. I mean, you're in the book business."

"Yes, but I'm a book*seller,* not an author."

"You could be — you have many talents. And besides, I think we should cultivate friendships with people in the publishing world. It'll be good for business in general."

Tricia studied her sister's innocent expression. Something was going on — something Angelica wasn't being open about. A quick glance at the clock told Tricia she didn't have time to pursue it just then.

The drive to the Manchester-Boston Regional Airport took less time than Tricia anticipated, and a glance at the arrivals screen informed her that Hamilton's plane was delayed. She browsed the airport bookstore with a judgmental eye, eventually bought the first book in Sheila Connolly's Orchard series, and settled down for a peaceful read, grateful to escape the stress she felt inside the Cookery. Half an hour later, a glance at her watch told her she'd better head for the security checkpoint and the arriving passengers. She pulled out the paper sign bearing Artemus Hamilton's name that she'd made earlier, and stood searching the faces for one she wasn't confident she'd recognize.

The crowd had pretty much thinned when a short, chunky, balding man dressed in a black turtleneck, suit jacket, and dark slacks strode toward her, his raincoat neatly folded over one arm, a briefcase in the same hand. "Ms. Miles?"

Tricia held out her hand. "Nice to meet you, again, Mr. Hamilton." They shook on it, his grip firm but not crushing.

197

"Can you direct me to the baggage claim? I would've preferred to travel lighter, but at least I was able to read most of a manuscript during my flight."

"A mystery?" Tricia asked eagerly.

He shook his head. "Sorry. It's a diet book. I really don't handle that much mystery."

"Then why — ?"

"Was Zoë Carter my client?" he finished. He shrugged. "She had a great book that transcended the genre, and I felt I could place it for her."

Evasive, but it was an answer.

"The baggage claim?" he reminded her.

"Follow me. While you wait for your bag, I'll bring the car around and meet you out front. It's a white Lexus."

Ten minutes later, Tricia pulled up to the curb, popped the trunk button, and Hamilton loaded his suitcase into it. It seemed a big bag for just an overnight stay. He climbed into the passenger seat and buckled his seat belt as Tricia eased the car back into the airport traffic.

"How far is it to Stoneham?" he asked.

"About twenty-five miles. It only takes about half an hour to get there."

He nodded, taking in what scenery was discernible in the rapidly fading light.

Conversation was light, and Tricia waited until they were off the airport property and well on their way toward Stoneham before voicing the question that had been on her mind for the past two days. Hamilton was a captive audience, and if he refused to answer, it could be a very long thirty-minute drive to Stoneham.

"Mr. Hamilton —"

"Call me Artie," he insisted good-naturedly.

Tricia forced a smile. "Artie, there's speculation around Stoneham that Zoë never wrote any of her books." She risked a glance at her passenger, whose gaze had turned stony.

"Why would anyone even think — let alone voice — that, especially now that she's passed on?" he asked. His voice had gone cold, too.

Tricia was glad to turn her gaze back to the road ahead of them. "Her background. Her lack of interest in fiction. Her lack of interest in much of anything, really." She risked a furtive glance at the man, but he'd turned away, and was staring out the passenger window.

"It would be —" He paused. "— disrespectful of me to even dignify that question with an answer."

"Mr. Hamilton," she tried again, trying to sound as respectful as possible, "as you pointed out, Zoë's dead. Whoever wrote those books probably killed her. He — or she — deserves the credit. And they — him or her — deserve to pay for the crime as well."

He sighed, still refusing to answer.

"If you don't know who wrote them, do you know who did the rewrites?"

"Rewrites?" he repeated dully.

"Yes. I've never heard of an editor who accepted a manuscript without making a few single-spaced pages of editorial suggestions."

"You've worked in publishing?" he asked, sidestepping the question.

"No, but I've talked to enough authors to gain a good deal of insight into the process."

Hamilton sighed, still refusing to meet her gaze.

She tried again. "Kimberly Peters told me the original manuscripts were written on an old manual typewriter. She never actually *saw* her aunt write the books." Okay, that was stretching the truth a bit, but it might be what it took to get answers. "Kimberly said she keyboarded some of the manuscripts into a computer."

Hamilton still said nothing.

"She never actually called the books her aunt's, always referring to them as 'the manuscripts.' Like they were separate entities. Not really a part of Zoë, but something foreign. Did you ever have that same feeling?"

Hamilton seemed to squirm in his seat. He didn't answer.

Tricia's hands tightened on the steering wheel, and the silence went on for more than a minute, until she thought she might want to scream from the almost palpable tension. Hamilton sighed again. "I did the rewrites on the first three novels," he admitted, voice low, almost embarrassed.

Trisha exhaled a *whoosh* of air, finally able to breathe once again.

"Mind you, Zoë never came right out and admitted she didn't author those manuscripts. She just made it clear that she was not open to rewrites or promotion."

"So you took them on because they were almost good enough for publication?"

He nodded. "Just reading her correspondence convinced me Zoë wouldn't know a verb from an adjective. She couldn't talk about the research necessary to pull off a historical novel. She had no knowledge of punctuation."

"And yet you represented those books."

"They were good. I was new to the business, but I knew I could sell them. At the time that's all I — and Zoë — cared about."

"Would you have made a different decision today?"

He didn't answer.

Tricia's grip on the steering wheel tightened once more as she thought about everything he'd said. "Who did the rewrites on the last two novels?" She thought she knew the answer before he even spoke.

"Kimberly Peters."

Aha!

"Kimberly has an English degree. She's written a couple of novels — women's fiction. I've read her work. It's good. It's publishable. But Zoë wouldn't hear of it."

"Why not?"

"She thought one author in the family was enough."

Which would seem to be a motive for Kimberly to get rid of her dearly "beloved" aunt.

"Why didn't you do the last two rewrites?"

"No time. Thanks to Zoë, my agency is one of the top twenty in New York. Kimberly offered to take over the rewrites, and she was good at it. She also took over Zoë's correspondence. She approved the cover copy and worked with the publisher's publicist.

Zoë hated any kind of promotion, but Kimberly talked her into a Web site. She put the whole thing together — coordinated the updates. She answered the fan mail. She made Zoë at least appear to be accessible. Somehow she even convinced Zoë to go on tour for the last book, coaching her all the way."

"Kimberly did all that for Zoë, and then the woman more or less disinherited her?"

"Zoë was not a logical woman. She rarely asked me for advice."

"Kimberly said that until recently you were named the executor of Zoë's will. Did you know that?"

"Yes."

"Do you know why she changed her mind?"

"Yes."

"And?"

"It's none of your business."

Touché. Time to try another tack.

"You knew there'd be no more Jess and Addie *Forever* novels. What's to stop you from helping Kimberly get published now?"

He exhaled loudly. "While Zoë was alive, it made sense to placate her. I now represent her estate. Those books will sell for another five, maybe ten, years. It wasn't like I totally ignored Kimberly's aspirations. I gave her a few of my colleagues' names, but I don't think she's yet found representation."

"I take it that you haven't spoken to Kimberly about her own manuscripts since Zoë died?"

He shook his head. "She did phone me, but that subject didn't come up."

"Would you consider representing her now?"

"I don't know. Maybe."

"She'll be at the dedication tomorrow. I'm sure you two will have a lot to talk about."

"Possibly."

They rode in silence for a good five minutes before Hamilton spoke again. "Ms. Miles —"

"Tricia," she insisted.

"Tricia, please don't talk about this to anyone. It would be —"

"Bad for business?"

"As you said, Zoë's dead. What good would it do to drag her name through the mud?"

"I'll make you a deal. I won't talk about this until after this weekend. It wouldn't do to embarrass my colleagues in the Chamber of Commerce, but if the real author of those manuscripts killed Zoë, eventually it will come out. You *do* see that, don't you?"

He shrugged, sounded resigned. "If it happens, it happens. I'll deal with it later."

By denying everything, Tricia thought bitterly. She pulled onto Route 101, steering toward Stoneham and the Brookview Inn. She'd be glad to be rid of Hamilton. And yet . . . for some reason, she didn't think he could be as cold and calculating as he'd come across. Or, despite his part in concealing the truth about Zoë's books, was she just hoping she'd see a better side of him?

Long minutes of silence later, she pulled into the Brookview's drive and stopped the car by the inn's welcoming front entrance. She popped the trunk as Hamilton got out, then retrieved his suitcase. He walked up to the driver's door. Tricia hit a button, and her window slid down and out of sight.

"Thank you for the ride, Ms. Miles. And thank you for giving me some time to —" He hesitated. "To come up with a plausible explanation for my actions. I hope I can be as creative as the person who wrote Zoë's books." With that, he turned and walked up the steps and into the inn.

The Cookery had been closed for more than an hour by the time Tricia made it back to Main Street. Dodging the goose droppings, she ended up in front of her sister's store. After the long day, she wanted nothing more

205

than a glass of wine, a soak in a tub, and to escape into an Agatha Christie story. That wasn't likely to happen. At least Bob's car wasn't parked at the curb, so she'd only have to contend with Angelica tonight.

She unlocked the door, trailed through the darkened store with only the dim security lamps overhead to light the way, and headed up the stairs. She got to the top and opened the door Angelica had left unlocked. "Hello!" she called.

"In the kitchen," came Angelica's muted voice.

The patter of little paws sounded, and before Tricia could hang up her coat, Miss Marple scolded her, at the same time rubbing her head against Tricia's legs. "I'm sorry I didn't come to see you all day, Miss Marple. You must have been terribly lonely," Tricia said, and scooped up the cat, which purred loudly, fiercely nuzzling Tricia's neck.

Tricia put the cat down and headed to the kitchen.

"I'm glad you're here," Angelica said, looking up from the stove, where she stirred some heavenly smelling concoction. "That cat has done nothing but make a pest of herself since I came up an hour ago."

"Did you feed her?"

"That's not my job."

Tricia sighed, grabbed the empty and well-licked food bowl, and took it to the sink to wash. Miss Marple kept rubbing against her slacks, which were soon coated in cat hair. She selected a can of tuna in sauce, supplemented the wet with some dry food, and set it on the floor. Miss Marple dug in gratefully. Tricia rinsed and refilled the water bowl before collapsing onto one of the kitchen stools.

"You look pooped. Ready to talk?" Angelica asked eagerly.

"You bet. More than that, though, I'm starved."

Angelica abandoned her spoon, took three steps and opened the fridge, grabbed a plate and peeled off the cling wrap before setting it on the island in front of Tricia. "I whipped these up yesterday afternoon in the store. Had a few left over and saved you some. They went over real well. Sold seven books on hors d'oeuvres because of them."

Tricia wrinkled her nose. "Ginny said she got sick eating them."

"Oh, don't be absurd. Nobody else did, and believe me, if any of my customers had gotten sick, I'd have heard. People love to sue. I use only fresh ingredients, and you know how meticulously clean I keep my workspace. I'm not afraid to use my digital thermometer, either."

No doubt about it, Angelica was a hygiene hound, and was especially careful not to cross-contaminate raw with cooked foods.

"Besides," Angelica said loftily, "I ate six of them for lunch, and they were delicious."

They did look appetizing, and Tricia *was* hungry. Throwing caution to the wind, she studied the delightful little morsels before her, choosing a baguette slice topped with cheese and what looked like homemade salsa. She took a tentative bite. Good, but probably needed time for the cheese to warm up to room temperature to truly be appreciated. "What are you making? It smells wonderful."

"Tlalpeño soup. Got the recipe on a trip Drew," her ex-husband, "and I made to Mexico City about three years back. You do like avocados, don't you?"

"Definitely."

Angelica grabbed another glass from the cupboard and poured Tricia wine from the opened bottle of Chardonnay, then handed it to her. "Margaritas would be a better choice, but I ran out of lime juice. So tell me all about Zoë's agent." Angelica wasn't above listening to gossip, and Tricia figured she could use a sounding board.

She took a sip, and sighed, letting herself relax for the first time in hours. "I had an interesting conversation with Mr. Artemus Hamilton."

Angelica resumed her position at the stove. "And?" she asked eagerly. "What's he like? Is he looking for new clients?"

Tricia blinked, taken aback by the question. "I didn't ask. He did, however, admit that Zoë Carter never wrote her best sellers."

Angelica snorted. "Yeah, and Santa comes down my chimney every Christmas Eve."

"I'm serious, Ange. I've been hearing rumors, and her agent confirmed it."

"But that's ridiculous."

"I talked to Zoë's next-door neighbor, the Stoneham librarian, and even Zoë's old English teacher. None of them ever believed she wrote the books."

"Then why didn't someone say something before now?"

"No one had proof."

"So what are you saying, that the real author stepped up and killed Zoë?"

Tricia nodded.

"But why would the author wait until now? The first book was published over a decade ago. I know. I bought it. In fact, I still have it." She waved a hand toward the stacks of unopened boxes that still littered her adjoining living room. "Somewhere in all this mess."

"I talked to Kimberly about it. She wasn't the author, but she knew Zoë didn't write them, either. Kimberly has an English degree and supposedly has some writing ability. Somehow she got Zoë to allow her to do the rewrites on the last few books. It's possible she could've felt at least a bit of ownership after she started doing that and approving the cover copy, et cetera."

"But who *did* write the novels?" Angelica asked.

Tricia shrugged. "We may never know. And speaking of books . . . why are you so interested in Artemus Hamilton?"

"Me?" Angelica said, sounding anything but innocent.

"Yes. Every time I mention him, you glow like a lightbulb. Come on, level with me."

Angelica bit her lip, looking thoughtful. "If I tell you, do you promise you won't make fun of me?"

Tricia sighed. "I promise."

Angelica turned to her pantry, opened the door, and took out a folding metal step stool. Setting it in front of the refrigerator, she stepped up to open the cabinet over the appliance. From it, she withdrew a sheaf of papers. She stepped down, closed the distance between them, and handed it to Tricia.

"Easy-Does-It Cooking," she read, "by Angelica Miles." She looked up at her sister. "You've written a cookbook?"

Angelica nodded. "Actually, I've written three. This is my latest."

Tricia flipped through the pages, noting the document wasn't formatted in accepted manuscript style. "What are you going to do with it?"

She shrugged. "I thought I might offer it to Mr. Hamilton. I kind of looked at his firm's Web site. Apparently they do take nonfiction. Now I just need an introduction to him."

Tricia handed back the papers. "Don't look at me."

Angelica frowned. "Why not? You did him a favor by driving him to the Brookview. He owes you."

"May I remind you, we did not part on happy terms. And" — she looked at the manuscript in her sister's hands — "you can't submit something like that without doing the upfront research."

"Are you kidding? I've been researching cooking my whole life. And during the past five months, when I've been working ten-hour days, I realized that what the world needs is recipes for delicious, easy, and quick-to make dinners."

"Ange, have you looked at the bookshelves in your own store? There are scores of cookbooks just like that already in print."

Angelica shook her head. "Not like mine."

"And it's not even properly formatted," Tricia pointed out.

"Oh, who cares about that? The quality will shine through."

"Fine. Find out the hard way. But one more thing: if I've learned anything talking to authors, there's nothing worse than shoving your manuscript at an agent or editor at an inappropriate time. It's the kiss of death."

"Oh, what do you know?" Angelica said, and held the pages to her chest as though they were a babe in diapers. "You'll see. I'm going to sell my cookbooks. I'll be fabulously successful, maybe even land my own TV show like Rachael Ray or Paula Deen. Lord knows I've got the personality."

And the ego, too.

"Fine. Don't listen to me." Tricia sniffed the air. "But, oh fabulous sister chef of mine, I think you'll find your soup is scorched."

Angelica dropped the manuscript on the counter as though it were on fire, and rushed to the stove. Grabbing the spoon, she stirred the pot, her expression souring. She took a taste. "Oh, no," she wailed. "My lovely, lovely soup."

Tricia shook her head, got up, and walked over to pick up the phone. "Looks like it's pizza again, after all."

TWELVE

True to his word, Mr. Everett was at the Cookery before opening on Saturday morning, just as Ginny and Tricia packed up the last of the books to take to Stoneham Square and the statue dedication. Tricia had questions for Mr. Everett, but this wasn't the time to voice them all. Perhaps later in the afternoon an opportunity would arise.

Still, she drew him aside to ask the most important one. "How did it go with Sheriff Adams?"

"She is not a very nice woman. I was glad Mr. Livingston did most of the talking; otherwise, I'm sure I'd be staring at the walls of a jail cell right now."

"Thank heavens for good legal counsel," Tricia agreed. "There's something else we need to discuss, Mr. Everett."

"Tricia, can you help me with these boxes?" Ginny called.

"Just a second." She turned back to Mr.

Everett. "We'll talk later."

He nodded, and headed for the back of the shop to stow his coat.

Tricia helped Ginny stack the boxes on two of the Cookery's dollies.

"I think I should go to the dedication," Angelica said, as she watched Mr. Everett don his yellow Cookery apron.

"You can't leave the store," Tricia said, putting on her coat.

"Why not? Mr. Everett is here to take care of things. And anyway, it's likely most of the village, and a lot of the tourists, will be at the square. The Cookery might not have any customers, anyway."

"Not if the weatherman is correct. He's predicting a high of only forty-six degrees today. That might just drive a bunch of the tourists into your toasty warm shop."

"I heard a couple of TV stations will be covering the dedication," Ginny said, and laughed. "It must be a slow weekend for news."

Angelica went behind her sales counter, came back with a big brown envelope, and handed it to Tricia. "Here, if you see Mr. Hamilton, will you give him this?"

Tricia handed the package right back to her. "I know what this is, and I already told you, the answer is no."

215

"What's in the package?" Ginny asked, curious.

"None of your business," Angelica snapped. She turned back to her sister. "Tricia, please? I'll make you a cheesecake — from scratch."

"I don't like cheesecake." Tricia pulled her gloves from the pockets of her jacket. "We'll tell you all about the dedication afterward."

"I can't wait," Angelica said, sarcastically.

Tricia tipped back her dolly of books and headed for the front door. "We'll probably be back about five, after striking the set."

"It's not showbiz," Angelica drawled.

"It is to me," Tricia said, and continued to the door, which Ginny opened for her. She'd already parked her car at the curb and had loaded the borrowed cash register and some boxes of books. Too bad all of it was new stock. Mystery lovers who traveled to Stoneham were expecting to find some of their long-out-of-print favorites. Curse Sheriff Adams and her stubbornness.

The atmosphere in the village square was more like that of a circus than a cemetery, considering the event had morphed from a celebration into a memorial service. As many as twenty tents lined the outside of the square, decked out in balloons and colorful wind socks madly waving in the brisk wind, while the aroma of fried dough, hot dogs, and kettle corn filled the air. Potential customers were already milling about as the vendors set up their wares.

Fifteen or twenty geese stood by, eyeing the crowd from the edges of the park's retention pond. Despite the DO NOT FEED THE GEESE signs posted all around, these birds knew that the presence of people often equaled food, and they looked ready to pounce should it appear.

Tricia stood at the opening of her three-sided tent. A gale blew through the canvas walls, threatening to make a box kite out of the whole contraption. Her generic "Thank You" plastic bags had to be weighted down with rocks Ginny found in one of the small park's gardens.

"Are you sorry you came?" Tricia asked.

Ginny had wrapped her arms around herself, the sleeves of her parka drawn over her fingers, her shoulders hunched until they touched the edges of the watch cap that covered her head and ears. She stamped her feet on the cold, damp earth. "I'd still rather be here, freezing off my behind, than working at the Cookery. I'm sorry to say I don't feel one bit guilty leaving Angelica and Mr. Everett alone together."

Tricia stifled a smile.

"Knock-knock. Anybody home?" Nikki Brimfield stood outside the tent, holding a white cardboard cake box in one hand and a grocery bag and the handle of an airpot coffee carafe in the other. "Thought you guys could use a bit of warming up."

"Hooray!" Ginny cheered, and turned to make room on one of the tables.

"I stopped at the store first, hoping you'd be open again by now. Then I went by the Cookery and Angelica said I'd find you here. Boy, she was grumpy."

Tricia ignored the last comment, but addressed the first. "We'd kill for hot coffee now, that's for sure."

"Yeah," Ginny echoed.

Nikki set the box and carafe on the table, handing the grocery bag to Ginny. She opened the box, revealing a white-frosted cake with a large splotch of red.

"Oh," Tricia said, afraid her lack of enthusiasm would be taken the wrong way.

Nikki laughed. "You're not seeing it complete," she said and dismantled two sides of the box to reveal the entire cake. "There's a fake knife in the bag, Ginny. Want to hand it to me?"

Ginny did as she was told. Nikki removed a cardboard sheath and plunged the plastic carving knife into the center of the cake.

218

Now the splotch of red made perfect sense: it represented a river of pseudo blood puddled around the knife and dripping down the sides. "It's a red velvet cake. It was my mom's recipe. I thought you might need some comfort food."

Why did everyone seem to make wrong assumptions about Tricia's definition of comfort food? So far they'd pretty much missed the mark. Couldn't they have just asked?

"That was thoughtful of you, Nikki. Thank you," Tricia said, trying to sound keen. Had Nikki forgotten it was less than a year ago that Tricia had seen a body with a knife in its back? The sight of the cake made the memory of that terrible evening all the more vivid.

"Now don't you go sharing that," Nikki cautioned, "it's just for you, Tricia." She indicated the bag. "I brought a couple of coconut cupcakes for you, Ginny."

"Thanks. They're my favorite."

"I really appreciate the gesture," Tricia said, taking the knife from the cake and shoving the box under one of the tables and out of sight.

"I feel so bad about everything that's happened this week," Nikki said. "Baking is my way of . . . well, coping."

"Has something else bad happened?" Tricia asked.

Nikki frowned. "Didn't you hear? The bank loan didn't go through. Apparently I don't have enough business acumen or assets or . . . anything."

Oh, yes, Frannie had mentioned the loan.

"But you have all that experience. You've run the patisserie for a couple of years, and you're a certified pastry chef trained in Paris," Ginny put in.

"I know. But it isn't good enough for the Bank of Stoneham." She let out a loud sigh, and for a moment Tricia thought Nikki might cry. But then she straightened, throwing back her shoulders. "I'm not giving up. I've already signed up for an online course on writing a business plan. I just hope Homer doesn't find another buyer before I can get my financing together."

"I'll keep crossing my fingers for you," Tricia said.

Nikki glanced at her watch. "Oh, I've got just enough time to go watch the unveiling. Are you going?"

Tricia shook her head. "We've got to stay here, not that we've been inundated with customers so far. I'm hoping that after the unveiling we'll see a few more sales."

"Okay," Nikki said, and turned to go.

"Oh, go ahead, Tricia," Ginny encouraged. "I can certainly handle things here. And I'm not all that interested in looking at a big old hunk of rock with a carved book on it, anyway."

"Come on, Tricia, it'll be fun," Nikki chided.

Fun? To go to a memorial service? Still, Tricia looked hopefully at Ginny. "Well, if you really don't mind."

"Go ahead," Ginny said, and took a Styrofoam cup from the bag Nikki had provided, then pumped coffee from the carafe.

Tricia removed her Cookery apron, stowing it under one of the tables. "Let's go!"

They left the vendor area circling the village square and headed for the center, where the gazebo sat amid a sea of short, stubby grass, still brown from its winter dormancy. This was no backyard variety structure, but a grand, freestanding granite edifice, its copper roof a mellow green with age. Mere feet away stood the short, tarp-shrouded statue, looking lumpy and ugly against such a stately pavilion. Bob had done a good job, ensuring that the sidewalk and grass surrounding the monument were devoid of goose droppings, although telltale stains still marred what had recently been pristine concrete.

A crowd had already gathered around the monument. Tricia recognized members of Haven't Got a Clue's Tuesday Night Book Club in the crowd, as well as Artemus Hamilton, standing with a subdued Kimberly Peters. She wore the same wrinkled suit she'd had on at the signing. Didn't she know how to use an iron? Tricia recognized several selectmen, a couple of the other bookstore owners, and Chamber members, who also stood by. Lois Kerr and Stella Kraft were standing with a knot of older ladies who'd gathered to one side.

Sheriff Adams and one of her deputies stood with a number of selectmen who'd shown up for the event — no doubt invited by the Chamber to give the ceremony some semblance of official sanction. Clipboard in hand, Frannie Armstrong flitted about the front of the gazebo, checking the names against her master list of invitees.

Among the missing was Grace Harris, not that Tricia had really expected Mr. Everett's close friend to attend without him. Or was there a reason she didn't want to be seen at Zoë's memorial service? Another angle Tricia would have to investigate.

News cameramen and still photographers had gathered to the left of the monument. Portia McAlister was also among them and, as a member of the press, so was Russ, his Nikon dangling from his neck, a steno pad clutched in his left hand. The rope, which earlier had been securely tied around the white canvas at the bottom of the monument, had already been removed.

Bob looked dapper, if partially frozen, in a kelly green sport coat that he always wore while showing real estate. The crowd quieted as he stepped up to the microphone, tapped it, then blew on it. "Testing, testing." Apparently satisfied with the sound quality, he consulted his notes, then raised his gaze to stare directly into the News Team Ten's video camera. Tricia squinted. Had he had his teeth whitened since the last time she'd seen him?

"It is with great pride and affection that Stoneham's Chamber of Commerce dedicates this statue to one of our own, *New York Times* best-selling author Zoë Carter, who helped bring fame to our little village. We hope Stoneham will remain a mecca to her millions of fans for generations to come." His words were greeted with a smattering of polite applause.

"Too bad Angelica is missing this," Nikki whispered, and giggled. "She might even swoon, seeing Bob in his green jacket."

"Shhh!" Tricia admonished.

"We had hoped Ms. Carter's niece," Bob nodded toward Kimberly, "might speak, but naturally she's quite distraught at her loss."

As though on cue, Kimberly dabbed a tissue at her dry eyes.

"Is there anyone here who'd like to offer a fond memory or words of praise for Zoë?" Bob cleared his throat, looking hopefully at the assembled audience, but no one stepped forward. "Mr. Hamilton?" Bob implored.

All eyes turned toward the literary agent, who blushed.

"Go on," Kimberly mouthed, and gave him a nudge.

A reluctant Hamilton stepped up to the microphone. "Uh . . ." He cleared his throat. "Uh, Zoë Carter was my very first client." His gaze wandered the crowd, lighting on Tricia. He frowned, no doubt remembering their conversation the night before. He looked away. "Zoë, uh, never missed a deadline. The world is a . . . a different place without her."

Different? That's all he could come up with? Perhaps he was afraid to gush, leery of what the press might say about him when the truth about Zoë came to light.

He nodded at those assembled and stepped away from the microphone.

"Thank you," Bob said to the sound of

weak applause. "Anyone else?"

Not a soul stepped forward.

"Anyone?" he begged.

As if on queue, the air was broken by the sound of flapping wings and the fierce honking of Canada geese as a portion of the flock took flight from the pond, making a low pass over the crowd, who seemed to duck as one.

When the cacophony receded, Bob cleared his throat, stepped away from the microphone, and moved over to the monument. He grasped the tarp with both hands and yanked dramatically. The wind caught the canvas, whipping it into the air like a sail. The crowd backed off as it came straight at them. Nikki gasped, and for a moment Tricia thought she might have been injured, but she stared straight ahead, her mouth open in astonishment. Tricia turned, and immediately her expression mirrored Nikki's.

The carving of the opened book had been shattered into several large chunks. Below, scarlet spray paint marred the brilliant white marble base, spelling out the word THIEF!

THIRTEEN

"What does it mean?" Nikki gasped.

"This is an outrage!" someone called out.

"What kind of security measures were taken to protect the statue?" said someone else.

Bob Kelly stood transfixed, his gaze focused on his brainchild, utterly flabbergasted at the devastation, while Wendy Adams and her deputy tried to keep the crowd away from the ruined marble.

The TV cameras continued to roll while photographers' flashes strobed. Russ scribbled madly on his steno pad.

Among those not speculating on the vandalism: Kimberly Peters and Artemus Hamilton, who stood staring mutely at the desecrated monument. Was it because they understood what the graffiti meant?

"Wendy," Bob bellowed, "how could you have let this happen?"

"You can't blame the Sheriff's Department — we never got a request to protect the statue."

"Maybe not, but it's your responsibility to keep the village safe."

The sheriff's brows inched menacingly closer. "My deputies and I have eight hundred and seventy-six square miles to protect. We can't be everywhere at once, Bob."

Bob turned to face Kimberly Peters. "I — I don't know what to say, how to apologize —" he stammered.

Tight-lipped, Kimberly replied, "Try, Mr. Kelly."

Bob stood there, mouth agape, his gaze returning to the defaced monument.

Tricia backed away. "I think it's time to go," she told Nikki.

"Yeah. To think I left Steve alone in the shop for an hour for this. Then again . . ." She let the sentence trail, looking thoughtful.

"You don't trust Steve?"

"Of course I trust him. He's got a lot of talent, and he works harder than anyone I've ever hired. But sometimes I just need a break from him. He doesn't have a lot of friends, so I'm afraid he sees me as a confidante, and I'd really rather not play that role."

"Have you let him know this?"

She sighed. "He doesn't always listen to me."

"Yet he wants to bend your ear?" Tricia nodded, knowingly. "I've met a few men like that myself."

Nikki looked to the south, toward the patisserie. "Well, I hope they find the creep who wrecked the statue and nail him. Then again, Wendy Adams couldn't find herself in a fun house mirror, let alone locate a vandal." She shook her head. "See you on Tuesday at the book club, if not before," she said, and gave Tricia's shoulder a quick pat before heading for Main Street.

Tricia headed in the opposite direction. At least she wasn't the only one in the village who questioned Sheriff Adams's qualifications.

Most of the crowd had already dispersed, deserting the square and definitely not visiting any of the vendor tents or food kiosks. Talk about a disaster. Her bottom line for the week was already red, and this event had plunged it into an even deeper scarlet.

Ginny stood at the tent's opening, arms wrapped around her, stamping her feet to keep warm. "I saw everyone leaving. What happened?"

Tricia explained while Ginny craned her

228

neck and stood on tiptoes, looking across the square in a vain effort to see the ruined statue. "I miss out on all the fun," she groused.

"We may as well pack up. I don't think we'll sell another book here today."

"Tricia, we didn't sell *any* books today."

Tricia grimaced at the thought, bending to grab one of the empty boxes from under the table.

"What will you do with Nikki's cake?"

"I can't take it to the Cookery. Ange doesn't want to serve anything she didn't make herself."

"Can I take a slice home to Brian? He could use a treat. With the stove on the fritz, he's pretty sick of sandwiches and microwaved soup."

"Take the whole thing. I'm not going to eat it. It's very sweet of Nikki to keep giving me sweet treats, but I'm just not into them."

"And that's how you stay so thin," Ginny said, and poked at the padding on her own hip.

Tricia grabbed another couple of books. "It would also aggravate Angelica if I brought it home."

Ginny laughed. "Well, that alone might be worth it. Are you sure you can't take even half of it?"

Tricia pushed the cake box toward her assistant. "No. Until the sheriff lets me back into my store, I have to live with Angie."

"It'll be a hardship, but I think between the two of us, we can eat the whole cake." Ginny set the cake aside and started packing books.

Fifteen minutes later, Tricia pulled her car in front of the tent, and they loaded it. She waved at her nearest neighbor, who was packing up her fried dough stand. "What a bust today turned out to be," she said to Tricia, who nodded and offered a wan smile.

Ginny decided to walk back to the Cookery so that she could put Nikki's cake in her car trunk. Mr. Everett met Tricia on the sidewalk with a dolly and helped her take a case of books from her car's trunk.

"Did you notice the crime scene tape is gone?" He nodded toward the door of Haven't Got a Clue.

"When did that happen?"

"Just after you left. I tried to call, but your cell phone must be turned off."

Roger Livingston's call to the Medical Examiner's Office must have done some good. "Are we allowed inside?" she asked, almost afraid to hear the answer.

"Yes," he said eagerly, and shot a glance at the Cookery, where Angelica stood behind the closed door, disapproval etched across her face.

Tricia flashed her a smile. "Mr. Everett, I know it's a terrible imposition, but would you be willing to stay at the Cookery, at least for the rest of the day, while Ginny and I get things going again next door?"

He sighed, as though he'd known she'd ask this question. "Yes. But, tomorrow is Ginny's day off, and you'll need me at Haven't Got a Clue." It wasn't a question; it was a statement.

"Yes, of course."

That was sure to start a fight with Angelica. But really, shouldn't she have been looking for a new employee during the past week anyway?

Tricia plucked the store key from among the others on her ring and placed it in the lock, savoring this moment. She opened the door and breathed in the scent of her store, a mix of old paper, furniture polish, and . . . *freedom.* How she'd missed days spent in the long, narrow shop with its richly pan-eled walls decorated with prints and photos of long-dead mystery authors, the comfy tapestry-upholstered chairs in the readers' nook, and the restored tin ceiling — the only original feature she'd been able to keep during renovation. She took in all her favorite features and sighed. She was home.

Mr. Everett cleared his throat, reminding her that he stood, coatless, directly behind her. "Where do you want me to put these?"

"Oh, anywhere. I don't think we'll be able to reopen today."

"Why not?" said Ginny, coming up from behind. "We've still got five hours. It won't take us that long to get the coffee on and the register open."

"Yes, but I need to give that washroom a thorough cleaning and I need to rescue Miss Marple," Tricia said, hearing the joy in her voice and realizing, for the first time in days, that she actually felt something other than angst.

"Come on, Mr. Everett, help me get these books inside while Tricia gets her cat," Ginny said. "It's time for us all to go back home."

Not exactly.

Angelica pounced on Tricia as she reentered the Cookery. "What are you doing with my employees?"

"*Your* employees?" Tricia said, taken aback.

"Yes. I'm paying them. At least, I'm paying Mr. Everett for today."

"And he will be right back, as soon as he helps Ginny unload my car."

"You can't have him tomorrow."

"Yes, I can. I'm going to reopen, and it's his regular day to work. It's Ginny's day off. Maybe you can talk her into working for you."

Angelica exhaled loudly through her nose, her mouth immediately settling into a pout.

"Ange, the minute Stephanie quit, you should've called the temp agency."

"I did. They . . . they've —" Her cheeks colored and she lowered her voice to a whisper. "They've blackballed me."

"What?"

"They said I have a bad reputation, and they will no longer supply me with candidates."

"What are you going to do?"

"Tricia, you've got to let me have Ginny or Mr. Everett. Just for a couple of weeks. Please. *Please!*"

"It's not up to me, it's up to them. And let's face it, you haven't exactly endeared yourself to them in the past couple of days."

"I've been a lot nicer to them than I was to my own employees."

"That's only because you were desperate."

Angelica opened her mouth to protest, apparently thought better of it, and closed her mouth once more.

"Mr. Everett has already told me he's

coming back to Haven't Got a Clue tomorrow. You can try and sweet-talk Ginny, but I don't know if you'll have any luck."

"I could offer her a bonus."

"That might work." Tricia turned and headed for the back of the store.

"Where are you going?"

"Upstairs to get my cat and the rest of my things. It's time for me to go home."

FOURTEEN

The circa-1935 black telephone by the register rang. From her perch on the sales counter, Miss Marple batted her little white paw at the offending jingle.

"Not again," Ginny wailed.

"You don't know it's Angelica," Tricia said, reaching for the receiver. The ringing stopped and she said, "Haven't Got a Clue, Tricia speak—"

"It's me," Angelica interrupted.

"Stop calling. Ginny told you she'd let you know in the morning. I'm hanging up now. Good-bye." She replaced the receiver and looked at her watch. "Whoa! Look at the time." It was nearly seven. "I've got a date tonight with Russ."

"And I've got a date tonight with a paintbrush," Ginny said. "We're working on the laundry room. Hopefully Brian got the right color this time. Men!" She reached for the duster.

"Leave that. You know it's Mr. Everett's favorite job. It'll give him something to do *and* make him happy tomorrow. Now, are you going to make Angelica happy and work for her tomorrow?"

Ginny sighed. "Yes. But she's going to have to sweat for it. I don't intend to call her until at least eleven tomorrow morning. Then Monday morning, I'm back here. That is, if it's okay with you."

"More than okay." Tricia smiled. "And thank you for helping Ange. She doesn't mean to be . . . mean —"

"She just is," Ginny finished.

Tricia shrugged. "Yeah." She reached for her coat, which still lay across the counter where she'd left it when she came in, and now sported a circle of cat hair where Miss Marple had made herself comfortable for most of the afternoon. Ordinarily Tricia wouldn't have allowed it, but the cat had been cooped up for days and Tricia felt she deserved a treat. And, besides, that's why she kept a sticky lint roller under the counter at all times, although she'd left it too late to use tonight. "Grab your coat, Ginny, we're out of here."

Tricia turned off all but the security lights. "You're in charge, Miss Marple," she said, and closed and locked the door.

Tricia and Ginny headed for the municipal parking lot. "They say it might snow tonight," Ginny said.

The streetlamps made it impossible to see much of the sky overhead. "Spring snow doesn't last long."

"We hope. See you tomorrow," Ginny said.

"You're going to the Cookery," Tricia reminded her.

"Shoot, I forgot already. It's just five hours. Every time Angelica makes me mad, I'm just going to tell myself it's only for five hours."

Tricia smiled. "See you Monday."

"Bye," Ginny said, and crossed the lot to her own car.

Tricia made it to Russ's house exactly on time. She hadn't even had a chance to raise her arm to knock on the front door before it was jerked open. "Tricia!" It sounded like he was greeting a long-lost friend. His hopeful expression and the way he practically bounced on his feet reminded her of a small child desperate to get back into someone's good graces.

"Hi, Russ." She stepped forward, planted a gentle kiss on his lips, then another, before he took her hand and pulled her over the threshold and into the brightly lit entryway.

"Let me take your coat," he said.

She handed him her coat and stepped into the living room.

No dim lights, no unpleasant aroma. In fact, no aroma at all. And, once again, the sound of the police scanner contributed to the lack of ambiance. Tricia sighed. Well, what did she expect? Maybe sending the flowers a few days before was all the romance Russ could muster. He was also probably dying to talk about the statue dedication, and she wasn't sure she was up to it. "What are we having for dinner?"

"Pizza. After last time, I figured it was a safe choice."

And easy. "Have you called it in yet?"

"I wanted to wait for you. I didn't want to take a chance on ordering the wrong toppings." And, unspoken, risking her ire. Okay, they would both be walking on eggshells with each other for a little while.

"I'll eat anything but anchovies . . . and maybe those terrible canned black olives."

"Veggies?" he offered.

"Always."

Squawk! "Dispatch to Two-A."

Russ's head snapped around as he listened to the police scanner.

"Two-A," said a disembodied voice.

"Respond to a noise complaint at seven-

238

teen Wilder Road. The complainant, who does not wish contact, is a neighbor directly across the street and reports loud music coming from the house for the last three hours."

"Two-A responding."

He turned back to Tricia, risked a smile. "Let's have a drink," he said, took her hand and led her to the living room couch. Scattered across the books and folded newspapers on the cocktail table were photographs of the vandalized statue he'd taken earlier that day, along with a bottle of white zinfandel and two glasses. He poured, offering her one of the glasses.

Tricia took it, but also picked up a photo. "What made you print them?"

"I thought you might like to see them."

She studied the picture. "It's a shame someone had to ruin the statue. If only Bob hadn't decided to dedicate it to Zoë." She wasn't about to elaborate on her theories to Russ. Let him find his own answers about the so-called writer's life — and her death.

"The whole thing was a fiasco, from start to finish," Russ said, leaning back against the cushions. "First of all, Bob should never have contracted with a Vermont quarry for the marble. He should've gone with granite. After all, New Hampshire is the Granite

State. And as the head of the Chamber of Commerce, he's the first one to complain when someone doesn't support local business."

"Oh, you're right. A major faux pas," Tricia agreed.

"And then they ordered the inscription too late for the dedication, which made it easy for them to change the focus of the celebration. Let me tell you, more than a few of the booksellers are annoyed the Chamber would honor a woman who refused to help the village get established as a book town."

Tricia hadn't had an opinion on that before now, but she had to admit she agreed with the sentiment.

"Added to that, a bunch of the locals are upset that the Chamber is honoring an 'outsider.' At least it wasn't public money that paid for the statue. That would've really landed the Board of Selectmen in hot water."

"You're a Stoneham native. What do you think of outsiders?" Tricia asked.

"I love them," he answered without hesitation. "You in particular." He leaned forward to kiss her nose. "They've saved this burg from dying."

She set the photo down on the table and

sat back on the couch, wishing they were in her own loft apartment. Was that what was wrong? In her own home she could control the atmosphere. Play soft music, dim the lights, light a few scented candles. Okay, she'd probably served pizza way too many times herself, but that was only because she wasn't very good at — or interested in — cooking, despite Angelica's offers to teach her a few basic recipes. Maybe she ought to reconsider that decision.

And maybe she should reconsider what she wanted out of the relationship. Russ was the only man she'd dated since her divorce less than two years ago. Could what they had even be called much of a relationship? Was she afraid to risk more heartbreak? If there was any spark between them, she'd spent little effort fanning what might burst into flames.

And he had been the first to say — in writing, no less — the word *love.*

"Did you read my top story in this week's issue?" Russ asked.

Tricia looked up at him. He wasn't at all like Christopher — and maybe that was something she found comforting. "Story?" she asked.

"Yeah, in the *Stoneham Weekly News.*"

It took a moment for the question to

register. Tricia hesitated before answering. She hadn't. The *Stoneham Weekly News* had arrived, but what with everything that had happened, it had been shunted into the trash — probably by Ginny. "Not yet," she said finally. "Didn't you say it concerned the geese problem?"

"Yes." He shook his head and frowned. "We have a murder right here in the village, and I come out with a story on goose shit."

"You're not psychic. You couldn't know someone would die," she said reasonably.

"Of course, the geese are just another one of Bob's problems."

"Surely it's up to the Village Board to deal with them, not the Chamber of Commerce."

"Yes, and privately Bob is advocating killing them."

"Frannie mentioned that was an option. She was pretty upset by the idea. But Bob seemed noncommittal when I spoke to him the other night."

"He knows you're a bleeding-heart animal lover — despite the inconvenience of cleaning up after the birds. He's not about to say what he really thinks in front of you."

"And what do you think?"

"About the geese?"

"No, about Bob."

Russ looked thoughtful. "Four years ago he almost single-handedly brought the village back from the brink of bankruptcy. That's pretty amazing."

"You didn't answer my question."

"Personally, I think the guy's a jerk. But you won't see that opinion in the *Stoneham Weekly News* any time soon."

A smile crept across Tricia's lips. Their eyes met, and she leaned in to kiss him.

Squawk! "Dispatch to Six-B."

"Six-B," came the reply.

She pulled back, lips pursed. "Russ," she said, speaking over the dispatcher, "do we have to listen to the scanner all evening?"

"Would you rather watch TV?"

"Not really. I want to sit and converse, although not about Zoë's death," she said adamantly. "Can't we talk about . . . I don't know . . . current events? Books? Music?"

"You're so interested in crime, I thought you were entertained by it."

"I'm interested in crime *stories* — fiction — not listening to noisy neighbor reports, or —"

"Fourteen Alpha and Six Charlie, respond to a burglary in progress at thirty-six Pine Avenue. Break."

"Thirty-six Pine Avenue?" Tricia repeated. "But that's Zoë Carter's house." She leaped

243

up from the couch, nearly spilling her wine.

"Fourteen Alpha en route," came a voice from the scanner, quickly followed by "Six Charlie en route."

"Are you sure?" Russ asked, not as quick on his feet.

"Yes," she called behind her, already heading for the front closet and her coat.

"Where are you going?"

"Kimberly's staying at the house alone. That's only two blocks away! We might be able to get there quicker than the sheriff's deputies. Come on!" she yelled and was out the door, running for her car.

Ginny's prediction of snow had already come true in the few minutes Tricia had been inside Russ's house. A dusting covered the grass and the windshield of her car.

She'd hopped in, had the engine revving, and the wipers going when Russ finally slammed his front door and jogged to the car. He'd barely closed the passenger door when Tricia jammed her foot on the accelerator and spun the tires.

The car fishtailed on the damp pavement as she rounded the corner.

"Slow down!" Russ implored.

Hands gripping the steering wheel, Tricia paid no attention to her panicked passenger, turned the corner, and took out a piece of the corner lot's grass.

"I'm going to report you to the sheriff if you don't slow down," Russ hollered.

Tricia jammed on the brakes and the car shuddered to a halt at the curb in front of number thirty-six. She yanked open the door and started running toward the house.

"Hey, you! Stop!" Russ yelled, and began running in the opposite direction.

Every light in the house appeared to be switched on, and the front door was ajar. Without a thought — and probably foolishly — Tricia entered. "Kimberly! Kimberly!"

The living room had been ransacked. Pillows and sofa cushions slashed, books dumped on the floor. The shelves on one wall had been cleared of everything breakable. Porcelain figurines and ginger jars lay smashed on the carpeted floor. Tricia cast about, but found no sign of Kimberly.

"Kimberly, where are you?"

She stepped over the detritus and headed down the well-lit hallway. The bedroom door on the left was open. She poked her head inside, saw the bed had been dismantled, the sheets and blankets in a jumble on the floor, the mattress and box springs standing against the far wall — just the metal frame and dust bunnies marked where they had once been. Except for a few clothes on hangers, the closet was empty. Not much else populated the space. Was it because the house was in the process of being sold, or was Zoë as spare with her possessions as she had been with the details of her life?

Tricia moved on. The bedroom on the other side of the hall was in much the same condition. A couple of empty suitcases lay open on the floor, the mattress stood against the wall, the box springs askew, revealing nothing had been stored beneath it. The dresser drawers all hung open, but there was nothing inside them, the contents — socks and underwear — were strewn across the floor.

"Kimberly?" Tricia called again.

Still no answer.

Tricia hurried on. The hallway dead-ended at what looked to be a home office — no doubt Zoë's inner sanctum — and it, too, had been turned upside down. Copies of the hardcover and paperback editions of the *Forever* books were scattered across the floor; a lamp lay smashed; pens, pencils, and other office supplies were spread among tapes and broken CDs and DVDs. The screen on a little television in an armoire was shattered. The glass from every picture had been smashed, the pictures themselves punched from the frames. Likewise, holes, three or four inches in diameter — from a sledgehammer? — marred the walls. And an old, battered trunk was upended in the corner, its contents dumped over the floor. It had suffered the same fate as the walls, with holes punched through its thin exterior.

A groan came from what appeared to be a bloody mass of clothes on the floor. "Kimberly!"

Tricia crouched and pulled back what had once been a white sweater. Kimberly's face was mottled, and her cheek was sunken; her blood-coated teeth hung broken, jagged in her gums. Tricia was glad she and Russ hadn't gotten as far as eating pizza, because her stomach roiled, but with nothing to bring up, she merely gagged.

Kimberly groaned again, and Tricia forced herself to turn back to the once attractive woman.

"The deputies are on their way," she managed, her voice catching.

Kimberly's hand groped for Tricia's, found it, her fingers slippery with her own blood. "Thone," she said through swelling lips.

"I don't understand."

"Thone," she tried again, almost frantic.

"I don't know what you mean."

Kimberly whimpered. "Thone," she said again.

Thone? "Phone?" Tricia tried.

Kimberly shook her head ever so slightly, a moan escaping.

Thone?

"Stone?" Tricia asked.

Kimberly nodded. For a moment her fingers tightened around Tricia's, and then went slack.

"Can't you ever mind your own business?" came a cold, hard voice from the open doorway.

Tricia started; she hadn't heard anyone approach. She looked up to see a grim-faced Sheriff Wendy Adams looming over her.

FIFTEEN

Zoë's tiny kitchen was about the only room in the house that had escaped the madman's wrath. And surely it had to be a man who'd inflicted all the damage.

Unlike the night of Zoë's death, when Angelica had thrust a sustaining cup of coffee into Tricia's hand, now she had only a damp tissue to clutch. She sat at the little Formica table under Sheriff Adams's unrelenting glare. "Let's go over it again."

Tricia sighed. "We heard the call come over the police scanner. We raced right over. Russ went running across the yard and I came into the house."

The sheriff shook her head in disgust. "A tremendously stupid act," she said under her breath.

"Russ was chasing whoever ransacked the place and injured Kimberly," Tricia continued.

"There could've been more than one assailant. You didn't know there wasn't."

That was true. Still, their showing up had probably frightened the attacker away.

At least, that was what Tricia chose to believe.

"Get on with it," the sheriff prompted.

"I hurried through the house and found Kimberly in the office. Bloodied but breathing. Is she still alive?"

"She was when the ambulance pulled out of here."

Tricia shuddered at the thought of Kimberly's bashed and bloodied face. "Where's Russ?" she asked, in an effort to distract herself.

"Talking with one of my deputies."

"I take it he didn't catch the robber."

"No. Too bad he was our high school newspaper editor. He might've caught the perp if he'd lettered in track."

Tricia blinked. *Perp?* Wendy Adams sounded like a caricature of a TV lawman . . . er, woman.

The sheriff crossed her arms over her ample bosom and leaned against the counter by the sink. "Now what was it Ms. Peters said to you before she lost consciousness?"

"Stone." Tricia frowned. "At least I think she said stone. It was hard to tell through those broken teeth."

"What do you think she meant by it?"

"The statue that was destroyed? What other explanation is there?"

"And she said nothing else?"

"She said it three times. I think she wanted to make sure I understood her."

Sheriff Adams's lips pursed. It didn't make her look any more attractive.

"Where did they take Kimberly?" Tricia asked.

"Southern New Hampshire Medical Center in Nashua. They've got a trauma center. If she makes it there."

A boulderlike weight seemed to rest on Tricia's chest. She hadn't been one of Kimberly's biggest fans, but she couldn't imagine how anyone could inflict such damage on another human being.

"Did you see any sign of a weapon?" the sheriff asked.

Tricia shook her head. "I assumed he —"

"Or she —"

"— used a sledgehammer. What else could've punched such holes in the walls and furniture?"

Sheriff Adams made no comment.

"I'll bet it was the same tool that smashed the statue."

Still no comment from the sheriff.

Tricia glanced at the clock over the sink

and wondered if she should volunteer her suspicions about why a hammer-wielding burglar would ransack Zoë's home and critically injure Kimberly. The sheriff hadn't wanted to hear Tricia's theories about the murder at the Cookery some seven months before; she'd probably be less receptive now. But how much longer could she keep her suspicions to herself?

She needed more information. But how was she going to get it?

Tricia sighed. "Are we about finished, Sheriff?"

"Not quite. I'm going to tell you this once and only once; you are never to violate a crime scene again. What did you think you were doing, playing hero?"

Heroine, Tricia mentally corrected. No way would she say it aloud and set off Wendy Adams's hair-trigger temper. "I've read enough mysteries and true crime to know not to do that. And I did not violate a crime scene. I walked through the house, and I touched nothing but Kimberly Peters's hand. Giving her that tiny bit of comfort was the least I could do for her — the very least I would expect from anyone."

Wendy Adams's expression was doubtful. "I also don't want you talking to the press about any of this."

Tricia raised her hands defensively. "No problem there. In fact, I'm glad to have your blessing *not* to speak to them."

The sheriff merely glared at her. "Go home, Ms. Miles. And stay there." She turned her head toward the doorway. "Placer!" Seconds later, a deputy appeared. "Please escort Ms. Miles to her car. And keep an eye on her. We wouldn't want her to get hurt." She ended her little speech with a sneer.

Tricia got up from her chair. The sheriff didn't budge, and Tricia had to sidle past her in the tiny kitchen. She was glad to get away from the disaster that was Zoë's former home. Glad to inhale deep breaths of the cold, invigorating air.

Glad to get away from Wendy Adams.

Tricia pulled up Russ's driveway and eased the gearshift to Park. "Are you sure you don't want me to come home with you?" he asked.

"No. I just want to go home."

"I could keep you company," he offered with a wry smile.

"Not tonight," she said dryly.

"Don't I even get a good-night kiss?" Russ asked, still strapped in the passenger seat and making no move to leave.

"Just one," Tricia said, and leaned forward, aiming for his cheek, but Russ took her face in his hands, planting a light, warm kiss on her lips before pulling back.

"Maybe two," Tricia said, and put a little more effort into that kiss, remembering why she liked to spend quiet time with Russ. But not tonight. Her nerves were too taut, and Russ would only want to rehash the evening's events for hours on end. She needed something different. Someone different to talk things over with.

Russ pulled back. "I'll call you tomorrow."

"Okay."

He unbuckled the seat belt and got out of the car, shutting the door. He stood, watching, as she pulled out of the drive. He waved as she took off down the road. At the corner, she could still see him standing in his yard.

Instead of heading home, Tricia steered for the convenience store on the edge of town. She parked the car and rummaged in her purse for her cell phone, selected one of the preset numbers, and waited as it rang, two, three, four times. "Hello?"

"Ange, it's Tricia. What are you doing tonight?"

Angelica sighed. "Unpacking boxes."

"Alone?"

"Yes," she said shortly. "And you don't have to rub it in."

"I'm not. I'd kind of like some company, and I was wondering . . . what kind of ice cream do you like?"

"Ice cream?" Angelica asked, her voice rising with pleasure. "Oh, anything. But I especially like butter pecan, pralines and cream, and — what the heck — rocky road. Do you need more suggestions?"

"That'll do."

"Get some of that canned whipped cream. And nuts. Maybe cherries, too. If we're going to splurge, we may as well go whole hog."

"See you in about twenty minutes," Tricia said, and folded up her phone.

True to her word, she arrived at the Cookery's door precisely nineteen and a half minutes later, and let herself in.

Angelica met her at the top of the stairs to the loft apartment. No Miss Marple greeted her. In all the excitement, Tricia had forgotten she'd taken the cat and all her equipment home.

Angelica led her back to the kitchen, where the light was better, frowning as she took in her sister's face. "What happened? You look pale. Did you and Russ have another spat?"

Tricia shook her head. "I had a bit of a shock this evening."

"Hang up your coat. I'll unpack the grocery sack, and we'll talk."

Tricia handed over the bag with its four pints of ice cream and all the trimmings. Angelica had its contents spread across the kitchen island, along with spoons and dishes, by the time Tricia returned to the kitchen.

Tricia looked around the room. The long line of boxes that had been stacked against the wall for months was considerably smaller. Several pictures had been tacked up on the walls, giving the kitchen a much homier appearance. Not prints, but antique oil paintings of fruits and vegetables — succulent strawberries, dew-kissed pears, and sun-ripened tomatoes. They reflected Angelica's love of food — her joy in its preparation and the care she took with its presentation. Tricia looked into the living room. There was actually a coffee table in front of the couch! Okay, it was still covered in boxes, but it was at least visible, and she saw pots of herbs on the sills in front of the street-side windows. "Wow, you've made a lot of headway with your unpacking tonight."

"Forget the decor; tell me what happened," Angelica demanded, removing the lid from a pint of butter pecan.

Tricia recounted her evening. From the lack of romance at Russ's home to finding a bloodied Kimberly to Wendy Adams's stern interrogation.

As Angelica listened, she plopped a big scoop of ice cream into her bowl, added some whipped cream, sprinkled it with crushed nuts, and topped it with a maraschino cherry. "Oh, you poor little thing," she cooed, not without sympathy, when Tricia finished.

Tricia scraped a small spoonful of French vanilla but didn't put it in her mouth. Suddenly the idea of all that sweetness was a turnoff. She set the container aside. "You should've seen that house. There was hatred in every swing of that hammer — sledgehammer — whatever it was."

"What were they looking for? The original manuscripts Zoë passed off as her own? Why would they think Kimberly would have them there? Didn't you say Zoë's main residence was down south somewhere?"

Tricia nodded. "And I can't imagine her keeping them. The woman was an accountant — or at least some kind of bookkeeper, which might indicate she had a logical mind. I'm sure she got rid of them years ago. Kimberly said she retyped a couple of them. And if Zoë was smart, she burned the originals so there'd be no paper trail."

Angelica shook her head, took another spoonful of ice cream. "And Russ had no clue who he was chasing?"

"Just someone in dark sweats and a hoodie."

Angelica frowned. "Didn't you say there was no sign of a hammer in the house?"

Tricia nodded.

Angelica shook her head, frowning. "That doesn't make sense. It would be pretty difficult, if not impossible, to run while carrying a sledgehammer. The handles are like three feet long."

"We're not sure it actually was a sledgehammer."

"From the way you described those holes in the walls, what else could it be? And you're no slouch when it comes to those kinds of details."

Modesty prevented Tricia from agreeing.

"So," Angelica continued, "where do you think the bad guy threw the hammer? In some bushes? Was this person already in the neighbor's yard when Russ took off after him — her — whoever?"

Tricia thought back. Everything had happened so fast. "I'm not sure. I ran straight for the open front door, and Russ didn't, so I guess maybe that could have happened. A couple of deputies followed the trail in the snow, but it petered out on the street. They talked about bringing in some dogs, but Russ said he lost the runner after about a block. He thought he heard a car start up on the next street over, but he couldn't be sure if it was just a neighbor or the person he was chasing."

Angelica added some more whipped cream to her bowl. "It's pretty cold out, but I've got plenty of long underwear and fresh batteries in my big flashlight. What say we take a field trip to Pine Avenue and have a look for that hammer?"

Tricia pushed her spoon and the virtually untouched container of ice cream aside. "Oh, no. Sheriff Adams warned me off, and I don't intend to disobey her. Besides, I'm sure she's already combing the neighborhood for it."

"Are you afraid of the sheriff?"

"Yes! She shut down my business for four days. I'm not going to give her a reason to do it again."

Angelica stuck out her tongue. "Party pooper!"

Tricia shook her head. "I think I'm just plain pooped." She stood. "Time for me to

259

go home. To my cat. To my *own* bed." The thoughts cheered her.

Angelica's expression was a cross between a frown and a pout. "I can't say I'm happy you're going home."

Of course not. If the store had been closed a few more days, she'd have a reprieve from finding permanent replacement workers as long as Ginny and Mr. Everett had nowhere else to go.

"I'm going to miss you, Trish. It was fun having you here. While I was alone here tonight, I realized I even miss Miss Marple."

Tricia swallowed, feeling guilty for her sarcastic thought. She felt even worse when Angelica came around the island and gathered her in her arms for a hug.

SIXTEEN

Tricia woke at seven the next morning to the sound of a flock of honking geese flying over her building. Why was it they made such a pleasant noise and such an unpleasant mess? As the sound faded, she threw back the covers and got up to revel in her usual Sunday morning routine: three miles on the treadmill, a shower, and then a satisfying breakfast of a microwave-thawed bagel with cream cheese and coffee. Miss Marple had been especially happy to return to her favorite haunts and eat her meals in her usual spot. All was right once again in Miss Marple's world, and she let Tricia know it with her continuous happy purring.

First on Tricia's agenda was tidying her shop. Although the store had been closed to customers, it had still accumulated an inordinate amount of dust. Dusting was Mr. Everett's favorite job, so she decided that she'd give the washroom another going over. Despite all her efforts the afternoon before, she feared she'd missed cleaning all the messy black fingerprint powder, and she wanted to give Haven't Got a Clue a thorough vacuuming before the store opened.

Then she remembered Artemus Hamilton was leaving Stoneham this morning. She took a chance, phoned the Brookview Inn, and found him still there.

"Mr. Hamilton? It's Tricia Miles. I'm glad I caught you before you checked out."

"By any chance are you related to an Angelica Miles?" he asked.

"Um . . . yes," she said, taken aback. "She's my sister."

"I just had a visit from her. She brought me fresh-baked muffins, hot coffee, and a manuscript." He didn't sound pleased.

"I'm so sorry. I tried to tell her she should query you, but she's very new to bookselling and knows virtually nothing about the publishing business."

"That much was obvious. Now why were you calling?"

"I'm afraid I have some disturbing news."

"News?" he repeated, dully.

"It's about Kimberly Peters. I'm afraid there's been —" Accident wasn't the right word. "I'm sorry to tell you she was attacked in Zoë's home last night. She was taken to Southern New Hampshire Hospital in Nashua. I'm sorry, I don't know what her condition is."

"Attacked?" he repeated, sounding much more interested.

"Yes." Tricia proceeded to fill him in on the previous evening's events.

"Oh, my," he said, sounding rather shell-shocked by the time Tricia finished her recitation.

"I know she's not your client or anything, but I thought you might like to know."

"Yes. Thank you. And you say she's at a hospital in Nashua?"

"Yes."

"Perhaps —" He stopped, and Tricia was surprised to hear a catch in his voice. "Perhaps I'll send her some flowers before I leave."

"That would be nice," Tricia said, and then mentally amended — *if she survives.* "Have you got a ride to the airport?"

"Yes. The inn's shuttle will take me. Thanks for asking. And thank you for calling, Ms. Miles." Hamilton hung up.

Tricia frowned, annoyed at his abrupt dismissal. She exhaled a long breath, but decided not to worry about it. She had other things to do.

Miss Marple danced around the door to

the stairwell, and Tricia was just about to head downstairs when the phone rang. She glanced at the little readout, but didn't recognize the number on caller ID. She picked up the receiver anyway, hoping it wouldn't be Portia McAlister. "Hello?"

"Tricia?" Whew! It was Ginny.

"You sound awful. What's wrong?"

"I'm just tired. I spent most of the night in the emergency room at Southern New Hampshire Medical Center in Nashua."

"How did you know about Kimberly?"

"Kimberly?" Ginny echoed, sounding puzzled.

"Yes, she was taken there by ambulance last night after being attacked in Zoë's home."

"That's terrible. But I wasn't there for her. I drove Brian in somewhere around midnight. He was so sick. He came over all pale and clammy early last evening. He was vomiting and had diarrhea. He wouldn't let me call an ambulance, but after three or four hours of this, he agreed to let me drive him to the emergency room."

"Appendicitis?" Tricia guessed.

"No. They think it was food poisoning. I admit I'm not that great a cook, but how can you ruin soup and sandwiches? The fridge came with the house, and I don't

264

think it keeps food cold enough. It was probably the sliced ham. We'd had it for almost a week."

"Were you sick?"

"No. But we didn't eat the same things. I had a slice of pizza from the convenience store down the road. The doctor said it will probably be tomorrow before the lab can identify what made Brian so ill."

"I'm really sorry about this, Ginny. Is Brian home now?"

"Yes, but he's so weak, I don't think I should leave him. Will you tell Frannie I can't make it to the diner?"

"Diner?"

"Yeah, the Tuesday Night Book Club is meeting there. A cheer-up brunch for Nikki."

"Oh, dear, I completely forgot about it."

"Can you do me another favor? I was afraid to call Angelica. I know she was counting on me to come in today."

"Don't worry about Ange. I'll explain it all. And if Brian needs you tomorrow, don't feel you have to come to work."

"But I do have to come in. Especially if we're going to have to replace the fridge now, too. And I don't know how we're going to pay the hospital bill. We don't have any insurance," she said with a small sob.

Tricia could well afford to give Ginny the money she needed to buy a refrigerator or pay the hospital bill, but she also knew Ginny was proud. Too proud to take what she hadn't earned. She'd have to think of some way to give her a bonus. But then she also knew Ginny would insist that Mr. Everett be treated in the same way. She'd been lucky in hiring two of the hardest-working, best employees in all of Stoneham. And why was it so hard to be generous and not appear to be fawning?

"Do what you have to do, Ginny. You know I'm behind you."

"Thanks, Tricia. I'm just worried that Angelica will think I'm trying to screw her. I'm not. Really. Please, make her understand."

"I will. Now you take care of yourself *and* Brian. And keep me posted."

"Thanks. I will." And Ginny broke the connection.

Tricia hung up her phone. Now the real work began. Convincing Angelica that Ginny *wasn't* just out to annoy her. The thing was . . . could she spare Mr. Everett, who did not want to work for Angelica, and since she hadn't been open in days, could she really do without any help?

Her mind raced. Mr. Everett had made it

plain he did *not* want to return to the Cookery. Tricia thought of everyone she knew in Stoneham — was there anyone she could call upon to lend a hand?

She grabbed her local phone book, flipped through the pages, and came up with the name of someone she thought might help. She punched in the number and recited a silent prayer.

The phone rang once, twice, and was answered on the third ring.

"Hello?"

"Frannie?"

"Is that you, Tricia?" came the oh-so-familiar Texas twang.

"Yes. Frannie, I'm calling to let you know Ginny can't make it to the diner for Nikki's brunch this morning. Her boyfriend is very ill and she doesn't want to leave him."

"Oh, that poor thing. I hope he'll be better soon."

"She thinks so. Frannie, I also have a very, very big favor to ask of you."

Frannie laughed, a joy-inspiring sound like that of an angel. "What's up?"

"You know my sister Angelica owns the Cookery — the cookbook store."

"Oh, sure. I was in there the other day, remember? She's got the most marvelous gadgets hanging up on her north wall. I swear I could've spent an entire paycheck in there."

"Well, she's got a really big problem. She's lost her sales force." Tricia had to bite her tongue not to say why. "If you're not doing anything this afternoon, would you consider spending a few hours helping her out?"

Tricia squeezed her eyes shut, held her breath, and crossed her fingers.

"If this was football season, I'd have to say no. I watch all the Patriots games — and the Dallas games, if they ever show 'em. But right now — I'm champing at the bit to do something I've never tried before! So, yes, I'd be glad to give your sister a hand."

"You would?" Tricia said, hoping she didn't sound too astonished.

"Yeah. I was just gonna sit around here and watch an Audrey Hepburn marathon on American Movie Classics, but it sounds a whole lot more fun to spend the day talking about food."

"So — so, you'll come to the Cookery?"

"Sure. What time does your sister need me?"

"Come about eleven thirty. That way she can give you a brief overview of the store and how she operates."

"Sure. We'll be done with brunch by that time."

Tricia winced, hoping that by Monday Frannie would not be her newest enemy. "Great," she managed. "I'll tell Angelica that you'll be there before she opens. I really owe you, Frannie."

Frannie laughed, the sound of her voice pure gold. "Not at all. I think this will be a blast. Woo-hoo! Today will sure be a lot more interesting than what I'd planned."

Yeah, and may you *not* live in interesting times, as the old Chinese curse proclaimed.

"See you at the diner," Tricia said. They said good-bye, and she hung up.

Tricia had to fortify herself with a very strong cup of coffee before she dared dial Angelica's number. She picked it up on the third ring.

"Ange, it's Tricia."

"Hey, what's up?"

"First of all, why did you take your manuscript to the Brookview Inn?"

"Because that's where Artemus Hamilton is staying. I figured this morning would be my only chance to get it to him before he leaves for New York."

"You could've mailed it to him."

"That's so tedious, and why bother when a personal visit is so much more —"

"Annoying? Presumptuous? Impolite?" Tricia interrupted.

269

"Personal," Angelica finished. "I think he was charmed by me and my presentation. I'll look forward to receiving an acceptance letter in the coming weeks."

She was absolutely clueless.

"Believe it or not, I didn't call to talk about your manuscript. Now don't get mad, but Ginny can't work for you today."

"What?" came Angelica's scorching voice.

"I said don't get mad. Her boyfriend has been hospitalized, and she needs to be with him today."

"Oh. Well, I guess I can understand that," Angelica said, not sounding at all convincing.

"He's going to be okay, but even better, I've found somebody willing to give you a hand for today at least."

"Who?" Angelica demanded, not in the least placated.

"Frannie Armstrong."

"Oh, Frannie?" She almost sounded pleased. "That sounds quite all right. Thanks, Trish."

Tricia resisted the urge to exhale a breath of relief. "Good. Well, I told her to show up half an hour before you open. That should give you all the time you need to train her." No, it didn't, but it sounded reasonable.

"Oh, Trish, you are a savior." No, she

wasn't, because she hadn't been willing to offer up Mr. Everett as a sacrificial lamb. And really, would Frannie hate her forever after several hours of unpleasant servitude at the Cookery?

Maybe. But right now she was willing to take the chance.

Miss Marple bounded down the stairs to the shop, eager to get back to work sunning herself on the counter, dusting the higher shelves with her fluffy tail, or just taking a nap on one of the comfy chairs in the nook.

Tricia crossed the store to open the blinds over the big display window. The sight of the News Team Ten van greeted her. Standing outside it, looking a bit windblown and partially frozen, was Portia McAlister.

Feeling a tad sorry for the woman, Tricia opened her door. "You look like you could use a cup of hot coffee."

"Could I ever," Portia said.

"Where's your cameraman?"

"At the diner. He wanted something a little more substantial."

Tricia held the door wide open and sighed. "Come on in."

Portia wasted no time.

Tricia shut the door. "Look, the sheriff says I can't talk to you about Zoë's murder or what happened to Kimberly Peters last night."

Portia frowned. "She's gotten to everyone. There *is* such a thing as freedom of speech in this country, you know."

"I'm a firm believer in it myself. I also firmly believe in not annoying Wendy Adams," Tricia said, and stepped over to the store's coffee station.

A sly smile crept onto Portia's lips. "Yes, I understand you've had a run-in with her before."

"Something else I'm not interested in talking about."

"Then why did you invite me in?"

"Because I'm tired of trying to avoid you."

"It's my job to be persistent. And you're making that job very difficult."

"Sorry. It can't be helped."

Portia straightened. "If you can't tell me about the crimes against Carter and her niece, at least tell me why you're so interested in them yourself."

"Initially I wanted to get my store open. Wendy Adams had me shut down for days. Longer than was technically necessary."

"And now?"

"Let's just say I'm not sure the Sheriff's Department is following every one of their leads." *And are clueless about some potential*

272

leads, she kept herself from voicing aloud.

Portia leaned her elbows on the counter. "You know, I could be a big help to you. I know things about the case you probably don't."

"Such as?"

"I'm not about to spill them without getting something in return."

Tricia hoisted the coffee grounds basket into the air. "I did offer you coffee."

"I can get that from the diner."

"You do have that option."

"Come on, Tricia, toss me something. Just a crumb."

Tricia thought about it. It might be better to get someone with the tenacity of a terrier in on the hunt. Someone who could ask questions and redirect Wendy Adams's anger away from Tricia's inquiries.

"How do you feel about revealing your sources?"

"I spent a week in jail back in the spring of 2003 to protect one. I have to tell you, those orange jumpsuits are ugly as hell, and the fabric chafes, but I'd do it over again if I had to."

Tricia poured water into the coffeemaker and hit the On switch. She'd promised Artemus Hamilton she wouldn't say anything about Zoë not writing the Jess and Addie books until after the weekend. That was before someone had gone after and nearly killed Kimberly Peters.

"Okay, I'm ready to dish. Years ago, several of Stoneham's citizens questioned whether Zoë Carter actually wrote any of the books she's credited with."

Portia's eyes widened. "Interesting. Did they have any proof?"

Tricia shook her head. "No, but their suspicions got me looking into things."

"And you don't believe she wrote the books, either?"

"I *know* she didn't write them. I've had it confirmed from two sources."

"Would one of them be Kimberly Peters?"

"I'm not saying. You asked me to toss you a crumb. That was it. Now it's your turn to give up something."

Portia straightened and smoothed back her hair. "Okay. Fair is fair. Like you, I've been looking into Zoë Carter's background. It seems she was indicted for embezzlement back in the 1990s."

Tricia waved a hand in dismissal. "I saw your report online days ago."

"Ah, but I didn't tell the whole story. She got off by turning in her boss — her ex-lover. The court was lenient because she had no prior convictions and had recently taken

274

in her orphaned niece. It was very unusual. She may have had some kind of political in, although I haven't been able to figure out the exact connection."

"It's still old news," Tricia said.

Portia chewed her lip for a moment, as though considering. "Zoë was being black-mailed."

"The person who wrote the letters has come forward. The sheriff investigated that angle and moved on to other things."

Portia frowned and sighed. "You *have* been persistent."

"I had good teachers," Tricia said, and waved a hand to take in all the mystery stories on the bookshelves around them.

"Okay, but this is the last thing I'm offering up." Portia leaned closer, lowered her voice. "As a girl, Zoë Carter wanted to be a nun."

"A nun?" Tricia repeated, surprised. Then again, Zoë dressed so conservatively, and her lifestyle was so . . . bland. But no one she'd spoken to had mentioned Zoë had deep religious convictions.

Portia nodded. "She got kicked out of the convent for improper behavior. With a little digging, I found out it was for stealing. Apparently she wasn't quite able to honor her vow of poverty. I guess her indictment for embezzlement several years later shouldn't have come as a huge surprise."

Maybe, but despite the millions she'd raked in as the so-called author of the *Forever* books, she hadn't lived the life of a millionaire, either.

"None of this seems to have anything to do with her getting murdered in my store."

"Nothing we *yet* know about. She had so many skeletons in the closet, I'm surprised no other reporters dug deep to find the truth about her before this."

"Yes, it would've been great fodder for the tabloids, especially as she was such a hermit when it came to book promotion."

"If you can't tell me about your run-ins with Zoë dead and Kimberly just attacked, tell me what you make of that ruined statue."

"Same thing as you do — that Zoë's killer did it."

"Any suspects?" Portia pushed.

Tricia shook her head. "Not so far."

"And why attack Kimberly?"

"To retrieve the original manuscripts?" Tricia suggested.

"Why?"

"To conceal who wrote them."

"Conceal or reveal?"

Tricia nodded. "Good question."

The coffeemaker stopped bubbling as the last of the brew dripped into the pot.

"If what you said about Zoë not writing the books is true, it's just another chink in her armor," Portia said.

"What are you going to do with that piece of knowledge?"

"I'm going to find out the truth. And I'm going to report it. Maybe I can even parlay it into a job in a better market."

"Better than Boston?" Tricia asked.

"Hey, winter in LA is a lot warmer than here on the East Coast."

"Can I count on you to tell me what you find out?" Tricia asked, pouring coffee for them both and handing one of the cups to Portia.

"Possibly. Can I expect the same from you?"

"Count on it."

They touched their paper coffee cups in a toast.

SEVENTEEN

Tricia always considered the Bookshelf Diner's name a bit of a misrepresentation. After all, she didn't know of many diners with a function room. Whether it was a diner or a family restaurant, it did indeed offer this amenity, and it was usually reserved for private parties, baby and wedding showers, and after-funeral-service occasions. The theme of its decor was unidentifiable; no doubt its creamy walls and the nondescript purple-gray floral border that ran just below the room's ceiling were deliberate choices, so that the room could be used for any purpose. In this instance, the occasion was more supportive than celebratory.

A long table had been set up in the center of the room, with unused smaller tables and extra chairs pushed off to the side. A stab at elegance had been attempted, but the linen tablecloth, though clean, had seen its share of spilled wine.

Tricia arrived later than she'd wanted, and was seated at one end of the table. The guest of honor was seated directly opposite her at the far end of the table, with at least four book club members and several of Nikki's other friends in between. Nikki's assistant, Steve Fenton, sat at her left, looking uncomfortable in the presence of so many women. He'd made an effort to spiff up, too. The do-rag was gone and the sleeves of his denim shirt were rolled up, revealing his heavily muscled arms.

Among the missing, Grace Harris and Mr. Everett. Tricia hadn't expected to see her employee — he never spent money frivolously — but she'd more than half expected to see his lady friend, who often acted as the book group's unofficial spokesperson.

"Glad you could make it," Frannie said, handing Tricia a menu.

"Where's Grace?" Tricia asked, noting an empty chair at the middle of the table.

"Grace Harris come to a diner?" Frannie asked, incredulous.

"Why not? I never got the impression she was a snob."

"Oh, I didn't mean that. She's the nicest woman on the face of the planet," Frannie hurriedly attested. "It's just that she's so

279

classy, what with her lovely clothes and jewelry. I would just never expect her to get down and dirty and eat eggs, bacon, and home fries with ketchup."

Tricia had to agree with that statement. And it was also true that, gracious as she was, it was the reading and the discussion of the books that she enjoyed, not necessarily the company of the people in the group. Except for Mr. Everett, that is.

Tricia glanced at her menu. She'd already eaten a bagel, and wasn't the least bit hungry. Maybe she'd just order toast and a cup of anything other than coffee. She set the menu aside.

"Anyway," Frannie started, addressing the others, "as I was telling you, if you don't want to be responsible for the deaths of innocent creatures, you've got to contact the Board of Selectmen and tell them."

"They wouldn't really kill the geese, would they?" Julia Overline asked.

"I don't care if they do," said a woman in a blue sweater, sitting farther up the table. "They're messy and they're noisy. Think of all the homeless people we could feed with them."

Oh, yeah, that's the answer, Tricia thought, considering all the health regulations that proposed solution would violate. Some

280

people just didn't have a clue . . . or were just woefully ignorant. She chose to think the latter.

At the head of the table, Nikki sat in animated conversation with a woman Tricia didn't know.

"Poor Nikki. I'm glad so many people showed up to cheer her up," Frannie said, changing the subject.

"She's worked so hard," Julia piped up. Of all the members of the book group, Tricia knew Julia the least. Gray-haired and plump, wearing a floral-embroidered sweatshirt, she was a voracious reader who'd recently joined the readers group, and had bought at least ten books, which certainly endeared her to Tricia. "She's had such a rough life. The family's home burned to the ground when she was just an infant. Her father died, too, but that was years after her mother's disappearance."

Tricia blinked. "Her mother's what?"

"Disappearance — when Nikki was just a young girl. It was the talk of Stoneham for months."

"And she was never found?"

Julia shook her head.

"Did the authorities feel it was foul play?" Tricia asked.

Julia shrugged. "She just disappeared. No

sign of a struggle, or blood, or anything. She didn't take any clothes. Her purse was still in her home. Her car was parked in the driveway. She was just gone."

"Didn't they suspect her husband?"

Julia shrugged. "Of course. After all, it was no secret he used to hit the poor woman. But they never arrested him for it. He was at work — with witnesses — the day she disappeared.

Tricia knew that in cases like the one Julia described, the husband was always suspected — especially if the relationship had involved domestic abuse. "How old was Nikki at the time?"

"Nine or ten. Years later they had her mother declared dead in order to settle the estate so Nikki could go to that fancy pastry institute in Paris."

"They? Who's they?"

"Nikki's grandmother and her aunt — Phil's mother and sister."

Poor Nikki. Tricia had never really been as close to her mother as she would've liked. Angelica had been the child her parents never thought they'd have. Tricia's arrival five years later had been a surprise, and perhaps not as welcome as that of the favored Angelica. But Tricia had had her grandmother to love. A grandmother who'd

282

imparted to her the love of books — especially mysteries.

"Sounds like Nikki's a real fighter," Tricia said.

"She sure is," Frannie agreed, and took a sip of her ice water. "Which is why I'm sure she'll bounce back from this loan disappointment. And speaking of fighting, just look at the muscles on that guy's arms," she said, with an admiring glance at Fenton.

"Oh, yes," Julia agreed. "It's so sad about him, too."

"Sad?" Tricia asked.

"He was once considered a shoo-in for the Olympic track team, until he hurt one of his knees."

"He used to be a personal trainer at the Stoneham gym." Julia gave Tricia a knowing glance. "You don't think he developed all those heavenly muscles lifting trays of cookies and cakes, do you?"

"Gym?" Tricia asked. There was no gym in Stoneham.

"It folded before you got here," Frannie explained.

Tricia studied the hunk at Nikki's side. He had to be a decade older than Nikki — more Tricia's age — reminding her of a younger, more handsome version of Bruce Willis. "Are they involved?"

"Not a chance," Julia answered, and laughed. "Nikki told me she was through with men after her divorce. They say she married a man just like her father — and just as abusive."

"I've seen Steve walking or jogging around the village or out on the road to Route 101," Tricia said.

"Of course. He doesn't drive, you know."

"Why is that?" Tricia asked.

Julia shrugged. "I guess because he's such a fitness nut. I've also seen him tooling around the village on a bike in good weather."

Frannie leaned closer, spoke with a hint of excitement in her voice. "I heard you were involved in some excitement last night."

"Me?" Tricia said, frowning.

"Yes, it's all over town that you and Russ Smith chased away a burglar and saved Kimberly Peters's life."

"Oh, that," Tricia said, and looked around, hoping to see the waitress and snag a cup of something hot.

"Did you really?" Julia asked eagerly. Obviously the whole town *wasn't* talking about it. Conversation around the table had stopped, all of them now looking at Tricia, waiting for her to spill the whole story.

"It wasn't that big a deal. Kimberly had already called nine-one-one. We just got there before the deputies did."

"What about the burglar?" Julia asked.

"Russ went after him, but he got away."

"Kimberly? Wasn't she that awful young woman at the signing with Zoë Carter?" Julia asked.

Tricia nodded.

"Why do you think someone came after her?" Frannie asked.

"I have no idea," Tricia lied.

"I heard Kimberly's in critical condition," Frannie said. Had she called the hospital to find out, or had she relied on her network of friendly informants to get this information?

"I didn't know that," Tricia said.

Frannie nodded. "She suffered head injuries. It's touch and go if she'll live." She shook her head and *tsk*ed. "I've been reading a lot of detective books lately, you know, and I think Kimberly's attacker was probably the same person who killed her aunt."

"Oh, that's obvious," Julia said. "But the funny thing is . . . it's probably someone we all know." Her gaze flitted around the table. "Someone who was in your store on Tuesday, Tricia."

As though she hadn't already considered

that fact one hundred times. Then again, there was no one she would even think could be capable of such a heinous act.

Still, she wondered about Grace. How she'd suddenly left town either the night of the murder or the morning after. And Mr. Everett had lied about it. But there was no way Grace had killed Zoë. She'd been accounted for during the entire ten or fifteen minutes Zoë had been absent from the group.

It couldn't be Grace. Grace, who'd had some as yet unknown beef with Zoë.

But what if the killer was someone Grace knew? Someone she'd tried to shield? What if — ?

"Can I take your order?" Janice, the Bookshelf Diner's weekend waitress stood by Tricia's elbow. She'd been so lost in thought, she hadn't even noticed her arrival.

"Just an order of wheat toast and a cup of tea, please."

Frannie tapped Tricia's arm. "No wonder you've managed to keep your figure. You never eat anything fattening."

"That you know of," Tricia said, and forced a laugh.

Janice continued circling the table until she'd taken all the orders, then retreated. The woman in the blue sweater tapped her water glass, gaining everyone's attention. She stood up and held her glass up in a toast. "Stoneham has, unfortunately, had a spate of serious crime. What one individual has done has shaken many of us. And yet it can't be argued that our little town isn't safe. It's outsiders that have attracted the wrong element." Her gaze momentarily settled on Tricia before moving back to the head of the table. "The real citizens of Stoneham know what true friendship is. That's why we're here this morning, to show our love and support to our dear friend, Nikki."

"Hear, hear," someone echoed.

Tricia's cheeks flushed. She glanced at Frannie to find her tight-lipped, and her complexion just as rosy.

The woman sat down.

"Of all the nerve," Frannie muttered under her breath.

Though this wasn't the first time Tricia had experienced the undercurrent of an us-against-them mentality from some of the denizens of Stoneham, she hadn't ever heard anyone voice that sentiment so blatantly.

Nikki stood and cleared her throat. "Thanks, Linda. I can't thank everyone — and I mean *everyone* — enough for coming here today." She focused her attention on Tricia and Frannie, and laughed nervously. "You guys *are* the best."

Everyone at the table broke into applause, with Frannie clapping the loudest.

It wasn't hard to get back into the groove of hand-selling mysteries, and Tricia fell in love with her store all over again. Mr. Everett was back to his cheerful self, and Miss Marple luxuriated in the afternoon sunshine that poured through Haven't Got a Clue's front display window. Trade was brisk for a Sunday, and only a few people loitered around the washroom, hoping for some titillating clue about Zoë Carter's murder. The fingerprint powder had been nearly impossible to fully clean, and every time Tricia shooed away some curious gawker, she saw another spot of the stuff that needed eradicating.

She'd just shut the washroom door for the fifth time when Mr. Everett signaled her from the register. "We're out of coffee, Ms. Miles. I made a pot before the last crowd of customers came in. It won't last until closing. Shall I go get another couple of pounds?"

Tricia shook her head. "I'll go. And I'll pick up a few goodies from the patisserie.

Can you handle everything here for ten or fifteen minutes?"

He nodded, always dignified. "Certainly."

"I'll just grab my coat, then."

Though the temperature was only in the forties, the sunshine felt warm on her cheeks as she stopped first at the Coffee Bean, then made her way down Main Street to the Stoneham Patisserie.

For the first time in a long time, the patisserie was not overflowing with customers. Nikki stood behind the counter, waiting on a customer who bought a loaf of cinnamon raisin bread. She rang up the sale. "Have a nice day," she said, and turned to Tricia.

"I'm surprised to see you here."

"Why?"

"Isn't Haven't Got a Clue back in business?"

"Yes, thank goodness. Mr. Everett is holding down the fort. I just came to get some cookies for our customers."

"I've got some nice raspberry thumbprint cookies." She leaned forward, lowered her voice to a whisper. "I think they're Mr. Everett's favorites."

"Then how about two dozen of those? If any are left over, he can take them home."

"Sure. Let me wrap them up."

The door opened and another customer

entered. "Nikki, I need three loaves of Italian bread — now! I've got guests arriving in ten minutes, and —"

Nikki looked from her new customer to Tricia, who waved a hand. "Take care of her first. I'm not in a rush."

"Thanks," Nikki said gratefully.

Tricia wandered the store, peeking through the display cases at the bread, cookies, cakes, and pies. Pretty pedestrian fare for someone who'd trained in Paris, but if that was what the local traffic demanded, that's what Nikki had to supply.

The door from the shop to the working bakery beyond was propped open with a rubber wedge, and Tricia noted the now-silent industrial-size mixer and bowl, which currently sported a bread hook. Angelica had a regular-size model on her kitchen counter. She recognized a bread slicer and saw a metal cabinet filled with trays of baked goods. It was from there that Nikki gathered the cookies. Steve stood at a counter with what looked like a nail in one hand and a pastry bag in the other, magically producing a beautiful rose out of pink icing. He plopped it on the frosted cake in front of him and started another.

Tricia's bored gaze wandered, but soon stopped on the floor against the far wall, focusing on something she hadn't expected to see in a bakery: a satchel of tools. Sticking out of the top were a can of spray paint and what looked like a . . . sledgehammer. But it couldn't be. Sledgehammers had long handles, and this hammer's head stuck out of a bag that could be only nine or ten inches in height. And why did Nikki have a bag of tools in the working part of her bakery?

Nikki finished plucking cookies from the tray and brought the bakery box back into the shop, setting it on the counter and tying string around it. Tricia handed her a ten and Nikki made change.

"Thanks," Tricia said, pocketing the money.

"Are you okay?" Nikki asked, concerned. "You look kind of funny."

Tricia forced a smile. "I'm fine."

"Thanks for coming to the diner this morning. Only I can't apologize enough for Linda's rude comments about 'the wrong element' here in Stoneham. Honest, Tricia, not everyone in the village thinks like her. I tried to give Frannie a call and apologize to her, too, but she wasn't home."

"No, she's helping Angelica at the Cookery this afternoon."

"She's got a big heart."

The door opened and another customer wandered in.

"I'd better go," Tricia said, sounding nervous even to herself.

"See you on Tuesday at the book club," Nikki called, as Tricia made good her escape.

"Is something wrong, Ms. Miles?" Mr. Everett asked as Tricia closed and locked the shop door on the last of their customers. The clock read five o'clock even.

"No." That wasn't true, especially not when her suspicions about Nikki had so recently been ignited. "Yes, there are several things wrong. One of them concerns you, Mr. Everett." It was time to clear the air at last.

"Me?" he asked, puzzled.

"Something you said the other day. You told me Grace had to leave town to take care of a sick sister. When I mentioned to her that I was sorry to hear about it, she told me she didn't have a sister."

Mr. Everett lowered his head so that his gaze was focused on the carpet.

"It's none of my business what Grace was doing or where she went, but I am concerned that you —"

She hated to say that four letter word.

He said it for her. "I lied. And I'm not proud of it."

"But why?"

"I didn't feel it was up to me to discuss another's personal business."

"I understand that. And I would never ask you to betray a confidence, Mr. Everett. But I don't appreciate it when someone I work with breaches my trust. You've been a businessman, I'm sure you can understand where I'm coming from."

He nodded. "If Grace wants you to know her business, she will tell you. I can't betray *her* trust."

Tricia nodded. "I accept that. But please, Mr. Everett, don't lie to me again. Next time, just tell me it's none of my business."

He nodded. "Then I must respectfully tell you that this is none of your business, Ms. Miles."

Tricia straightened to her full height. "Thank you, Mr. Everett. We won't speak of this again."

"Thank you, Ms. Miles." Mr. Everett turned away.

And Tricia knew no more now than she had before they'd started the conversation.

EIGHTEEN

Not ten minutes after Mr. Everett had left for the evening, a knock on the door caused Tricia to look up from her paperwork. Angelica stood outside. Tricia crossed the front of the shop and opened the door. "Why didn't you use your key?"

"It's upstairs. I thought I'd invite you over for dinner."

"Bob busy tonight?" Tricia asked.

"Yes, but I also figured you might want some company. Unless you have plans with Russ, that is."

Tricia shook her head. "He hasn't called. Besides, I was thinking about going to the hospital in Nashua to visit Kimberly."

"Great idea. I'll come with you."

Tricia stacked her papers, and tucked them under the counter. "You don't have to."

"No, I insist. You don't want to be driving there all alone in the dark."

"It won't be dark when I leave — which will be any minute," she said, and headed for the back of the store to retrieve her jacket. "Besides, I'm a big girl. I can handle it."

"Oh, you know what I mean. Hey, we can stop and get a bite to eat on the way up there."

"Okay. I'll drive."

"Fine. Just let me go back to the Cookery to get my purse."

As Angelica disappeared through the door, the old telephone rang. Tricia headed back to the sales counter, tossed her jacket on it, and picked up the receiver. "Haven't Got a Clue, Tricia speaking. Sorry, but we're closed."

"Tricia? It's Russ."

"Hey, I was hoping I'd hear from you."

"You busy tonight?"

"I wasn't, until five minutes ago. But now Angelica and I are going to Nashua to visit Kimberly Peters at the hospital. What did you have in mind?"

"Dinner, of course. I was hoping the third attempt might be the charm."

"No such luck, darling. At least not to-night. Ange and I are getting a bite on the way."

"You might be wasting your time and gas

by driving to Nashua. When I checked earlier this afternoon, Kimberly was still out of it. They're keeping her heavily sedated."

"I thought hospitals didn't give out personal information on patients anymore."

"I'm a reporter. I have my sources. So why go visit? She's not your friend."

"As far as I know, she hasn't got anyone else. No family, and no friends that I know of — at least not in Stoneham. If she *is* awake, she might be grateful to see at least one familiar face. I thought I might buy a plant or something on the way. That way, when she does wake up, she'll have something pleasant to look at."

"You're hoping she's going to tell you who attacked her and ransacked Zoë's house," he accused.

"Don't be absurd," Tricia said, although that was exactly what she'd hoped, and was extremely grateful he couldn't see her face at that moment. "And what if I do? Am I supposed to call you so you can add that to your story?"

"Play nice," he warned. "If she *is* awake, I suspect you'll have to vie for her attention with Sheriff Adams or one of her deputies. If the woman has any smarts at all, she'll have a guard posted at Kimberly's door."

"I did think of that," Tricia said, not

bothering to hide her disdain.

"The thing is," he said, his voice softening, "have you considered that you could be in danger?"

"What are you talking about?"

"Don't play dumb with me, Tricia. At every turn, you've been one step behind the killer. That means you're likely to be the next target."

"May I remind you I'm not the one who chased the robber?"

"No, but you were the last one to speak to Kimberly. Zoë's killer might think she said something of significance to you."

"But she didn't."

"The killer doesn't know that."

Why did he always have to be right?

"I'll be perfectly safe with Angelica."

"Only if she's packing heat in her handbag."

"Now who's been reading too many old detective stories?"

He laughed. "You have contaminated me," he conceded. "Let me come with you two."

"You just want to tag along in case Kimberly's awake and *does* tell me something. That way you can put it in your next issue."

"Tricia, there's no such thing as 'breaking news' when you publish a weekly. And could you try to think the best of me once in a while instead of the worst?"

Whoa, that hurt. But he was right.

"I'm sorry, Russ. That was uncalled for."

"Thank you. Now what about my offer to take you to Nashua?"

"I don't know. Angelica might feel the need for bonding. And she'll probably want to dish on Frannie."

"Frannie?"

"She worked with Ange today. I arranged it. Frannie will probably never speak to me again."

Russ laughed. "Angelica's reputation does precede her."

"Sadly, you're right."

"Look, why don't you give me a call when you get back? Or maybe you could drop Angelica off and come see me."

"We'll see." She glanced at the clock. "Ange will be here any minute. I'd better be ready. You know she doesn't like to be kept waiting."

"Okay, but don't forget me."

"How could I?" she said, her voice softening. "You sent me a card that says you love me."

"Yes, I did."

Tricia couldn't help but smile. "I will definitely call you later."

"I'll hold you to it. Bye."

"Bye." She hung up the phone.

The shop door opened and Angelica entered, her gigantic purse slung over her shoulder and a smile plastered across her lips. "Let's get this show on the road."

Tricia and Angelica headed down the sidewalk to the municipal parking lot.

"Cold again," Angelica said, and shivered. "Doesn't winter ever end around here?"

"Give it another month and we'll have plenty of spring flowers," Tricia said as they approached her car. She pressed the button on her key ring and the doors obediently unlocked. They got in.

"Where can I find some daffodils or a plant to take to Kimberly?" Tricia asked.

"Hey, you've lived here longer than me. Shouldn't the hospital sell some in their gift shop?"

"Possibly, but they may close early on a Sunday evening."

Tricia started the car and pulled out of the parking lot and into Main Street, steering north for Route 101.

"Do you know where we're heading?" Angelica asked.

"I looked at a map earlier this afternoon. Do you want to eat first or go straight to the hospital?"

"Visit first. Eat later. I'd like to try a new little French bistro not far from the hospital. One of my customers told me about it the other day."

"If you've got the address, I'm sure we can find it," Tricia said, as the last of the village fell behind them. Though it wasn't yet dark, the trees that lined the road cloaked it in deep shadow. Tricia turned on her headlights. Theirs was the only car on the road.

"By the way, I can't thank you enough for sending Frannie to me today, Trish."

"What?" Tricia asked, disbelieving.

"We just had the most fun all day long. And I sold a ton of books. The woman's a natural-born salesperson. Too bad she's got a regular job, because I would hire her in a heartbeat. In fact, she's coming back to work for me next weekend. She suggested I order some Hawaiian cookbooks, and we could make some appetizers or dessert and pass it around next Saturday. Have you ever had poi?"

"No. Isn't it some kind of messy, green goop from a root, that's beaten to a pulp — and looks not unlike goose droppings?"

"Frannie swears it's delicious."

"I think I'd just swear if I had to eat it," Tricia said, glancing into her rearview mirror. A car coming up from behind flicked on its headlights, blasting her retinas with its high beams.

"You have absolutely no culinary adventure in your soul," Angelica went on.

They zipped past a deserted vegetable stand. "So says you."

"Are you kidding? I've eaten eel, whale blubber — highly overrated in my opinion — and once I even ate a box of chocolate-covered ants."

"On a dare, I'll bet."

"Of course. I was about eleven. Nowadays I can think of plenty of better uses for luscious dark chocolate."

The lights of the car following seemed to grow bigger in the rearview mirror. Tricia stepped on the accelerator a little harder, but the too-close car kept pace. A growing anxiety caused her to press down even more.

"Should we be going this fast on this road?" Angelica asked.

"Someone's playing with me," Tricia said, and eased up on the gas.

The car following them bumped her.

"Hey!" Angelica called, bracing her hands against the dashboard. "That's not playing. That's serious stuff."

Tricia steered for the side of the road, the spinning tires sending gravel flying.

The car behind did the same thing.

"What do they want from us?" Angelica cried, grabbing for her purse.

"Playing chicken. But it's not a game, and I won't play." Tricia slowed even more, and the car rammed the back end of her vehicle.

Angelica withdrew her cell phone, frantically pushing the buttons. "Why is there never a cell tower around when you need one?"

"Keep punching those buttons," Tricia hollered as the car bumped them again, harder this time. The driver meant business.

"Do something!" Angelica wailed.

"What?"

"I don't know. You're the one who reads all those mysteries. What would Miss Marple do now?"

"She never drove a car," Tricia said, and swerved to the left, hoping to shake their tail, but the car swerved right behind her like a shadow.

Tricia wrenched the wheel again, desperately hoping they wouldn't go into a spin. The road was some four or five feet above the surrounding terrain, drainage ditches running along both sides of it.

"If mysteries won't help — think of what James Bond would do."

"James Bond?" Tricia repeated, grimly

holding onto the steering wheel while flashing on a sexy, young Sean Connery. Yes, James Bond would've gotten out of this easily — by dumping oil on the road, or nails to puncture the bad guy's tires. But Tricia didn't drive an Aston Martin; she'd purchased the white Lexus without the "licensed to kill" package.

As she struggled to maintain control, a dark shape came whizzing overhead — a Canada goose — and then another.

"We're going to die!" Angelica wailed, shielding her face with her hands.

Tricia's gaze bobbed from the road to the rearview mirror. The car behind swerved — and Tricia heard the screech of brakes.

"It's falling behind!" she hollered.

"Behind what?" Angelica wailed, her hands still plastered to her face.

"The car, it's —"

But their pursuer regained control, the car's headlights growing bigger and bigger.

It rammed them, this time sending the Lexus careening off the road and into a ditch with a shuddering crash.

NINETEEN

The flashing lights of the police cruiser cast weird shadows against the pines. Tricia watched as the winch on the back of the flatbed tow truck pulled her car up the makeshift ramp. The Lexus might've been drivable, but she wasn't about to take the chance. While Angelica had called nine-one-one, Tricia had extricated her own cell phone and called the one person in Stoneham she knew would mourn her.

Russ stood beside her, collar pulled up around his neck, his hands thrust deep into his jeans pockets, his ears already beginning to go pink. It wasn't until he'd shown up that she'd stopped shaking.

"I should have listened to you when you said Zoë's killer might come after me," Tricia said.

"And I should have insisted on driving you to Nashua." He withdrew his right hand from his pocket and wrapped his arm around Tricia's shoulder, pulling her close. She allowed herself to rest her head against his chest.

If it hadn't been for that goose . . . Russ had found its remains by the side of the road some hundred or so feet behind them.

Her gaze drifted to where the Lexus had come to an abrupt halt, the tall brown grass flattened and grooves cut into the thawing earth where the wheels had dug in from being towed out. Beyond that was Miller's Pond, with a lone mute swan, silhouetted by moonlight, serenely sailing across the still water. Not a goose in sight.

"This stupid thing," Angelica growled, shattering the quiet moment. She leaned against the tow truck's bumper as she stabbed the buttons on her phone. "I still can't get hold of Bob."

"Maybe his phone is turned off," Tricia offered.

Deputy Placer ambled up, clipboard in hand, pen poised to write. "And you said you couldn't identify the make of the vehicle?" he asked, as though their conversation hadn't taken a ten-minute break.

Tricia shook her head. "I told you. The car's headlights were on bright."

The deputy turned his attention to Angelica. "What about you, ma'am?"

"I was too shook up to notice anything — except that we were probably about to die."

"Check the collision shops in the morning," Tricia suggested. "I'm sure it hit a low-flying goose. That's the only thing that saved us."

"Right," the deputy said, his voice filled with sarcasm.

"Hey, Jim, what's going on with the Carter murder investigation?" Russ asked.

"What's that got to do with this accident?"

"Tricia's the common denominator. She was there at the murder; there at the scene of Kimberly Peters's attack. And now this."

Placer shook his head. "No link that I can see," he said, jotting something down on the paper on his clipboard.

"No," Tricia muttered, "and I don't suppose Wendy Adams will, either."

Placer looked up, distracted. "Huh?"

"Nothing." It was all Tricia could do not to lose her temper.

The tow truck driver from the Stoneham Garage hooked chains to the bashed and dented Lexus, securing it to the truck. He dusted off his hands and turned to Tricia. "Just tell your insurance adjuster where to find it."

"Thank you." Tricia made a mental note to call the shop in the morning to see if anyone brought in a car needing a new windshield or other damage repaired. She doubted the Sheriff's Department would.

The trio stood back as the driver got back into his rig and pulled onto the highway.

Placer stepped forward. "Tell your insurance company to call on Tuesday or Wednesday for the accident report. We're always backed up with paperwork after a busy weekend. This is my third accident today." He shook his head and muttered, "Women drivers."

He made the accident — and what Tricia and Angelica had gone through — sound so trivial, the chauvinist pig.

"Come on, girls, I'll take you home," Russ said.

"No way," Tricia said. "I want to visit Kimberly." She turned to her sister. "That is, if you don't mind, Ange."

"Not at all. And I really do want to try out that new French bistro. I'm not letting a little thing like attempted murder spoil my dinner plans for the evening."

Tricia winced: the phrase "attempted murder" hit a little too close to home.

"I hope you don't mind, but I brought the pickup, so it'll be a snug fit," Russ said.

"I only worry about those things after I

eat a fabulous meal — not before," Angelica said.

Russ opened the passenger side door and Tricia piled in, with Angelica squeezing in beside her. After buckling up, they were back on their way to Nashua.

As Russ had predicted, a uniformed deputy stood outside Kimberly Peters's private hospital room. "Uh-oh," Tricia muttered, clutching the vase filled with colorful tulips. "Do you think he'll let us in?"

"Probably not," Russ said.

The deputy's name tag read BARCLAY. His broad shoulders and imposing height made him look more like a former linebacker for the New England Patriots than a cop.

Tricia strode up to face him. "Excuse me, sir, we're here to visit Kimberly Peters."

He looked down at her from his six-four or six-five height. "No visitors. Sheriff Adams's orders."

She tried again. "The medical staff wouldn't tell us how she's doing. Privacy laws or some such. Can you at least tell us if she's regained consciousness?"

"She hadn't, last I looked."

Not very talkative, either.

"And when was that?" Russ asked, shoving his press credentials in front of the deputy.

The deputy glanced at them, but they made no impression. "Half an hour ago."

"Is there a chance she can recover?" Angelica asked.

"I'm no doctor, ma'am."

"Can we at least leave our flowers for her?" Tricia asked, offering up the tulips. The vase was clear glass, so it was evident that it contained only green stems — and nothing lethal. She handed him the vase.

He poked at the flowers and took a tentative sniff. "I'll put them on the bedside table," he said, turned, and opened the door to Kimberly's room.

What Tricia saw took her breath away: Kimberly, her face bruised and swollen, looking more like a jack-o'-lantern than a human being. Crowding the over-bed table and the windowsill were vases of flowers: roses, gladiolas, tulips, and daffodils, and at her bedside sat a well-dressed, chunky man, his hand wrapped around hers, his attention focused only on Kimberly, his expression filled with worry and grief.

"Artemus Hamilton!" Tricia cried.

The literary agent looked up at the sound of his name, just as the door to the room *whoosh*ed quietly shut.

"Zoë's agent?" Russ asked.

"Yes."

"What's he doing here?" Angelica asked, no doubt delighted that she could give her cookbook manuscript another heartfelt testimonial.

A moment later the deputy reappeared with Hamilton right on his heels. "Ms. Miles, what you doing here?" Hamilton asked, sounding incredibly nervous.

"The same thing you are." She turned her attention back to the deputy. "I thought you said Ms. Peters was allowed no visitors."

"Mr. Hamilton is Ms. Peters's fiancé," Barclay said.

Tricia felt her jaw drop — then quickly shut her mouth.

"Why don't we go get a cup of coffee or something?" Hamilton said and grabbed Tricia's arm, pulling her away from the deputy, with Russ and Angelica bringing up the rear. Down the corridor, they stopped beside an empty gurney that had been parked near a storage closet.

"Ms. Miles —"

"Tricia," she insisted.

"Tricia, I had to tell the sheriff I was Kimberly's fiancé. It's the only way they'd let me visit her. She hasn't got anyone else."

"Yes, I know. How is she?"

He let out a sharp breath. "Doing better than they'd originally expected, but she's got a few hard days ahead of her and a lot of reconstructive work to come."

"Did you buy her all those flowers?" Angelica asked.

He nodded. "I felt so bad for her. She won't want to see her face when she wakes, and she deserves to have something beautiful to look at after what she's been through."

There was no arguing that.

"I take it you'll be staying in Stoneham for another night?" Tricia asked.

"Not at the Brookview Inn. I've booked a room at a hotel not far from here. I'll pick up a rental car tomorrow."

"Sounds like you're planning on staying for the duration," Russ said.

"I've asked my assistant to clear my schedule for the next few days."

"Very generous — especially since Ms. Peters *isn't* your fiancé," Russ added.

"Kimberly and I have known each other for several years. We even dated for a while. I consider myself her friend. And isn't being with her now the least a friend can do?"

"Yes," Tricia agreed. Or had simply seeing Kimberly's battered face reawakened whatever feelings he had for her — of friendship, or otherwise? She wasn't about to second-guess his motives.

"You must be exhausted after spending the day here. We're going to dinner when we leave. We'd love to have you join us," Angelica chimed in, ever the gracious hostess.

Hamilton shook his head. "I got something from the cafeteria an hour or so ago. But thanks for asking."

Tricia nodded, understanding completely. Angelica, however, looked annoyed.

"When Kimberly wakes up, I'll let her know you came to visit — and that you brought flowers," Hamilton said.

"Thank you."

"The sheriff told me you found her. Did she tell you who did this to her?"

Tricia shook her head. "Sorry." She wasn't about to tell him what Kimberly had said — and risk Wendy Adams's wrath. Besides, the information hadn't pointed to whoever had attacked Kimberly and why.

"Look, I'd better get back to Kimberly. If she wakes up, I want to be there for her." He gave them a wan smile and turned toward the main corridor.

Tricia, Russ, and Angelica looked at one another.

"Well, that was certainly unexpected," Angelica said.

"It sure was," Tricia agreed.

"But it doesn't mean anything, either," Russ said. "I mean, so the guy feels sorry for the poor woman — or maybe he even discovered he cares about her. It doesn't give us any more information."

"No," Tricia agreed, "it doesn't."

TWENTY

The ambience at La Parisienne reflected its cuisine, from its textured plaster walls to its gilt mirrors and the shiny copper-bottomed pans that hung as decoration. Angelica had pronounced the coq au vin adequate, but assured Tricia and Russ that in her own hands it would've been magnificent. And, in fact, it would make a wonderful addition to her *European Epicurean* manuscript. Russ was about to ask her to explain when Tricia gave him a warning look. He kept quiet.

"Let's face it, I missed my calling," Angelica said, as she swirled the last of her pinot noir in her glass and Russ dipped into his wallet to pay for the dinner. "I should've opened a restaurant instead of a cookbook store. It sure would've been a lot easier."

"On whom?" Tricia asked, thinking about her sister's continuing employee problems. "And what's going to happen at your store tomorrow? You're still short staffed."

"Frannie said she'd put out the word that I need help. She has a lot of contacts over at the Chamber of Commerce, you know."

No doubt about that.

"Of course, if you don't need Ginny —" Angelica hinted.

"I don't even know if she's coming in tomorrow. It depends on how Brian's doing and if she feels she can leave him."

Angelica waved a hand in dismissal. "Oh, what's a little food poisoning?"

"I'm sure you'd feel differently if it was your intestines tied in knots," Tricia said.

"Let's change the subject," Russ said. "Like what are you going to do to protect yourself, Tricia?"

She stared at him, surprised. "From whom?"

"Exactly," Angelica quipped.

"Come and stay with me," he said.

Angelica shook her head. "Nope. It's too far from her shop. And don't forget about your cat, Trish. You can stay with me. I loved having you this past week. It was just like being back in college with a roomie."

"Sorry to disappoint you both, but I have my own home, and I have a perfectly good security system. If somebody breaks in downstairs, they've got to come up three flights. I have a sturdy door in between, and a cell phone if my landline goes dead."

"You can't count on someone having a coronary trudging up those three flights. And remember, Kimberly was bludgeoned with a sledgehammer. That could knock down a door, no matter how sturdy," Russ said.

"You're not going to frighten or bully me into anything. Either of you."

Angelica sighed and turned her attention to Russ. "Doesn't she sound like the heroine in a bad movie or novel? You know, the stupid character — usually a woman — who goes into a darkened basement or attic when there's a serial killer on the loose?"

"May I remind you that I have no basement, and whoever killed Zoë is not a serial killer?"

"Unless Kimberly dies," Russ pointed out.

For a second — and only a second — Russ's argument made sense. "But Artemus said Kimberly will recover. I have faith in the doctors at Southern New Hampshire Medical Center to pull her through, and in no time she'll be her smiling self again." She cringed. Kimberly rarely smiled, and now with no front teeth, she'd be even less apt to flash her gums.

"There's no argument. If you won't come stay with me, I'm going to stay with you."

Angelica patted her massive purse. "I just happen to have brought along my toothbrush and nightie. I'm all set."

"But —"

"Good," Russ said. "Then it's all settled."

"It's not settled."

"Would you prefer we drop you off at a motel here in Nashua to stay the night?" Russ asked.

"Oh, come on, guys, you're paranoid — both of you."

"And you ought to be," Angelica said.

Tricia thought about how frightened she'd been when the car had forced them off the road. Was she being foolish?

"Okay, Ange, you can stay with me. But only for tonight."

Angelica eyed Russ. "We'll see."

A lot had changed in the six months since Angelica had come to live in Stoneham. The biggest change, of course, had been in Tricia herself. They'd returned from Nashua and Angelica had made herself comfortable on Tricia's couch. They'd opened a bottle of wine, and Miss Marple had deigned to join them, even contemplating sitting on Angelica's lap, which, upon further reflection, she decided not to do.

For more than an hour the sisters had

chatted and laughed, sticking to subjects that did not include murder, cookbook manuscripts, or personal criticisms. It occurred to Tricia that somewhere between their squabbles and disagreements, the two women had added something else to their ofttimes troubled relationship: they'd become friends.

Angelica acquiesced to sleeping on the comfortable leather couch, and peace reigned during the night.

Tricia awoke the next morning to the heavenly aromas of coffee and bacon coming from her kitchen. She found Angelica standing over the stove, a dishtowel safety pinned to her nightgown, and Miss Marple sitting smartly at her feet, licking her chops.

"Did you know your cat likes bacon?" she asked.

"Where did you find bacon?"

"In the back of your freezer. You really should clean it out more often, Trish. This meat was on the verge of freezer burn."

"I don't cook very often," she defended herself.

"Excuse me; you don't cook at all."

Tricia grabbed a mug from the cupboard and poured herself a cup of coffee. "I've been thinking about that. I think I'd like to take you up on your offer to teach me a few simple things. Just so I could have Russ over now and then and not have to rely on Angelo's Pizzeria or spaghetti sauce from a jar."

Angelica paused in turning the crispy slices, her mouth dropping open. "You want me to — ?"

Words seemed to fail her.

"If you don't mind. Maybe on a Sunday morning — before we have to open our stores."

Angelica's eyes began to fill. "I'd love that," she managed, turned away, and cleared her throat. "And as a start, I could let you read my cooking manuscripts — use you as my guinea pig."

Tricia set her cup down, not bothering to hide the smile that touched her lips. "Sure thing. In the meantime, how about I get the toaster out? I've already perfected the recipe for toast."

She'd just plugged it in and taken bread from the fridge when the phone rang. "Tricia?" Portia McAlister asked.

"I didn't give you this number."

"I'm not a reporter for nothing," she said. "Look, I thought you said you'd keep me in the loop."

"Loop?" Tricia asked, gazing into the toaster to check on the toast's progress.

"That incident last night. You know, the

one that dented your car and nearly did the same to you and your sister."

"How did you find out about that?"

"Uh-uh. I told you, I protect my sources."

The police report wasn't supposed to be available until at least Tuesday. Could it have been the tow truck driver from the Stoneham Garage who'd squealed?

It didn't matter.

"We weren't hurt, just shaken up."

"Where were you going at the time?"

"Is this off the record?"

"Maybe."

Did that matter, either?

"We were on our way to visit Kimberly Peters at the hospital in Nashua."

"Did she say anything enlightening? I can't get to her, and her fiancé won't talk to me."

That snippet of information made Tricia smile. "No. She wasn't awake when we got there, so we went out to dinner. Would you like to know what we ordered?"

"That won't be necessary." The line went quiet for long seconds. "I can still use this," Portia muttered.

"How?" Tricia asked, as the toast popped up.

"I'll let you know," Portia said, and hung up.

■ ■ ■ ■

Mr. Everett was waiting at the door when Tricia came down to prepare Haven't Got a Clue for another day of commerce. The day was overcast, the clouds hanging low and threatening. Another perfect day for retail!

"Good morning, Ms. Miles."

"Good morning, Mr. Everett. Lovely weather."

"Yes, we should have a good day." Mr. Everett headed for the pegs in the back of the store to hang up his coat. "Shall I straighten up the back shelves? Someone pawed through them yesterday, stuffing the books in every which way." He shook his head in disapproval.

"That's fine," Tricia said, and bent down to open the safe to collect and count out the bills to start the day. She thought about calling the Stoneham Garage to see if anyone had brought in a damaged car, but decided it was probably too early. And anyway, perhaps whoever had come after her the previous evening was smart enough to take their damaged car to Nashua or even Manchester for repairs. It wasn't likely the Sheriff's Department would be interested enough to make a few calls to try and locate it.

A knock at the door caused her to look up. She pushed the cash drawer shut with her hip and went to answer it. She lifted the blind; Ginny waited in the cold. Tricia opened the door.

"I think I should've brought my umbrella from the house."

"Yes, but it's too warm for snow, so that's something in our favor."

"Only if you believe the low forties are warm," Ginny said, pulling off her knit hat and stuffing her gloves into her pockets.

"How's Brian?" Tricia asked.

"Much better." Ginny took off her coat, and headed toward the back of the store to hang it up.

The phone rang. Although the store didn't officially open for another ten minutes, Tricia wasn't a stickler for such details and picked up the receiver. "Haven't Got a Clue, Tricia speaking."

"Hi, it's Brian. Is Ginny there yet?" He still didn't sound well.

"Brian, Ginny says you're better."

Ginny stopped at the sound of Brian's name.

"Lots. Can I speak with her, please?"

"Sure."

Ginny hurried to take the phone from Tricia. "Hey, sweetie, what's up?"

Tricia went back to sorting the bills for the cash drawer, trying not to listen to Ginny's conversation, which appeared to consist of only three phrases: "Oh, God!" "You're kidding?," and "I don't believe it."

When she finally hung up, she was ashen faced.

"What's wrong?" Tricia asked, concerned.

"The lab report came back," Ginny said, her voice shaking.

"That was quick. How did you get them to turn it around so fast?"

"Brian's aunt works at the hospital. She pulled some strings. They said it was salmonella that made him sick."

"It was the ham from the fridge, right?" Tricia asked.

"No, Trish, it could only be Nikki's cake."

"What?" Tricia said. Astonished didn't begin to express what emotion coursed through her.

Ginny nodded. "Brian was so caught up working on the laundry room, he didn't eat lunch, so when I brought the cake in on Saturday night, he ate a huge piece. Not long after, he was sick."

"Salmonella," Tricia repeated. "It often comes from eggs. Nikki's been in the food service business a long time. I don't under-stand how she could accidentally —"

"I don't think it was an accident. Remember I took home some of those cut-out cookies she sent over to the Cookery? I didn't make the connection until I talked to Brian just now, but they made me sick. And now this."

Tricia shook her head in denial. "I just can't believe —" That Nikki would want to hurt her? Make her ill? Why? Unless what Russ had been saying all along was true. That Zoë's killer thought she was getting too close to the truth — too close to tracking down him or her. Tricia remembered the bag of tools containing the sledgehammer and the can of spray paint sitting on the bakery's floor. But what possible motive could Nikki have for killing Zoë? True, it was she who'd asked Tricia to invite the so-called author. Nikki left the signing early . . . and came in through the back door to strangle Zoë?

"What do you remember from the night of Zoë's signing?" Tricia asked.

"What do you mean?"

"I wasn't paying attention when Nikki left, but she did leave early. And neither of you remembers disarming the security system, nor does Angelica."

"It doesn't matter. It wouldn't be hard for Nikki to do," Ginny said.

"What do you mean?"

"I've worked in several stores in Stoneham. Half the merchants on the street have the identical system we do. Even the Cookery."

"You think the Stoneham Patisserie might have the same system? That Nikki disabled our system and came in the back of the store to kill Zoë?"

"It's possible."

"But what's her connection, her motive?"

Ginny shrugged. "The only way we'd know that is to ask her. And I doubt she'd say a word."

Tricia thought about the awful scene at Zoë's home on Saturday evening. "The last thing Kimberly Peters said before she lost consciousness was 'stone.' "

"Stone," Ginny repeated, looking thoughtful.

"I thought she was talking about the statue that got ruined."

"But it's marble, not stone."

"Technically, marble is stone."

"Stone," Ginny repeated again. "It seems like I should remember something about that word."

Tricia looked across the room. "Mr. Everett?"

Mr. Everett paused in straightening the shelves to join the two women. As a lifelong resident of Stoneham, he was a font of useful information. "Is there a family in the area named Stone?"

The old man shook his head. "Hasn't been for years. Stoneham was named after Hiram Stone, who opened a quarry back in the mid-eighteenth century, although the village wasn't incorporated until 1798."

"So they died out generations ago?"

"Oh, no. One of my favorite customers was Faith Stone. Wonderful woman," he said. "Very generous with her time. I occasionally saw her when my grocery store donated dented canned goods to the local food pantry where she volunteered. I believe she and Grace were acquainted. Something to do with the library."

"What happened to her?"

He shook his head. "No one seems to know. She just disappeared one day."

A shiver ran through Tricia as she remembered what Julia Overline had said the day before at Nikki's brunch.

"Her family had her declared dead so that the estate could be freed up and fund her daughter's further education," Mr. Everett continued.

"Who was her daughter?" Tricia asked, dreading the answer.

"The manager of the Stoneham Patisserie: Nikki Brimfield."

"Nikki?" Ginny repeated.

Mr. Everett nodded. "Brimfield is her married name, although I believe she's now divorced."

"And her maiden name?" Tricia asked, already knowing the answer.

"Stone, of course."

Since Mr. Everett had mentioned that Grace and Faith had been acquainted, Tricia's first impulse was to call Grace. She did, but there was no answer. Grace didn't have voice mail or even an answering machine, so Tricia could only slam down the phone in frustration.

Her next thought was to talk to Stella Kraft. Unlike gadabout Grace, Stella was pretty much a homebody, and answered the phone on the first ring. "I'd be glad to talk with you again, Tricia."

"Can I come over now?"

"Now is fine. I'll put on a pot of coffee."

Tricia left Ginny and Mr. Everett with a few hurried instructions, donned her coat, and started down the sidewalk. In a moment she heard her name being called.

"Tricia, Tricia!"

Tricia turned, delighted to see Grace Harris waving to her. She waited until the older woman caught up with her. "Grace, what brings you out so early on a Monday morning?"

Grace looked down at the sticky goo on her shoe. "Oh, dear, not again," she muttered, and tried to scrape the goose poop from her sole. "I've run out of the Coffee Bean's superior blend. When I saw you, I wanted to tell you how much I admire you for helping that Peters woman the other night."

"News certainly gets around."

"She wasn't very nice, but I can't imagine the cruelty it took to inflict those injuries."

Tricia shuddered, remembering the amount of blood that had soaked into Kimberly's clothes and pooled on Zoë's office floor. "It was the least I could do."

Grace nodded.

"Do you mind if I ask you a couple of questions?" Tricia asked.

"Of course not, dear."

"At Zoë's signing, you said you were glad to speak to her under 'happier circumstances.' What did that mean?"

Grace bowed her head. "Had I known she

was destined to die within minutes, I never would have brought it up. It was thoughtless of me."

"You couldn't have known she'd be murdered."

"Yes, well, I like to think of myself as a good person. And bringing up an unpleasant incident from the past is just plain bad manners."

This was maddening. "What was it?"

"A confrontation — in public — over her not supporting Stoneham's efforts to promote ourselves as a book town."

"Oh, that," Tricia said, blowing it off. "Bob Kelly mentioned it to me last week."

"He did? Why — that — how could he?" Grace sputtered.

"Grace, it was years ago, and I'm sure everyone — everyone but Bob," she amended — "has forgotten about it."

"I hadn't forgotten it, but whatever feelings I had about it, they didn't stop me from supporting her as an author."

Finding out the truth about who actually had written the books would have done it, for sure.

"It's all in the past now. I think you should just forget about it," Tricia said.

"I have tried," Grace admitted. "I was sorry I couldn't make it to her memorial service on Saturday, but it sounds like that was a fiasco as well."

"Yes, it was."

"I had an appointment at the New Hampshire Medical Center," Grace volunteered.

"Oh, dear, I hope nothing's wrong."

Grace smiled. "Luckily, no. Thank you for your concern."

"Is that also where you were early Wednesday morning?" Tricia asked, pushing the boundaries of polite conversation, but she wanted to know what Mr. Everett felt so strongly about that he would lie to her.

"Yes. In the past I had some female problems," Grace said, without elaborating.

"I see," Tricia said, and nodded. "Well, I'm certainly glad you're all right."

"Thank you."

"I had another question for you, too. It concerns Faith Stone."

Grace laughed. "Good grief, I haven't thought about her in years."

"Mr. Everett says you were friends."

"Not really. We were acquainted. We belonged to the same book club — not unlike the one you host at Haven't Got a Clue, only this was sponsored by the Stoneham Library. A nice little group. Mostly retirees and stay-at-home mothers."

"Did you know Faith wanted to be a

writer?" Tricia bluffed, wondering where the idea had even come from.

"Oh, yes. She used to carry a notebook around with her, scribbling down thoughts and ideas for some great saga she said she hoped to write one day."

"She didn't say she was actually writing it?"

Grace frowned. "She didn't talk a lot about herself, poor thing."

"Poor thing?"

"Her husband was the jealous kind. I can't say I was surprised when she went missing, although they were never able to pin anything on that brute Phil Stone. More than once she came to our meetings with bruises on her arms or legs."

"Her husband was the controlling type?"

Grace nodded. "She ultimately stopped coming to the meetings. It wasn't long afterward that she disappeared."

"And no one's ever heard from her?"

"I think her body was probably dumped in the woods somewhere. Perhaps some hunter will find her bones one day."

"Perhaps," Tricia said.

Grace put a hand on Tricia's arm. "You were obviously on your way somewhere, and I'm holding you up."

"No, I'm just running an errand."

"Well, I'll let you go. I'll see you tomorrow evening at the book club meeting. I'm grateful we won't have a guest," she said with a laugh.

"I'm so glad what happened last week hasn't scared you off," Tricia said.

"Oh, I think you'll find that we'll return. After all, don't we love a good mystery?" Grace asked.

Tricia laughed. "Yes, but I prefer mine between the covers of a book."

"Good-bye, dear," Grace said with a pleased smile, and continued on her way.

Tricia pushed forward, glad to have one more mystery cleared up . . . and another still facing her.

Stella Kraft opened her back door before Tricia could press the bell. "I knew you'd eventually figure it all out," she said smugly, her pale blue eyes sparkling.

Tricia pursed her lips, annoyed. "Why didn't you just come right out and tell me about Faith Stone?"

"Come in, come in. I'm not paying Keyspan to heat the great outdoors," Stella chided.

Once again the smell of boiled potatoes and mothballs filled the immaculate kitchen. Stella had set the table with mugs, spoons, and napkins, and a plate of gingersnaps. "Let me take your coat."

"I don't want to be a bother. I'll just drape it over the back of the chair," Tricia said, and settled at the table.

Stella moved to the stove, picked up the coffeepot, and poured. "Now, what led you to Faith?"

"A number of things." Tricia told Stella about her conversations with Kimberly and Artemus Hamilton; Nikki's tainted cookies and cake; Mr. Everett's revelation; and Grace's confirmation. "Nikki sure had me fooled. She always seemed so even-tempered at our book club meetings, always bringing the refreshments and all. Did you have her for a student?"

Stella nodded, taking her seat. "She's another one who slid through my class without making much of an impact. Such a disappointment after having her mother."

"And you lied to me when you said you had no idea who really wrote Zoë's books."

"I didn't actually lie," Stella said. "I kept the truth to myself. That's not lying. Exactly."

Tricia wasn't about to debate her. Instead, she said, "Tell me about Faith Stone."

Stella sat back in her chair, a smile lighting her face. "Faith was the best student who ever passed through my classroom. She had a real thirst for learning. Even in high school she had a wonderful gift for story-telling."

"You said you didn't keep any of your students' work."

"That was no lie, but it wasn't easy to forget her way with words, even at that age. I hoped she'd go far. Obviously, she would have, if the books had been published before her disappearance. They would have set her free." She shook her head sadly.

"But how did Zoë get hold of Faith's manuscripts?"

Stella reached for a cookie. "Near as I can figure, it was from the estate sale."

"Estate sale?"

"After she disappeared, Faith's former in-laws pushed to have her declared dead."

"Her in-laws, not her husband?"

Stella nodded. "Five or six years after she disappeared, her good-for-nothing husband, Phillip Stone, died in a work accident. He was a lineman for PSNH." The local power utility. "Faith's daughter went to live with her grandmother. I don't know if the in-laws ever legally had Faith declared dead, but they made a big show of it and had a big sale at the house. I believe Zoë got the manuscripts at that sale. Faith's in-laws wouldn't have known what they were — and would have cared even less. They considered her writing a frivolous waste of time. Her ex-mother-in-law was dead by the time the books were published. Her sister-in-law never recognized Faith's work, or I'm sure she would have tried to get her hands on some of the money Zoë raked in."

"How long after Faith disappeared was the first book published?"

"Oh, maybe ten years. I'm assuming Zoë had the manuscripts for a couple of years before she figured out what to do with them. Not the sharpest pencil in the box, that one."

"Why didn't you say something? Why didn't you let people know Zoë didn't write those books?"

"I told you, I did hint about it to my colleagues, but I had no proof. All I could do was be enraged on Faith's behalf. Eventually —" She shrugged. "I got over it."

"But what about Nikki? Didn't she deserve compensation? Imagine what she must have felt like. It's certainly motive enough to kill someone."

Stella frowned. "The only one who deserved to benefit from Faith's work was Faith herself."

"Which was impossible. She was dead."

Stella blinked, then smiled. She picked up her coffee mug and took a sip. "Faith's not dead. She just lives in Canada."

TWENTY-ONE

"Not dead?" Angelica murmured in disbelief.

Tricia had left Stella's home in a fog. The ex-teacher wouldn't say much more, leaving Tricia with far more questions than she'd had before she'd arrived. Armed with new knowledge, she knew she'd burst if she didn't tell someone, and her first thought was to call her sister. She had pulled the cell phone from the pocket of her jacket and dialed.

"Well, where is she? Where's she been?" Angelica asked, when she'd heard the tale.

"In Canada. Somewhere."

"And no one knows she's still alive — not even Nikki?"

"As far as I know, only you, me, and Stella know. She wouldn't tell me more. She said it wasn't up to her to out her former student."

"But what about Faith? Why doesn't she

want her daughter to know she's not dead?"

"Stella wouldn't say. But if I had to guess, I'd say because it's been over twenty years. Maybe she doesn't want to intrude on her daughter's life. Maybe she's ashamed she left without taking Nikki with her. I know that would be my reaction."

"So what are you going to do?"

"Look for Faith myself."

"In Canada?"

"No, on the Internet. The only clue Stella would give me was that Faith is still writing, and has been published."

"Under her real name?"

"Apparently not."

"That's going to make finding her a little difficult, don't you think?"

"Difficult, but not impossible."

"Ha! Who died and made you Sherlock Holmes?"

"Hey, I've read enough police procedurals and true crime novels to have picked up a few tips."

"Well, all I can say is 'go for it.' And tell me everything as soon as you know, will you? I feel like I've just put down a book I can't wait to get back into."

"You and me both."

Tricia arrived back at Haven't Got a Clue

just in time for the afternoon rush, which kept her from her laptop for another hour. By then she was ready to jump out of her skin. But between customers she'd thumbed through the Sisters In Crime and Mystery Writers of America membership directories she kept near the sales register. Not surprisingly, there was no Faith Stone listed. She'd searched for last names that began with S that had first names beginning with F. There were no published authors she recognized.

"What am I thinking?" she said, and gave her forehead a slap. "I'm not going to find her in a U.S.-based group."

"Find who?" Ginny asked.

"A writer," Tricia said.

"Maybe I can help."

"I need the laptop. I've got to check the Crime Writers of Canada Web site."

"Crime Writers of Canada? We don't carry any books from Canadian publishers, do we?"

"Not really. To make any kind of a living, most Canadian authors have U.S. publishers."

"So what's the name of this Canadian author?"

"I'm not sure."

"Then how can you look him — or her — up? Or do you have the book title?"

Tricia shook her head. "No author, no title, no ISBN."

Ginny spread her arms wide. "Then — how?"

"I'm going to take a good guess." Tricia headed for the back of the store and the stairs to her loft apartment. "I'm going to go online to check. Call me on my cell if things get hairy down here."

"You got it," Ginny said.

Miss Marple saw Tricia heading for the stairs and jumped down from one of the bookshelves to lope after her. Tricia opened the door to the stairs and the cat took off like a shot.

Less than a minute later, Tricia had powered up her computer and waited as it found the Internet connection. At the Google site, she typed in "Crime Writers of Canada," and in seconds was taken to the CWC home page. She clicked on the button labeled Member Bios, selecting S. A fast perusal came up with only one name that had the initials F and S: Fiona Sample.

Tricia was already familiar with that name. She'd read at least one, perhaps two, books in the Bonnie Chesterfield librarian "cozy mystery" series. She remembered she'd liked them, but hadn't kept up with the rest of the series — simply because she'd been preoccupied. By her divorce, by opening Haven't Got a Clue, and by the hundreds of other mystery books vying for her attention . . .

The question was: Could Fiona Sample actually be Faith Stone?

She clicked on the link to the author's bio. Fiona Sample was born in the U.S., but came to Canada in the early 1990s to live and work in Toronto. She married a Canadian citizen and lived happily outside of Kitchener, Ontario, with her two children, twins Jessica and Andre, and a house full of cats and dogs, as well as a yard full of chickens.

Chickens? Addie Martin from the *Forever* book series had kept chickens, too.

Tricia tried to remember the Bonnie Chesterfield books. They were contemporary novels set in western New York. Had Faith originally come from that state and transplanted herself to New Hampshire, as Tricia had done, or was the locale just enough over the border to interest an American publisher?

Tricia left the computer long enough to search her own bookshelves. It took ten minutes, but she did find the first book in Fiona Sample's series: *Death Turns a Page,* published some seven years before.

She flipped through the pages, reading paragraphs at random. The book was well written, and memories of it came back to her almost at once, but it didn't resonate like the Jess and Addie *Forever* historical mysteries. Could this be the same author who wrote the books Zoë took credit for?

Tricia just wasn't sure.

She went back to the computer and scanned the rest of the entry, then clicked on the link to Fiona's Web site. The site had only four pages. The About Fiona page had little more on it than the CWC site, and no picture, either. Tricia clicked the Contact button. That page gave her yet another link, which she clicked, and up popped an empty note addressed to Fiona@FionaSample.com with a subject line of From the Web site.

Tricia thought about what she could write in the message area, something that would elicit a fast reply. After a few moments she erased the subject line and typed in "Nikki's in trouble." In the message area, she added, "She needs her mother." Tricia signed it with her standard signature line of her name, the store name, and the telephone number; clicked the Send button; and sent it flying through cyberspace.

With her laptop tucked under her arm, Tricia returned to Haven't Got a Clue, set the computer up behind the sales counter, and wondered when — or even if — she'd get a reply to her e-mail. For now, there was nothing to do but wait. And since the store was quiet, she decided to surf the Internet.

What she'd seen Sunday night at the scene of her car — chase? wreck? — had stayed with her: an open body of water with no geese. She Googled the words "swan" and "geese," and hit the Enter key. Within seconds, a list of Web sites appeared on her computer screen.

The first few sites weren't helpful. But on the fourth one, she hit pay dirt. It suggested that mute swans, like the one she'd seen on Miller's Pond, had been used successfully as goose deterrents. Apparently swans aggressively protect their young, chasing away any creatures — including man — that dare to intrude on their breeding grounds. Bob hadn't mentioned swans during their talk some days before. Did he even know about this?

Hitting the Compose button, Tricia keyed in a quick note, including the Web site's URL, addressed the note to Bob at his Chamber e-mail address, and hit the Send key — just as a customer opened the door and entered. Tricia didn't get back to her computer for another ten minutes. The note she found waiting her attention wasn't from Fiona Sample or Bob, but from Portia McAlister.

"Did you see my latest report? Catch it online," and she gave the URL.

Tricia clicked on the link.

The report was dated that morning, and she waited impatiently while the video loaded, then hit the Play button.

Portia stood along a bare patch of road, tall pines the only backdrop. The location looked suspiciously familiar. The door opened, admitting three potential customers. Ginny sprang into action, welcoming them as Tricia strained to listen to the report.

"— on this lonely patch of road. Stoneham merchants Tricia Miles, owner of the mystery bookstore Haven't Got a Clue, and her sister Angelica, who owns the Cookery bookstore, were two sisters on a mission of mercy when tragedy almost struck."

"Is this the only Agatha Christie book you have in stock?" asked a white-haired woman in a purple ski jacket.

"Uh —" Tricia tore her attention from the laptop's screen. "No." She cast about. "Mr. Everett, could you help this customer?"

Mr. Everett signaled the woman to follow him.

Portia had continued with her report, heedless of her lack of an audience. "—Kimberly Peters, in critical condition at Southern New Hampshire Medical Center —"

"There's no more coffee in the pot," said a gentleman customer, thrusting his empty cardboard cup at Tricia.

She gritted her teeth, trying to hold her temper. "One of us will take care of that in just a minute. Please excuse me for a moment." She turned back to the screen.

"Are these three incidents linked?" Portia asked earnestly.

The old telephone on the cash desk rang.

"With murder and attempted murder," Portia went on.

The phone rang again.

Tricia clicked on the video, stopping Portia in mid-sentence. She grabbed the phone. "Haven't Got a Clue mystery bookstore. This is Tricia, how may I help you?" she asked, sounding anything but helpful.

"This is Fiona Sample. What did you mean by your e-mail, Ms. Miles?"

"Oh, it's you!" Tricia said, startled, and had to catch her breath. "Uh, as I said in the note, I think your daughter Nikki's in

345

terrible trouble. She needs her mother."

"I don't have a daughter by that name."

"You did when your name was Faith Stone."

Silence.

"Did you write the five Jess and Addie *Forever* historical mysteries attributed to Zoë Carter?" Tricia asked, point-blank.

"What?" Fiona said, sounding breathless. "What did you say?"

"Did you write the Jess and Addie historical mysteries?"

"Who are you? Where did you get that idea?"

"Miss, Miss!" the woman in the purple jacket insisted, holding up two volumes in her hands. "These aren't the Agatha Christie books I want. Don't you have a back room with other titles?"

"Mr. Everett!" Tricia called.

"Ms. Miles?" Fiona Sample insisted from hundreds of miles away.

"Excuse me," Tricia told Fiona, and turned to Mr. Everett. "We may have other titles, but they haven't been inventoried. I wouldn't know where to find them right this minute."

The woman slammed the books onto the glass counter. "What kind of customer service is this? I want *Murder at Hazelmoor.*

I was told your store stocked every mystery book ever written!" she said indignantly.

Was she crazy?

"Ginny!" Tricia called.

Ginny looked up from her customer, excused herself, and hurried to the cash desk.

"Ginny, I'm on a very important phone call. Can you please help this customer?" she asked, pleading.

Ginny turned to the irate woman. "How can I help you, ma'am?"

"Ms. Miles," Fiona said firmly.

"I'm sorry," Tricia apologized. "It's organized mayhem in the store today. Would you be open to me calling you right back from a more quiet location?"

Tricia heard the woman on the other end of the line sigh. "Yes." She gave Tricia her number.

"Please call me right back," Fiona said. "I want to get to the bottom of this."

TWENTY-TWO

"Wow," Ginny murmured, not for the first time. "You're practically a living, breathing Miss Marple to figure all that out yourself."

Hearing her name, Tricia's little gray cat jumped onto the cash desk, immediately nuzzling her head on Ginny's chin. "Not you," she chided, petting the purring cat.

Tricia shook her head. "I had a lot of help. And a lot could still go wrong. That's why I need your help to set this up."

"Hey, all you have to do is ask," Ginny said. "But do you really think you can pull it off by tomorrow? And what are your safeguards?"

"Good question."

Ginny beamed. "Hey, in the last year, I've read a lot of mysteries. I can't wait to see how this goes down," she said, perhaps a bit too eagerly.

Tricia shook her head. "You aren't going to be here. I won't put you or Mr. Everett in danger."

"Oh, but you being in danger is okay, right?"

"I won't be in danger."

"Doesn't that kind of contradict your previous statement?"

"It all depends on how much cooperation I can get from the Sheriff's Department."

Ginny snorted. "I think you can count on one hundred percent total noninvolvement from our local law enforcement."

"I hope you're wrong, but it will mean pulling in a few favors from friends and acquaintances."

Ginny crossed her arms over her chest. "Okay, I'll do as you ask, but if I don't get all the juicy details, I will commit serious mayhem."

"And you won't be the only one, I'm sure."

Ginny sobered. "What do you want me to do?"

"Tomorrow, late in the afternoon, you and I will call all the members of the Tuesday Night Book Club and tell them the regular meeting's been canceled."

"All but one member?" Ginny asked.

"Yes."

"And what if she calls or comes in asking about it?"

"There's only one person who could spill the beans."

"Frannie?"

Tricia nodded. "I'll handle her myself."

"Okay. That doesn't seem like much work to me."

"I'm sure I'll think of something else for you to do. In the meantime, there's a box of Agatha Christie books to shelve. I want to be ready in case our irate customer decides to come back and berate us again."

Ginny smiled. "You got it," she said, and trotted to the back shelves.

Tricia looked down at the notepad in front of her. The logistics of pulling everything off in just about twenty-four hours were frightening, but she felt she needed to gather all the players and have an old-fashioned showdown, just like in a Rex Stout Nero Wolfe Story.

First up was talking to Artemus Hamilton. She called his office and was told he would be out of town for at least the rest of the week, and no, she could *not* have his cell phone number. The Southern New England Medical Center told her that Kimberly Peters's room had no phone hookup. Okay, if that meant she'd have to make another visit to the hospital to track down Hamilton, she would.

Next on the agenda: backup for herself. She didn't feel like making the lonely ride to Nashua all by herself. Another phone call later and she'd lined up Russ to ride shotgun, but only if she promised to tell him the whole story. This time she readily agreed. There were just two people she didn't want to make a party to her plans: Angelica and Frannie. As she told Ginny, although without malice, Frannie was liable to blather, and Angelica was likely to put herself in danger trying to protect her baby sister. Tricia wasn't about to put her plan at risk by telling either woman more than she needed to know.

Still, the twenty-four-plus hours until her own private D-Day seemed like a lifetime.

Tricia let out a sigh and hoped she could orchestrate her plan. If the whole thing soured, Zoë Carter might not be the only fatality.

The elevator doors *whoosh*ed open. Tricia stepped into the quiet hospital corridor, with Russ right on her heels. He hadn't ridden shotgun after all, leaving that spot for her, and their trip to Nashua in his beat-up old pickup truck had been uneventful. The journey, that is. The conversation had been lively.

"Are you nuts?" Russ had asked when Tricia told him her plans for the next day. His next question had been "Can I be there?"

The answer to that was a flat "No! If you want to watch the store — either from across the street or behind in the alley, I could use someone out in the field on guard, just in case something goes wrong."

"Okay, but only because I'm getting that exclusive."

They turned the corner, passing the nurses' station and heading down the hall. The door to Kimberly's room was open, with no deputy on duty outside it. They peeked inside. The TV was switched on, with some decorating program from HGTV playing for background noise. Kimberly sat propped up in bed, her face still alarmingly swollen and bruised, a trail of bloody drool leaking from the corner of her mouth. Artemus Hamilton held a small plastic cup of dark liquid in one hand, and a spoon in the other. A blood-stained cloth lay on the bedside table. On the floor, parked against the wall, was Hamilton's opened briefcase with manuscript pages poking out of it. Angelica's manuscript?

It was Hamilton who first noticed their arrival. "Oh, look, Kimberly, Tricia and Mr. Smith have come to visit."

Kimberly blinked and slowly turned her face toward the doorway. What seemed like eons later, her eyes brightened and her lips parted into a toothless smile. "Tre-ah," she managed in greeting.

Tricia swallowed the urgent impulse to cry. She gave into emotion and surged forward to capture the frail Kimberly in a gentle hug, grimacing as she took in the fetid odor that seemed to surround her. A long moment later she felt a soft pressure on her back and realized Kimberly's free hand was patting her.

She pulled away. "Are you okay, Kimberly?"

A very dumb question.

Kimberly fell back against her pillows and a mix of grunt and laugh escaped her lips.

"She's much better today," Artemus said, his voice faltering, his eyes bright with unshed tears as he gently wiped away the bloody spittle that leaked from Kimberly's slack mouth.

Tricia braved a smile. "Yes, I can see that."

"I goh no teef," Kimberly mouthed, pointing at the stubs of knotted black suture that stuck out at angles from her scarlet gums.

"The dental surgeon came by today," Hamilton said. "He looked at the X-rays, and tomorrow he'll tell us what we can expect for treatment."

What *we* can expect?

"Kimberly could be eating steak again in just a few months," Artemus continued, his voice breaking.

Kimberly clapped her hands together like a small child, the gesture bringing Tricia close to tears once again. She cleared her throat, swallowing the onslaught of emotion that threatened to overwhelm her.

"Where's the deputy?" Russ asked.

Hamilton glowered. "The sheriff has decided that whatever danger Kimberly was in has passed, and she pulled the guard earlier this afternoon."

"Is that wise?" Tricia asked.

"I don't think so, but she wasn't interested in my opinion," Hamilton said. "That's why I've decided to spend the night. Someone needs to look out for Kimberly's interests."

Kimberly blinked, her brow furrowing as she tried to follow the conversation.

Tricia waggled a finger at Hamilton, who got up from the bedside chair to follow her.

Russ reached over to take the cup of cola and spoon from Hamilton's hands. "Hey, Kimberly, did you ever play dinnertime airplane when you were a kid?"

She looked at him quizzically. He dipped the spoon into the flat soda and waved it back and forth in front of Kimberly's face, her gaze joyfully following.

"Yee-ow, yee-ow," he intoned, mimicking a small aircraft, and gently landed the spoon onto her tongue.

She swallowed and laughed. "A-gah!" she said.

Russ obliged.

Hamilton followed Tricia into the corridor, his hands plunged deep into his pants pockets, his shoulders slumped. "She's pretty high on painkillers," he said, glancing back into the room. "They're planning to wean her off them in the next couple of days."

Tricia nodded. "I'm so glad she's making progress, but it was really you I came to see."

"Me?"

"I found the woman who wrote the Jess and Addie books."

He frowned. "Why am I not surprised?"

"It really wasn't that hard. But I will admit I had some help."

"And what do you expect me to do about it?"

"Help me expose Zoë's killer."

"You know who killed her?"

"I'm pretty sure I do. And I'm pretty sure I know why, too."

"He wants a cut of the money."

"She."

He turned, looked back into the hospital room. "And you think this person is the one who attacked Kimberly, too?"

"I do," Tricia said, and nodded.

"Then, yeah, I'll help you. I'll do anything to put that bitch behind bars."

TWENTY-THREE

Angelica was already ensconced in Tricia's loft apartment by the time she and Russ returned to Stoneham. They knew this even before they opened the door because the heavenly aroma of something delicious met them on the stairs.

Miss Marple greeted Tricia at the door, looked up at Russ, and turned away in disgust. Luckily, he was used to her reaction and took no offense.

"Finally!" Angelica called from her position at the stove. Decked out in peach sweats and fluffy pink slippers, there was no doubt she felt totally at home in Tricia's digs. "How was Kimberly?"

"Awful. I mean, she'll recover, but I hope she's got good insurance. She'll be seeing a lot of her dentist in the next few months. You should've seen Russ with her. Her mouth smelled awful, but he spoon-fed her warm cola."

"*Ewww.* She's a stranger. How could you do that?" Angelica asked.

Russ shrugged. "I used to help my mom by feeding my grandmother after she had a stroke. It never bothered me."

"You're a very nice man," Angelica said, and pointedly stared at Tricia, mentally transmitting the words *Who you don't appreciate enough.*

Maybe she was right.

"Ange, you didn't have to cook for us," Tricia said. "We were going to call for a pizza."

"You two live on pizza. You need *real* food."

"I agree," Russ said. "What smells so great?"

"Chicken cordon bleu."

"Homemade?" he asked hopefully.

"Sort of not. But this shortcut version is really tasty. Now that you're here, I can pop them back in the oven," she said, and removed a plate from the fridge, transferring the contents to a baking sheet and into the oven.

"What are we having with it?" he asked.

"Caramelized carrots and stuffed baked potatoes. Is that okay?"

Russ nodded. "I'll say."

"I appreciate the effort, but aren't you

358

tired after working alone all day?" Tricia said, already feeling guilty.

"I wasn't alone," Angelica said, and stirred the carrots on the stove. "At least not the whole day. You want a beer or something, Russ?"

"You bet," he said.

Angelica turned toward the fridge.

"You've hired someone?" Tricia took off her coat and handed it to Russ, who hung it, plus his own, on the oak hat tree in the corner.

Angelica handed Russ his beer and a pilsner glass from the cupboard. "I contacted another employment agency. They sent over a woman who'd never worked retail a day in her life," she said, and turned up the heat under the carrots.

"And she's already quit?"

"No, but I wouldn't be surprised if I have to call them to send me someone else before the end of the week. I just can't get competent help."

Tricia ground her teeth together to keep from speaking.

"Then again, I wonder if there's any way I could wrestle Frannie away from the Chamber of Commerce."

"Wouldn't that just upset Bob?" Tricia asked.

Angelica waved a hand in dismissal. "Oh, he'd get over it . . . eventually. It's just that he can offer her benefits like health care and the like." She sighed dramatically, truly the epitome of the put-upon small business owner.

"It might be a stretch, but you could offer benefits," Russ pointed out. "Of course you'd have to pay for it. I do it for my two employees through a group plan."

"Oh?" Angelica said, actually sounding interested. "Doesn't the Chamber offer insurance? I know some do in New York."

Russ shook his head. "It's not legal here in New Hampshire. But I'm pretty sure the Chamber stocks a few brochures on local group plans for their members. Ask Frannie for one. She doesn't have to know why you want it."

Angelica raised an eyebrow. "I might have to offer benefits just to keep an employee for more than a few weeks." She shook her head. "People these days have such an entitlement complex. They think everything should be done for them. Tricia — set the table," she ordered, her tone full of entitlement.

Tricia did as she was told. Chicken cordon bleu made a far better dinner than pizza. It made one more affable to commands from someone else in one's own kitchen. She only half listened as Russ and Angelica discussed the pros and cons of group health insurance plans. She needed to keep Angelica away from Haven't Got a Clue tomorrow night. Perhaps she could enlist Bob's help — get him to take Angelica out of the picture and keep her safe from any potential harm.

Or was she just getting paranoid? Was it likely Nikki would pull out a gun and shoot whoever was in the store at the time? *Don't be silly,* she chided herself, yet worry continued to worm through her. Her grand plan was hit-and-miss at best. She was counting on the element of surprise.

Nikki was the unknown, possibly explosive, factor. If she was capable of murder — and attempted murder — what else was she capable of?

"Would you like a glass of wine, Trish?" Angelica asked.

Tricia looked up, took in her sister's face. Angelica was here, in her kitchen, cooking a meal for her, because she didn't want Tricia to be alone — to possibly face a murderer with no backup. That was a form of love she'd never expected to receive from Angelica.

Tricia gave her sister a sincere smile. "Yes, Ange, I would."

■ ■ ■ ■

The phone rang the whole next day, and tour buses disgorged hundreds of tourists looking for bargains, rare books, and the volumes missing from their personal libraries. Haven't Got a Clue hadn't been this busy since the week before Christmas. Even the weather had seemed to break, bringing warmer temperatures and a flood of customers.

Besides being kept busy by the minutiae of running her own business, when others weren't on the phone to Tricia, she was on the phone contacting the players for the little drama she expected to produce that night. Only Sheriff Adams balked at the idea. It was time to implement Plan B.

Back in her loft apartment, Tricia dialed Grace Harris's number, crossing her fingers that she'd find Mr. Everett's companion at home.

"Hello?" Grace answered.

"It's Tricia Miles. I've got two reasons for calling. First, I've had to cancel tonight's meeting."

"Oh, and I was so looking forward to it."

"I'm a little pressed for time, so I'll let Mr. Everett explain everything."

362

"Secrets?" Grace said thoughtfully.

"For the time being."

"Just like a good mystery. I shall look forward to seeing William tonight. But what's your other reason for calling?"

"As I think you're aware, Sheriff Adams and I aren't the best of friends."

Grace laughed. "I think the entire village knows that."

"You, on the other hand have a lot of clout in this town. I need to get the sheriff to come to my store at six p.m."

"Does this have anything to do with Zoë Carter's death?"

"Yes, it does."

"Will the sheriff be making an arrest?"

"If someone can persuade her to come. The problem is, she's already rebuffed my invitation to join us. She wasn't happy last fall when I tried to point her in the direction of Doris Gleason's killer, and she isn't open to my suggestions now, either."

"I'll do my best to persuade her, and get back to you after I speak with her."

"Thank you, Grace. I can't tell you how much this means to me."

"Dear, it doesn't begin to repay you for what you did for me last fall. I'll call you as soon as I speak to her."

"Thank you, Grace. Good-bye."

Tricia was getting more antsy by the minute. At almost three o'clock, when she could stand the inactivity no longer, she grabbed her coat and escaped the shop, heading for the Chamber of Commerce. This mission was too important to accomplish via telephone.

As usual, Frannie was on the phone when she arrived. She waved a less-than-cheerful hello and continued talking, her voice lower, less boisterous than usual. In fact, she almost sounded depressed — something Tricia hadn't thought Frannie was capable of.

Knowing this might take time, Tricia wandered into the cabin's main room, bypassing the free coffee and heading for the brochure rack. As Russ had mentioned, in addition to tourist material covering the bulk of southern New Hampshire, Tricia found a folder for the local group health insurance plans. She glanced through it before pocketing it for Angelica. On impulse, she grabbed one for herself, too.

At last, Frannie hung up the phone. "What brings you out to visit during work hours?"

"I had an errand to run," Tricia lied, "and thought I'd kill two birds with one stone. You're the last one on my list."

"List?"

"Of members. I wanted to personally let you know that I had to cancel the book club meeting for tonight."

"Oh, and I was so looking forward to it. I thought it might be good for all of us to get together to, you know, kind of heal after what happened last week. But maybe it's better for us to just take a break. Has something come up?"

"Yes. I've already spoken to everyone else to let them know."

"And?"

"And?" Tricia echoed.

"What came up?"

"Oh. Well . . ." Her mind scrambled. "It's . . . it's Angelica. She's had such a hard time keeping workers that she's fallen terribly far behind in her paperwork. I felt so bad for her I volunteered to help her out this evening — what with it being early closing and everything."

"That is so sweet of you."

Tricia nodded. "Well, that's what being a sister is all about."

Frannie sighed. "I just had the best time helping Angelica out on Sunday. I wish I could do it again."

"Oh? I thought she said you'd be coming back next weekend."

"I'd love to, but Bob won't let me."

"He won't let — why?"

"He doesn't think it looks good for the Chamber's only paid employee to be moonlighting at a second job."

"But helping Ange isn't like a real job. It's helping out. Okay, so maybe she paid you — she did pay you, didn't she?"

"Oh, yes. And very well, too."

"But that isn't a regular job."

"According to Bob it is."

"But he knows how swamped she is. How could he begrudge you helping out his girlfriend?"

"I don't know. I've known Bob for over a decade, and I've never seen him so angry." Her lip trembled. "It really hurt my feelings."

"I don't blame you for being so upset," Tricia said. "Does Angelica know about this?"

"I didn't think it was my place to say anything. But I do need to let her know I can't help her out this weekend. And I was so looking forward to it."

"Do you mind if I speak to Bob?"

"That's up to you. But don't be surprised

if he reams your ears out good, too."

He'd better not, Tricia thought.

Frannie let out a breath and straightened. "I'd best get back to work. I don't want Bob angry with me if I don't get the monthly flyers folded, stuffed, stamped, and to the post office before the end of the day."

"Okay. I'll see you soon."

Frannie sniffed, and for a moment Tricia thought she might cry. She reached out and gave her friend a hug. "It'll work out," she said.

"I hope so," Frannie said, and pulled back from the embrace. "Until yesterday, I loved my job. I hope I can feel good about it again in a week or so." She turned back to her desk.

Tricia left the Chamber office and marched next door to the Kelly Real Estate office. By the time she yanked open the door, steam threatened to escape from her ears.

Bob sat at his cluttered desk. He looked up at her entry and smiled. "Hey, Tricia, I was just about to call you on —"

"What have you done to poor Frannie?" she demanded, cutting him off.

"Done?" he asked, and stood, his plastered-on grin faltering.

"Yes, I just spoke to her, and she said

she'd gotten in trouble for working at the Cookery on Sunday."

"Yes."

"Why?"

"Because it looks bad for the Chamber."

"How?"

"Frannie is the public face of the Chamber. She gets paid a decent salary to work for us."

"Minimum wage?"

"No. We pay her better than that. A bit better."

"A bit better? What does that mean?"

"Two dollars an hour over minimum wage."

"And you expect her to live on that? I'm surprised she hasn't had to find a second job before now. Oh, wait, you'd probably fire her if she did."

"Now, Tricia, she gets health care benefits, too."

"And how much does she have to pay toward that?"

"Fifty percent."

"Fifty percent?" she repeated, hardly believing what she'd just heard. "On two dollars an hour over minimum wage?"

"There aren't that many clerical jobs in Stoneham. Frannie's lucky to be with us.

She's only got a high school diploma, you know."

"Doesn't ten years of experience with the Chamber count for anything?"

Bob shook his head, his expression insufferably patient, as if he was about to speak to someone with a low IQ. "We're paying a wage commensurate with her education and comparable jobs within the community."

"Then obviously the community isn't paying its female workers a living wage."

Bob shook his head again and looked at his watch, as though she was taking up too much of his time.

"Who's going to tell Angelica about this?" Tricia demanded.

"Angelica?" he repeated, a note of alarm entering his voice.

"Yes. She's expecting Frannie to show up to help her out on Saturday. I don't think it ought to be Frannie who tells Angelica why she can't be there. And I don't think it should be me who tells her, either. That leaves only one person."

"Me?" he asked, appalled.

"Yes, Bob, you. And the sooner, the better. In fact, this evening would be perfect. It's early closing night. You could take her to dinner and break the news to her. Take her someplace nice, too, won't you?"

"I'd planned to take her to this little seafood place I know in Portsmouth."

"That's wonderful. And I'll make it my business to talk to her tomorrow morning to make sure this little situation has been resolved."

"You'd check up on me?"

"Yes. And if she doesn't know the reason why Frannie can't work for her on Saturday, I *will* tell her myself, and you can bet I won't put the same spin on it you would."

"That sounds like a threat."

"You bet it is," Tricia said. She turned, grabbed the handle, and made sure she slammed the door on her way out.

Tricia worked off most of her anger on the chilly walk back to her store. She stopped off at the Cookery to find a harassed Angelica overwhelmed with customers. Whipping off her coat, she held down the register for fifteen minutes while her sister helped patrons. Thankfully, the bus that awaited most of the customers had a tight schedule, and the store soon emptied out.

"Thanks for showing up when you did. It's been like this all day," Angelica said, breathless.

"What happened to your new employee?"

"She didn't show up." Angelica studied

Tricia's face. "Why are you here?"

Tricia wriggled back into her coat sleeves. "I brought you this," she said, taking the health care brochure out of her pocket. "I haven't had a chance to look at it, but you might want to study it carefully. Hiring Frannie away from the Chamber might not be as difficult as you thought."

"What do you mean?"

"That's for you to find out. I'm sworn to secrecy."

"Intriguing," Angelica said with a smile. She looked down at the brochure in her hand. "I will study it. Thank you."

The phone rang, and Angelica practically jumped on it. "The Cookery, how can I help you?" She paused. "Oh, Bob, it's you! Sure, I'm free tonight."

Tricia forced a smile and waved as she let herself out. At least one part of her plan had been set into motion. She continued down the walk to Haven't Got a Clue. It was full of customers who were in need of assistance.

As the rest of the afternoon wore on, and still no word from Grace, Tricia's anxiety multiplied. As she checked her watch for the hundredth time, she hoped Nikki had been kept as busy over at the Stoneham Patisserie. At the same time, if she was run

371

ragged, Tricia worried Nikki might opt out of attending the weekly book club meeting — which would spoil everything.

At T minus one hour, she dialed the number.

"Stoneham Patisserie, this is Nikki. How can I help you?"

"Hi, Nikki. It's Tricia over at Haven't Got a Clue. I just wanted to make sure you'll be attending the book club meeting tonight. I managed to line up a special guest — someone in publishing who was here for Zoë's memorial service. He stayed in town an extra couple of days just so he could talk to the group. I'd like to have as many warm bodies as possible in the store to make him feel welcome."

Nikki sighed, and Tricia flinched, afraid her plans might already be on the verge of unraveling. "I guess I can make it, but I can't pull off a cake on this short notice. Can I bring something else? Cookies?"

It was Tricia's turn to sigh — with relief. "You don't have to bring anything," she said. "I've got everything covered."

"Oh. Well, okay. I'll be there around six."

"See you then," Tricia said brightly and hung up the phone. No sooner had she set the receiver down than it rang again. "Haven't Got a Clue, this is Tricia."

372

"Tricia, it's Grace."

"Thank goodness. I was getting worried. Do you have good news for me?"

"It took some persuasion, but I've convinced the sheriff to arrive at precisely six o'clock."

"What excuse did you give her?"

"None at all. I just reminded her of her duty, that she's a public servant, and that it would be in her best interest to be there on time."

"And she bought it?"

"I believe she respects my reputation and the authority I used to wield. I wonder if I could use that same tactic to get the Board of Selectmen to step up their efforts and find a humane solution to the geese problem."

"Grace, I'm sure you could."

"Thank you for your faith in me. Ah, I think I hear William at the door. I'm looking forward to hearing all about the intrigue that's going on at your shop."

"And I'll be glad to update you later myself."

"Thank you, dear. Good-night."

Tricia hung up the phone.

"Aha! The stage is set," Ginny said, as she wrestled into her jacket a full half hour earlier than usual. Mr. Everett had been dismissed early after flawlessly performing his part of Tricia's scheme.

"Stage?" Tricia asked, pretending she hadn't thought of what lay ahead in the same terms.

"Didn't Shakespeare say that in one of his plays?"

"Not that I'm aware of. Now scoot, will you?"

Ginny hesitated halfway to the door, her expression growing serious. "I don't like this, Tricia. I think you should cancel the whole thing."

"It's too late now. And anyway, I'm not a bit worried," she lied.

"Well, I am."

No way did Tricia want Ginny hanging around and possibly spoiling everything. She came around the cash desk and put an arm around Ginny's shoulder, guiding her toward the door. "Look, if it'll make you feel better, I'll call you at home later tonight, okay?"

"Well, okay."

"Now go home. Relax."

"I'll go back to our house, but it's not yet a home."

"It will be one day." Tricia opened the shop door, gently pushed Ginny through.

"I'll see you tomorrow. Say hi to Brian for me."

"Good night," Ginny called, and shuffled down the sidewalk toward the municipal parking lot.

Tricia shut the shop door, turning the cardboard sign around to CLOSED, but she didn't lock the door. Nor did she shut the blinds along the big display window. If something unforeseen was destined to happen, she wanted Haven't Got a Clue to stand out like a lighted stage with the curtains drawn for the whole world to see.

She looked out over the street. Several of the other bookstores were already darkened. Tuesday was early closing night for most of the booksellers and other merchants. It was no joke that they rolled up the sidewalks of Stoneham a little after six p.m. If something unusual did happen, would there be anyone around to notice?

That's when she saw Russ across the street, standing in the doorway of History Repeats Itself, trying to blend in with the shadows. She raised a hand to wave, but he ducked out of sight. He'd promised he'd be there, cell phone in hand, to call nine-one-one in case of an emergency.

There will be no emergency, Tricia told herself. And if she was lucky, this whole fiasco with Zoë's murder and Kimberly's attempted murder would be over and done with within the hour. Tricia glanced at her watch. She was still two players short for her little production: Artemus Hamilton and Wendy Adams.

A silhouetted form paused in front of the shop. The door opened and Hamilton stepped inside. "Am I too late?"

"No," Tricia said, relief flooding through her. "Let me take your coat."

He stuffed his leather gloves in his pockets, unbuttoned his coat, and shrugged out of it. Tricia took it to the back of the shop to hang with the others.

"What do you want me to do?" he asked, when she returned.

"Why don't you stand over by those shelves? I'll make all the introductions once the sheriff gets here."

Hamilton looked around the shop, his gaze resting on the nook for a moment. "Whatever," he said.

The door opened, the bell above it jangling. Angelica stepped inside, dressed to the nines in her pink-dyed rabbit fur coat, another enormous purse, and matching magenta stilettos. "Why is your CLOSED sign up?" she said, noting the two people in the store and turning it around to say OPEN again. "It isn't six o'clock yet."

"And why aren't you in your own store?" Tricia said, charging forward.

"I closed early and didn't want customers pounding on my door. I'm meeting Bob here. He's taking me to Portsmouth for dinner overlooking the harbor."

"That's all very nice," Tricia said, pushing her sister back toward the door, "but I think you should just go back to the Cookery and wait for him."

"What's the big deal?" Angelica protested, digging her heels into the carpet. She caught sight of Artemus Hamilton lurking further back in the store. "Oh, Mr. Hamilton!" she called brightly and waved.

"Ange, you've got to go. Now!"

Before Tricia could maneuver her sister to the exit, the door opened again, but instead of Wendy Adams, it was a coatless Nikki who stood in the open entrance, still dressed in the white waitress garb and thick-soled shoes she wore at the patisserie — a full twenty minutes early. "What's going on, Tricia? Frannie just stopped by the shop and told me the meeting had been canceled. But you called me not half an hour ago to say there was a special guest coming in. What gives?"

Rats! Her worst fear had come to pass.

"We do have a guest. In fact, we have two."

"Then what — ?"

The woman who'd been quietly sitting in the nook, her back to the door, finally stood. Slight, with shoulder-length graying blond hair, she turned, face taut, arms rigid, and fists clenched at her sides.

"Nikki, this is Fiona Sample. She writes the Bonnie Chesterton librarian mystery series," Tricia said.

Nikki gave the woman a quick once-over. "Oh, sorry. Nice to meet you." She turned back to Tricia. "What's going on? What gave Frannie the idea the meeting had been canceled?" She looked around the room, her gaze settling on the only other person in the shop. Nikki took him in, and Tricia wondered if she'd remember Hamilton standing next to Kimberly at the statue dedication.

"I could've brought some cookies or cupcakes if I'd known," she said, distracted. "I should go home — change. Where is everyone else? Will they be here at six?"

"This is a private signing," Tricia said, and turned to her guest. "Fiona, I'd like you to meet Nikki Brimfield."

Fiona held out her hand. Nikki took it, shook it impatiently. "Nice to meet you," she said again.

"But we've met before," Fiona said, her voice shaking.

"Before?" Nikki echoed, puzzled.

"Yes. I'm your mother."

TWENTY-FOUR

Nikki's jaw dropped. "My mother's name was Faith. She died over twenty years ago."

"She left Stoneham over twenty years ago," Fiona said. "But here I am." Her right hand dipped into the pocket of her long, dark skirt. She pulled out an old photograph, handed it to her daughter.

Nikki stared at the image of a little girl on a bicycle.

"I have more in my purse. Your seventh birthday. Even then you liked to bake. Remember, together we made a three-layer chocolate cake with marshmallow frosting?"

Nikki looked up from the photo to glare at the woman before her. "My mother is dead."

Fiona swallowed. "Your father's mother and your aunt told you that. Did they ever offer you any proof?"

Nikki opened her mouth to answer, then closed it again. "What are you doing here?

Why now?"

Fiona's eyes filled with tears. "Because . . . I'm afraid. Afraid you've done something very, very bad."

"Me? I didn't abandon anyone. I didn't stay away for years and years," Nikki accused. "You let me believe you were dead. Where have you been all these years?"

"Believe me, I didn't want to leave. I told you —"

"But you did nothing to let me know you were alive, either."

"Your father gave me an ultimatum: leave without you — without anything — or he'd kill me. I believed him. No one told me when he died. Many years later, I was told his mother and sister had had me declared dead."

"You could've come back."

"To what? I had no home — no one, except a daughter who probably hated me. And I had a new life, a new family in Canada. Was I supposed to abandon them?"

"Family?"

"Yes, you have a half sister and brother. Twins. They're sixteen now."

"Don't tell me Jess and Addie," Nikki sneered.

"No, Jessica and Andre. My husband's French Canadian."

Nikki crossed her arms defiantly over her chest. "So what do you want me to do, embrace you all with loving arms?"

"I came to ask you to do what's right. To give yourself up."

"What?"

"You've done a terrible, terrible thing."

"Just what is it you think I've done, killed someone?" She took in the faces of the people surrounding her, focusing on Hamilton's penetrating, hateful stare. "Good grief! You don't think I killed Zoë Carter, do you?"

Fiona's gaze swung toward Tricia.

"Tricia? What have you been telling people?" Nikki asked.

Tricia stepped forward. "I'm sorry, Nikki, but the evidence is pretty overwhelming."

"You wouldn't like to let me in on some of this *evidence,* would you?"

"You knew who the real author of the Jess and Addie *Forever* books was when you asked me to invite Zoë Carter to sign here at Haven't Got a Clue. She hadn't returned to Stoneham in several years, but an invitation to speak in her hometown as the last leg of her first and only book tour was an opportunity you could use."

"And what was I supposed to use it for, blackmail?"

"Zoë made millions off your mother's work."

The anger drained from Nikki's face, replaced by annoyance. "How was I supposed to shake her down for money? I didn't have any proof my mother wrote the books. I didn't even know they'd been published until a few months ago when I was browsing in this store."

"And what was your reaction when you found out?" Fiona asked.

"Okay, I was angry. It wasn't right that someone made money off of your work. But so what? I thought you were dead."

"So why didn't you out Zoë?" Tricia asked.

"What proof did I have? Was I going to tell a lawyer that Addie was afraid of thunderstorms? That was mentioned in the second book. I could tell them that in *Forever Banished,* when Jess had to kill his horse, Prince, because he'd broken a leg, my mom cried buckets. But guess what? By the time I knew of the books being published, they'd been in print for years. Why would anyone ever believe some down-and-out baker in the boonies of New Hampshire? It would sound like sour grapes — or some kind of greedy envy."

"There's more," Tricia said. "The attack on the statue in the park. I saw a satchel full of tools in the patisserie on Sunday."

"So what? Steve knocked out an old closet so we could have more space for the baking trays."

"There was a can of red spray paint in the bag as well."

"Is it against the law to possess spray paint?"

"And Kimberly was attacked by someone wielding a sledgehammer," Hamilton said, finally joining in the conversation.

"Did she point the finger at me?"

"She doesn't remember what happened that night," he admitted.

"Very convenient," Nikki said.

"Someone forced Tricia's car off the road Sunday night. We could've been killed," Angelica said.

Nikki rounded on her. "What proof do you have that it was me?"

"None," Tricia said, "but you did give me poisoned food."

"Are you delusional?"

"The cut-out cookies and the red velvet cake you gave me were laced with some foreign matter that contained salmonella. A lab in Nashua has confirmed it — at least with the cake."

"You don't look sick."

"It wasn't me who ate them. Ginny Wilson and her boyfriend Brian did. Brian was so ill he was hospitalized on Saturday night."

"That can't be. I baked them myself, I —" She stopped short, her eyes growing wide in horror, her face blanching.

The door to Haven't Got a Clue opened, and Steve Fenton stepped inside. "What's taking so long, Nikki? I got the bakery cleaned up, but you know I can't cash out without you."

Nikki turned to face her assistant. "What have you done?" she asked, her voice shaking, frightened.

Steve shrugged. "Cleaned the bakery, like always."

She raised her left arm, pointed abstractedly at the people behind her. "They think I put something in those cookies and that cake I gave Tricia. They say they have proof."

"What are you talking about?"

"I assembled the ingredients for that cake, but you put it together and iced it. I baked those cookies, but you frosted them."

"You'd take their word that something was wrong with them?"

"Yes, because what they're saying makes a lot of sense. My God, I'm surprised the Health Department hasn't swooped in and closed me down." She clasped her head in her hands, looked at Steve in panic. "What am I thinking — they all think I killed Zoë Carter. They think I destroyed the statue in the park." She inched closer to him. "They think I attacked and nearly killed Kimberly Peters."

"You would never do that," Steve said, his gaze softening as he looked at her. "You could never hurt anybody."

Nikki closed her eyes and swallowed hard before speaking. "Please tell me you couldn't, either."

Steve looked away, his mouth flattening into a straight line, exhaling short breaths through his nose, sounding like an angry bull.

Tricia stared disbelieving at the couple before her. Steve the murderer? Not Nikki?

Then she remembered what Kimberly had told her the morning after the murder: that a man had called to tell her Tricia was spreading rumors about Zoë Carter's death, and Kimberly's supposed part in it.

With his focus still only on Nikki, Fenton clenched his fist, punched himself in the chest. "I take care of my own."

"Excuse me, but I don't belong to you. I don't belong to anyone. Not now. Not ever again."

"Nikki, it's just a matter of time," he said,

oblivious of the others standing by in stupefied silence. "It's always been a matter of time before you turn to me. We were made to be together, babe."

"Why would you think that?"

"You hired me. You gave me work when no one else would. You and me. We're a team at the bakery. We can be a team in life."

"You killed Zoë Carter," she accused.

Steve didn't deny it.

"Why — why did you do it?" she cried, horror-struck.

"For you. I did it for you."

"But why?"

"I felt so bad when you told me about the books and your mother and all. The money that woman made off those books should have been yours. That woman was a liar and a thief. You could've had a better life — owned the bakery without bank loans. You wouldn't have had to work so hard."

"Stop calling it a bakery. And I *like* working hard."

"And what did you gain by killing Zoë and attacking Kimberly?" Tricia asked him.

"Gain?" he asked, blinking.

"Nikki could never prove her mother wrote those books. She'd never get her hands on any of that money. What was the point?" Tricia said.

Steve stood straight, looked her in the eye. "If Nikki couldn't have that money, I didn't want those bitches to have it, either."

The shop door opened once again, the little bell jangling cheerfully as Wendy Adams stepped inside. "What's this all about?" she asked Tricia, ignoring the others standing there like mannequins at the edges of the action taking place in the center of the store.

"What're you doing here?" Steve demanded, staring at the uniform and the badge on Wendy Adams's jacket.

"Apparently, I'm here to arrest someone. That is, if what I'm about to hear isn't yet another cock-and-bull story."

"You called the cops on me?" Steve demanded of Nikki.

"No. Tricia called them on me!"

Steve turned, his eyes blazing. He charged forward, yanked back his right arm, and punched Tricia square in the face. She fell back against the sales counter, clutching her bleeding nose as the room seemed to explode in a cacophony of noise. A raging pink blur launched itself at Steve, clawing and screeching like a banshee.

"Steve!" Nikki yelled.

"Nikki!" Fiona screamed.

"Stand back, stand back!" Sheriff Adams

388

called, and yanked the handgun from its holster at her side.

"Angelica!" Tricia cried through the blood gushing over her lip.

The shop door banged open. "Tricia!" Russ howled, as Angelica and Steve rolled over and over across the carpet, Angelica punching him with the power of a pile driver.

"That's. For. Hitting. My. Sister. You. Stinking. Little. Coward!"

"Stop it! Right now!" Sheriff Adams ordered.

Russ jumped forward, grabbing Angelica's arms and pulling her onto her feet. She wasn't about to give up, and though she'd lost her shoes, she kicked at Steve again and again.

He lunged for her, but Wendy Adams's voice stopped him. "Don't make me shoot!" she hollered.

Fiona pressed a handful of tissues into Tricia's hand while Nikki hauled her to her feet. "Are you all right?" Fiona asked.

Angelica continued to struggle in Russ's arms.

"Stop it!" Sheriff Adams yelled once more, this time aiming the gun at Angelica.

"Wendy!" Russ yelled, outraged.

Steve lunged again, and Sheriff Adams

charged up to him, planting the barrel of the gun against his temple. He froze.

"Don't make me shoot," she repeated, this time her voice low and menacing. "Firing a weapon means an awful lot of paperwork, and quite frankly, you're not worth it, scum."

Sirens screamed outside.

"Lie down on the floor. Now!" the sheriff ordered.

Fenton did as he was told as two deputies barreled through the door.

"Placer, take care of him," the sheriff said.

Another vehicle pulled up — the News Team Ten van. Portia hopped out before it came to a complete halt.

Angelica broke away from Russ, hurrying to her sister. "Trish, Trish, are you okay?"

"Ange, your coat is torn," Tricia said, her voice sounding high and squeaky.

"That doesn't matter. Let me see," she said, pulling the tissues away from Tricia's face. She recoiled. "Oh, Trish, I think your nose is broken."

The deputies pulled a handcuffed Fenton to his feet.

"Get him out of here," Sheriff Adams said.

"What's the charge?" Placer asked, as Portia stuck a microphone into the store.

"Apparently the murder of Zoë Carter

and the attempted murder of Kimberly Peters. I'm sure we'll have a few more charges to add before the night is over."

"Wonderful!" Portia squealed, as the cameraman's lights flashed behind her. "Why did you kill Zoë Carter?" Portia asked Fenton. "Did you attack Kimberly Peters? Did you —"

"Get out of my face!" Fenton roared.

Wendy Adams straightened her uniform jacket, stood an inch or two taller, and prepared to meet the press.

"She's going to take credit for finding Zoë's killer," Angelica said, annoyed.

Tricia held the bloody wad of tissues to her nose and winced. "She can take all the credit she wants." She turned to face Nikki. "I'm so sorry I thought you —"

Nikki held up a hand to stop her. "Not now, Tricia. It's all too new. I need some time to think about it." She gazed at her mother. "To think about a lot of things." She moved to stand near the wall.

"Fiona, I'm afraid I've ruined whatever relationship you could've recaptured with Nikki."

Fiona glanced after her daughter, who stood, arms folded over her chest, looking lost and forlorn. "I'm not ready to give up yet," she said, and crossed the room to stand beside her daughter. Nikki didn't turn away, so perhaps there was some hope of reconciliation, after all.

Yet another vehicle rolled up across the street from the store. The rescue truck from the Stoneham Fire Department. Two EMTs hopped out, gear in hand, and jogged across the road, headed for Haven't Got a Clue.

"I think your dates have arrived," Russ said.

"I don't need —"

"No arguments," he said, grabbed her arm, led her to the nook, and forced her to sit before he signaled the paramedics to come over.

Angelica consulted her watch. "Where is Bob? Our reservations are for seven."

"You're going to leave me?" Tricia cried, clutching for Angelica's hand.

"Of course not. Bob will have to cancel them. I hope they send you to Southern New Hampshire Medical Center instead of that rinky-dink hospital in Milford. Then we can order off the take-out menu from that little French bistro we went to the other night. At least the onion soup was palatable." She glanced down at her manicured fingers. "Oh, darn, I've broken a nail."

"Good grief," Russ said, "Tricia's gushing blood, her nose is broken, and you're worried about a broken nail?"

Angelica frowned, looked down at her shoeless feet. "I've got a run in my stockings, too."

"Angelica," Russ said sharply.

"Don't, don't," Tricia pleaded. "She saved me from Steve."

Angelica smiled. "All in a day's work, my dear sister, all in a day's work."

TWENTY-FIVE

"I thought you were going to call me last night," Ginny scolded Tricia before she'd even shucked her jacket the next morning. She'd arrived at Haven't Got a Clue half an hour before the store was to open — much earlier than usual. She took in Tricia's bruised face, and winced.

"It was late when I got home from the hospital. I didn't want to wake you," Tricia said, and tried to sniff. She couldn't breathe, at least not through her swollen nose. Already the skin around both of her eyes was turning a lovely shade of purple. The concealer she'd applied wasn't meant for that degree of discoloration and failed to disguise it. "I didn't get home until nearly midnight. And I have to go back in two days for them to reset my nose."

"I had to find out all about it from the eleven o'clock news last night. You picked the wrong killer," Ginny accused. "Wasn't that really embarrassing?"

"You bet," Tricia said. "I don't see how Nikki can ever forgive me. If I was her, *I'd* never forgive me. And to make the accusation in front of her long-estranged mother . . ." She shook her head in disgust.

"So, are you okay?" Ginny asked.

"I feel like I've got a really bad head cold because of all the gauze packing my sinuses. But as I handed over my insurance card before I got treated, I remembered that you and Brian have no insurance. That's why —" Tricia reached under the cash desk and handed Ginny an envelope.

Ginny stared at it. "What's this?"

"Open it."

Ginny worked at the flap, removed the check that was inside. "Oh, Tricia — a thousand dollars." She looked up, tears filling her green eyes.

"I promised you a bonus for all your help this past week, and I wanted to make good on it."

Ginny shook her head. "I can't accept —"

"Oh, yes, you can. And not only that, I don't want you and Brian ever to be in a situation where you might put off a hospital visit because of the cost. That's why I've decided to get health insurance coverage for you and Mr. Everett through a local group health plan."

"Tricia, I don't know what to say. Thank you seems so inadequate." She threw her arms around her boss.

"It's enough," Tricia said, trying to swallow the lump in her throat.

Ginny pulled back, wiping tears from her eyes.

"I'll tell Mr. Everett as soon as he gets in," Tricia said.

"What a wonderful surprise. I can't wait to tell Brian," Ginny said, and put the check into her purse.

The door opened and Angelica burst into the shop, balancing a tray. "My poor baby sister. How are you feeling this morning?" she cooed. On the tray was a plate covered with a clean dishtowel. "I'll bet you didn't have a thing for breakfast, so I've made you some muffins."

"Ange, you know I don't like sweet —"

"Who said they were sweet? These are sausage and cheese muffins." She removed the towel, allowing the aroma to escape. "Like to try one, Ginny?"

"Sure," she said, and plucked the top muffin from the plate.

The door opened again. This time it was Russ, carrying two insulated cups from the Coffee Bean. "Hey, if I'd known you guys were here, I'd have brought some more," he said, and paused beside Tricia, bending to give her a soft peck on the cheek. "Wow, you look terrible."

Tricia faked a smile. "You sure know how to sweet-talk a girl."

"And she sounds like Rudolph the Red-Nosed Reindeer when he had the false nose on," Ginny chimed in. "I'll get the coffee going. You want a cup, Angelica?"

"I'd love one. Try one of these muffins, Russ."

"Thanks, don't mind if I do."

Tricia took a muffin as well, brought it up to her nose, and tried to sniff it. "I can't smell anything. I don't think I can taste, either."

The door opened again, this time admitting Mr. Everett. "Ms. Miles! I heard on the news you'd been hurt," he said. In his hands he held a brown paper sack. "I brought you some poppy seed bagels. I know they're you're favorite. I even brought you some dental floss to get the seeds out of your teeth."

"That's very sweet, of you, Mr. Everett, but —"

"I've already brought fresh-made muffins," Angelica broke in. "Would you like to try one?"

Mr. Everett removed his gloves. "Thank you, Mrs. Prescott."

"Miles," she reminded him. "I'm Ms. Miles again. And I think I'm going to remain Ms. Miles, no matter how many more times I get married. Did you bring butter or cream cheese with those bagels?"

"Both."

"Excellent. Give me that muffin, Trish, I'll butter it for you."

"But I don't think —" The door opened again. "What is this, Grand Central Station?" Tricia muttered, straining to turn to see who'd arrived this time.

Nikki and Fiona each held a tray as they descended on the nook. "Looks like a party," Nikki said. "And what's better than partying on fresh-baked Danish? Mom and I made them together."

"I brought bagels," Mr. Everett said, brandishing the paper sack.

"Nikki, I —"

Nikki held out a hand to stop her. "Tricia, don't you dare apologize. Mom and I talked until almost one last night. Added all together, the evidence —"

"All circumstantial —" Tricia interrupted.

"Was pretty convincing," Nikki finished. "Sheriff Adams called me this morning. Steve made a full confession. He admitted he handled goose droppings before he frosted those cookies, and when they didn't make Tricia sick, he actually put some in the red frosting on the cake."

Ginny blanched. "Oh, Lord! No wonder Brian was so sick."

Nikki nodded. "The Health Department came in first thing this morning and shut me down. I'm afraid the patisserie is closed for the time being."

"Oh, no," Tricia said.

"To tell you the truth, I'm surprised they didn't do it yesterday. Apparently there was a paperwork holdup, or they would have. And it might actually be a good thing in the long run — at least for me," Nikki added, trying not to smile. "You see, I got a call from the owner this morning. He's already lowered the price, and if the patisserie stays closed for any length of time — which means no income for him — he'll be really eager to unload it. By then I should have my new finance package assembled."

"Then at least one good thing has come of this," Tricia said.

"There are still some things I don't get," Angelica said. "Everybody knows Steve doesn't drive. So who tried to run Tricia and me off the road?"

"It *was* Steve," Nikki said. "It wasn't that

he couldn't drive — he just didn't. He lost his license years ago from a DWI conviction. He never tried to get it back."

"But whose car did he use?"

"Apparently he stole one in Milford, then returned it to the same house he'd taken it from. If it weren't for the smashed windshield —"

"From where the goose hit it," Tricia piped up.

"The owner probably wouldn't have known it was even taken."

"Don't tell me Sheriff Adams figured that out."

Nikki shook her head. "Once Steve got talking, he couldn't shut up. He told the deputies *everything*."

"Can I try one of those Danish?" Russ said, dusting the muffin crumbs from his fingers.

"Oh, sure." Nikki held up the tray, offering him the pastries.

Angelica was still shaking her head. "But I don't understand where Zoë got the manuscripts. Tricia, didn't you say she got them at an estate sale? Did they come in a box lot?"

"I can answer that," Fiona said. "My husband didn't approve of my writing, so I had to hide the manuscripts. I lived in fear he'd destroy them, so I kept them in an old trunk. It sounds stupid and corny, but I put a false bottom in the trunk. If he'd ever thought to look carefully, he would've found them."

"Did you know about the trunk?" Tricia asked Nikki.

She nodded. "And I told Steve about that, too."

"The night Kimberly was attacked, I saw an old trunk in Zoë's home office. Steve did a real number on it. I doubt it can be repaired."

"I don't care about that. I left it — and the manuscripts — behind a long time ago," Fiona said.

"But aren't you furious that Zoë took the credit and made all that money from your work?" Ginny asked.

"Of course. I've got two kids who will head off to university in two years. I'll probably consult a lawyer, but I don't have the kind of money to wage a long legal battle — and that's most likely what would end up happening."

"So no happy ending there," Ginny said.

"Perhaps not, but I'll never regret you sent me that e-mail, Tricia. It gave me a way to reconnect with my daughter." Fiona gazed at Nikki with loving eyes.

Nikki, however, wasn't as easily placated. "We've still got a lot of issues to resolve. A one-night chat-a-thon can't solve everything."

"But at least we've agreed to talk everything through and try to remain civil," Fiona added.

Nikki nodded. "Hey, it takes some getting used to, finding out the mother you thought was dead is still alive, and you've got a whole new family you never knew about. I've got a brother and sister to meet sometime in the near future."

Fiona gazed at her watch. "And I've got an interview in less than half an hour. Tricia, that friend of yours, Portia McAlister, wants to make me the feature on her newscast tonight, talking about how I wrote the Jess and Addie books, and what I think of all that's happened in the last week."

"That ought to give your Bonnie Chesterfield series a push, too," Tricia said.

Fiona laughed. "At the very least, I'm determined to prove that there's no such thing as bad publicity."

The door opened yet again, this time admitting Artemus Hamilton, whose leather-gloved hand held Kimberly's. Her face was still swollen and bruised, but her toothless smile would've brightened a cold, dark night.

"Tri-ah," Kimberly managed, "Oo loo li me."

"Not too much talking, now," Hamilton warned her gently. "Kimberly got released from the hospital first thing this morning, and we made a stop before coming here," he said.

Kimberly pulled off her left glove. "-ook!" She wiggled her hand, showing off what was probably a two-carat diamond on the ring finger of her left hand. "An Ar-ie's gonna sell my ook."

"I'm going to try," he said, glancing at her with fondness, seeing past her temporary ugliness to the beautiful soul beyond.

"Would you like a muffin?" Angelica said, proffering the plate.

Kimberly shook her head.

"For now, she can only drink room temperature liquids," Hamilton explained.

"An -oy, am I -ungry," she said, laughing.

"I have some good news for you, too, Ms. Miles."

"For me?" Tricia said.

He shook his head, then turned to look at Angelica. "I read your manuscript yesterday. It's well done. There's a market out there for time-stressed working women who want to feed their families healthy foods. I think I could sell it — at least, I'd like to try."

"Well, of course you would," Angelica said, her smile as wide as Tricia had ever seen it, and she gave her sister an "I told you so" glance.

"We'll need to talk more about it, and you'll need to do some rewriting before I can start rounding it to publishers. But it doesn't have to happen today. I'll give you a call early next week."

"You have my number," Angelica said brightly.

"I've got a question," Russ said, directing his gaze to Kimberly. "The night you were attacked, you said the word 'stone' to Tricia. Did Steve Fenton tell you that was the name of the author of the Jess and Addie books, or were you talking about the desecrated statue?"

"Boph," she said. "He hur- me — hittin- me. Saying I wou- pay for wha- happen to Fayfe Thone."

"The thing is," Hamilton said, "Kimberly didn't have a clue who Fenton was talking about."

"I'm so sorry he put you through that," Fiona said.

"I sorry my aun- -tole you wok. Fo- a lon- time, I din know."

"Everyone thought you were dead," Hamilton added.

"That doesn't make it right, but I do understand," Fiona said.

Ginny brought over a tray of Haven't Got a Clue paper coffee cups, the carafe, sugar, and cream, setting it all down on the nook's table. She picked up a cup, raising it into the air. "Why don't we all cheer up?" she suggested. "We've got a lot to celebrate this morning."

"I sure do," Angelica said.

The door opened yet again, this time admitting Frannie Armstrong. "Come on, boss, we've got a store to open," she said, her smile so wide it showed off most of her teeth.

"Boss?" Tricia asked, in awe.

Frannie entered the store, closing the door behind her.

"In a minute," Angelica told Frannie. She picked up the carafe, poured coffee into all the cups. "Bob and I had a long discussion last night after we left the hospital." She shook her head. "Sometimes I don't know what I see in that man."

Amen, Tricia felt like echoing; instead, she bit her tongue.

"When I found out what he was actually paying Frannie, I knew I could do better, and even give her benefits. I called her last night the minute I got home. Woke her from a sound sleep, too."

"But that was one call I was glad to take," Frannie said.

"What about the Chamber?" Russ asked. "Who'll be manning the reception desk?"

"I offered to give Bob two weeks' notice, but he seemed in rather a big hurry to get rid of me. So much for a decade of dedicated service." Frannie shrugged. "I start today at the Cookery." She glanced at her watch. "We're supposed to open in twelve minutes, Angelica. Don't you think we ought to be going?"

Before Angelica could answer, the door opened once again. "It worked, Tricia, it worked!" Bob called, his voice jubilant. Then he caught sight of his former employee standing in the middle of the crowd, and his face fell. "What's going on?"

"Just a gathering of friends," Angelica answered. "And what worked?"

Bob tore his gaze from Frannie, focusing his attention on Tricia. "Wow, you look terrible."

"Thanks, Bob."

"I just stopped by to tell you your suggestion about introducing swans to the geese worked. When I couldn't come up with a live swan, I bought four or five decoys.

Yesterday afternoon I installed them around the pond in the park. I haven't seen a goose since. I've called the Stoneham Golf Course and the Board of Selectmen. They're going to install swan decoys at every place the geese gather. That ought to fix them. And it's a happy ending for everybody."

Except that the geese would just move to other wetlands. Oh, well. That wasn't Stoneham's problem.

Ginny raised her cup once again. "We've all got something to celebrate this morning. I want to propose a toast." She turned and faced her boss. "To Tricia."

"Me? What for?"

"For solving a murder," Ginny said.

Fiona raised her cup, gazing fondly at Nikki. "For reuniting a mother and daughter."

Angelica handed her new employee a cup. "For helping me get a new job," Frannie said.

"And me a new employee," Angelica said. "Not to mention my new literary agent."

"For giving me an exclusive," Russ said.

"For not firing me," Mr. Everett said.

"For brin-ee Ar-ie to me," Kimberly said.

"And making me realize how much I cared for Kimberly," Hamilton confirmed.

"For telling us how to get rid of the

geese," Bob said.

Tricia took in the smiling faces of all her friends, a lump rising in her throat. "Oh, well," she stammered. "If that's all, then." She raised her own cup. "I'll drink to that."

ANGELICA'S RECIPES

SHRIMP SCAMPI

1 1/2 to 2 pounds large shrimp (about 16
  to 24), peeled and deveined
1/3 cup clarified butter or olive oil
2 cloves minced garlic (I often toss in more)
6 green onions, thinly sliced
1/3 cup dry white wine or vermouth
2 tablespoons lemon juice, fresh if possible
3 tablespoons chopped fresh parsley
salt and pepper, to taste

Rinse shrimp and set aside. (If they're frozen, defrost them first.) Heat butter or oil in a large skillet over medium heat. Add garlic; cook 1 or 2 minutes or until softened; do not brown. Add shrimp, green onions, wine, and lemon juice. Cook until shrimp are pink, about 1 to 2 minutes on each side. Sprinkle with parsley and salt and pepper.

Serve over linguini or your favorite pasta.

Serves 4.

TLALPEÑO-STYLE SOUP

6 1/2 cups chicken stock
1/2 chipotle chili, seeded
4 skinless, boneless chicken breasts
1 medium avocado (slightly underripe for easier handling)
6 scallions, finely chopped
14-ounce can chickpeas (garbanzo beans), drained
1 cup cooked rice
salt and fresh-ground black pepper
1 cup grated cheddar cheese
1 tablespoon chopped fresh cilantro (optional)

Pour chicken stock in a large saucepan, and add the chili. Bring to a boil. Add the whole chicken breasts, then lower the heat and simmer for about 12 minutes or until the chicken is cooked. Remove the chicken from the pan and let it cool a little.

Shred the chicken into small pieces and set it aside.

Cut avocado in half, remove the skin and pit, then chop into 1/2-inch pieces. Add it to the stock, with the scallions and chickpeas. Return the shredded chicken to the pan, add rice, and heat through. Add salt and pepper to taste.

Ladle into bowls, sprinkle with grated cheese. If desired, top with cilantro. Serve immediately.

Serves 6.

PASTRY CHICKEN CORDON BLEU

2 sheets frozen puff pastry
4 boneless chicken breasts
2 tablespoons butter
salt and pepper (optional)
8 slices Swiss cheese
4 slices deli ham (I like mine sliced medium to thick)

Thaw pastry at room temperature for 30–40 minutes. Season chicken with salt and pepper if desired. In a medium skillet over medium-high heat, heat butter; add chicken and cook until browned. Remove chicken from skillet. Cover and refrigerate at least 15 minutes.

Unfold pastry and place it on a lightly floured board; roll it out until it is 1 inch wider and longer. Cut pastry in half and layer 1 slice each of cheese, chicken, and ham, and second slice of cheese. Fold over top half and press the sides closed with your fingers. Repeat the process, making a total of 4 pieces. Bake on an ungreased cookie sheet.

Bake in 400° oven 20 minutes, until pastry is puffed and golden.

Serves 4.

STUFFED BAKED POTATOES

3 large baking potatoes (1 pound each)
1 1/2 teaspoons vegetable oil (optional)
1/2 cup sliced green onions
1/2 cup butter, divided
1/2 cup half-and-half
1/2 cup sour cream
1/2 teaspoon salt
1/2 teaspoon black pepper
1 cup shredded cheddar cheese
Paprika

Rub potatoes with oil if desired; pierce with a fork. Bake at 400° for 1 hour and 20 minutes, or until tender. Let stand until cool enough to handle.

Cut each potato in half lengthwise. Scoop

out the pulp, leaving a thin shell. Place pulp in a large bowl and mash it. In a small skillet, sauté onions in 1/4 cup butter until tender. Stir into potato pulp along with half-and-half, sour cream, salt, and pepper. Fold in cheese.

Spoon mixture into potato shells. Place on a baking sheet. Melt remaining butter; drizzle it over the potatoes. Sprinkle with paprika. Bake uncovered at 350° for 20–30 minutes, or until heated through.

Potatoes may be stuffed ahead of time and refrigerated or frozen. Allow additional time for reheating.

Feel free to add other toppings, such as chopped chives, chopped mushrooms, or crumbled bacon to the mix.

Makes 6 servings.

PEANUT BUTTER BLONDIES
2 cups all-purpose flour
1 1/2 teaspoons baking powder
1/2 teaspoon salt
2/3 cup butter
2 cups firmly packed brown sugar
2 large eggs, beaten slightly

10 ounces peanut butter morsels
1 cup chopped peanuts (optional)

Combine flour, baking powder, and salt in a bowl and set aside.

Melt butter in a large saucepan over medium-low heat. Add brown sugar and eggs, stir well. Gradually add to flour mixture. Add morsels and nuts, stirring well. (Batter will be stiff.) Spread batter in a lightly greased 13″ × 9″ × 2″ pan. Bake at 350° for 30 minutes. Cool completely in the pan on a wire rack. Cut into squares.

Makes approximately 30 brownies.

SAUSAGE-SWISS CHEESE MUFFINS

1/4 pound mild or spicy ground pork sausage
2 cups all-purpose flour
2 teaspoons baking powder
3/4 cup shredded Swiss cheese
1/4 teaspoon ground sage
1/4 teaspoon dried thyme
1/2 teaspoon salt
1/2 cup milk
1/4 cup vegetable oil
1 egg, lightly beaten

Preheat oven to 375°.

Brown sausage in a skillet over medium heat, stirring until it crumbles. Drain well. Combine sausage, flour, and next 5 ingredients in a bowl; make a well in the center of the mixture.

Combine milk, oil, and egg; add to dry ingredients, stirring until moistened. Spoon batter into greased (or paper cup-lined) muffin pans, filling 2/3 full. Bake for 20–22 minutes or until golden. Serve warm. Store leftovers in the refrigerator.

Makes 1 dozen.

NIKKI'S RECIPES

EASY-TO-MAKE WHITE-CHOCOLATE GANACHE

1 1/2 cups heavy cream
8 ounces white chocolate chips

In a saucepan heat the cream and bring it to a boil. Remove from the heat. Place white chocolate chips in a large bowl and pour hot cream into the bowl. Let sit for 1 minute or so, then whisk until smooth. Transfer to the refrigerator to cool, stirring occasionally.

When mixture is cold and thickened, beat with an electric mixer into soft peaks, then beat the last few strokes by hand with a whisk until thick and firm. Do not over-whisk, or mixture will become grainy.

For flavored ganache, use 1 ounce less of cream (or 2 tablespoons) and add 1 1/2 ounces (3 tablespoons) of rum or your favorite liqueur. Or add 1/4 teaspoon vanilla extract, or other flavoring.

Ganache can stay at room temperature for 2 days, as long as it's kept in a cool place.

Makes about 1 cup.

BUTTERMILK SUGAR COOKIES

1 1/2 cups sugar
1 cup vegetable shortening
2 eggs
1 teaspoon vanilla
4 1/2 cups flour
1/2 teaspoon baking soda
3 heaping teaspoons baking powder
1 cup buttermilk (or commercial eggnog)

In a large bowl, cream together sugar and shortening until fluffy. Add eggs and vanilla. In a separate bowl, mix flour, soda, and baking powder. Alternate adding buttermilk and dry ingredients to the creamed mixture.

Refrigerate overnight.

Divide dough into 4 equal pieces. Roll out a portion on floured surface to 1/4 inch thickness. (To keep dough from getting tough, use confectioner's sugar instead of flour.) Cut out with your favorite cookie cutters. Place on lightly greased or nonstick cookie sheets or parchment paper-covered baking trays.

Bake at 350° for 8–10 minutes, until they just start to brown.

Cool in pans for about 5 minutes; transfer to cooling/wire racks, and cool completely before decorating.

Makes (approximately) 4 dozen.

Frosting
1/2 cup confectioner's sugar
1 1/2 tablespoons water
3 to 4 drops food coloring (or more as needed)
Colored sprinkles (optional)

In a small bowl, mix sugar and water to form a thick, smooth icing. Stir in food coloring to reach desired shade. Use separate bowls for additional colors. Frost cookies. Add sprinkles before icing dries.

RED VELVET CAKE
1/2 cup shortening
1 1/2 cups sugar

2 eggs
2 tablespoons cocoa
1 1/2 ounces (or 3 tablespoons) red food coloring
1 teaspoon salt
2 1/2 cups flour
1 1/2 teaspoons vanilla
1 cup buttermilk
1 teaspoon baking soda
1 tablespoon vinegar

Cream shortening; beat in sugar gradually. Add eggs, one at a time; beat well after each addition. Make a paste of cocoa and food coloring; add to creamed mixture. Add salt, flour, and vanilla alternately with buttermilk, beating well after each addition. Sprinkle soda over vinegar; pour the mixture over batter. Mix well.

Bake in 3 prepared 8-inch pans or 2 9-inch pans for 30 minutes at 350°, or until toothpick tester comes out clean.

12 servings

Frosting
1 package (8 ounces) cream cheese, softened
1 1/2 cups butter, softened
3 3/4 cups confectioners' sugar

3 teaspoons vanilla extract

In a large mixing bowl, combine ingredients; beat until smooth and creamy. Spread between layers and over top and sides of cake.

Frosts one cake.

Blood Glaze

You can color your cream cheese frosting with red food coloring, or make your own "stage" blood.

1 cup white corn syrup
1 tablespoon red food coloring
1 tablespoon yellow food coloring
1 tablespoon water (optional; it'll "thin" the "blood")

Mix well, drizzle over one side of cake.

Makes 1 cup (or 1/4 pint).

We hope you have enjoyed this Large Print book. Other Thorndike, Wheeler, Kennebec, and Chivers Press Large Print books are available at your library or directly from the publishers.

For information about current and upcoming titles, please call or write, without obligation, to:

Publisher
Thorndike Press
295 Kennedy Memorial Drive
Waterville, ME 04901
Tel. (800) 223-1244

or visit our Web site at:

http://gale.cengage.com/thorndike

OR

Chivers Large Print
published by BBC Audiobooks Ltd
St James House, The Square
Lower Bristol Road
Bath BA2 3SB
England
Tel. +44(0) 800 136919
email: bbcaudiobooks@bbc.co.uk
www.bbcaudiobooks.co.uk

All our Large Print titles are designed for easy reading, and all our books are made to last.